OUR LAST RESORT

# OUR LAST RESORT

### A NOVEL

Clémence Michallon

ALFRED A. KNOPF
NEW YORK
2025

A BORZOI BOOK

FIRST HARDCOVER EDITION PUBLISHED BY ALFRED A. KNOPF 2025

Published by Alfred A. Knopf, a division of Penguin Random House LLC, 1745 Broadway, New York, NY 10019.

Knopf, Borzoi Books, and the colophon are registered trademarks of Penguin Random House LLC.

Library of Congress Cataloging-in-Publication Data
Names: Michallon, Clémence, author.
Title: Our last resort: a novel / Clémence Michallon.
Description: First edition. | New York : Alfred A. Knopf, 2025.
Identifiers: LCCN 2024045795 | ISBN 9780593802762 (hardcover) |
ISBN 9780593802779 (ebook) | ISBN 9781524712921 (Canada)
Subjects: LCGFT: Thrillers (Fiction). | Novels.
Classification: LCC PS3613.I344475 O97 2025 |
DDC 813/.6—dc23/eng/20241001
LC record available at https://lccn.loc.gov/2024045795

penguinrandomhouse.com | aaknopf.com

Printed in the United States of America
2 4 6 8 9 7 5 3 1

The authorized representative in the EU for product safety and compliance is Penguin Random House Ireland, Morrison Chambers, 32 Nassau Street, Dublin D02 YH68, Ireland, https://eu-contact.penguin.ie.

*For Tyler, again,*
*and for the readers*

*Was I not the whole world, and would not the universe crumble away when I was no more?*
    —Émile Zola, "The Death of Olivier Becaille"


*One sits down on a desert sand dune, sees nothing, hears nothing. Yet through the silence something throbs, and gleams . . .*
    —Antoine de Saint-Exupéry, *The Little Prince*

# OUR LAST RESORT

# 1  ESCALANTE, UTAH

## THE FOURTH NIGHT

There are times when joy settles perfectly inside my body. I notice.

The world twisted out of shape around me, years ago. My brain rewired itself to keep me safe. *Check your door before bed,* it tells me. *Once, twice, three times. Unlock the door to make sure it was locked. Then lock it again.*

*Look through the peephole. Make sure the stove is off. Is the dog okay? Is he breathing? Doesn't matter that you've already checked. Do it one more time.*

My mind: always anxious. My whole world like a dollhouse. I know where everything is, how everything works. No surprises.

Which makes the exceptions all the more vivid. Happiness sprouting in the unlikeliest places—a green spray of ivy curling around barbed wire, flowers blooming on the grassy surface of a shallow grave.

Like now. Gabriel asleep in our shared suite, me on our private patio. Above, the desert sky.

In a few hours, the sun will rise. The hotel, our unlikely oasis of straight lines and modern architecture, will flood with natural light. Morning smells will waft through the air, the rich aroma of coffee, the fresh bursts of perfume, the sweet mist of sunscreen.

The pool will shimmer, golden blue, like a mirage. Guests will head to breakfast in a sleepy shuffle.

But for now, it's all quiet. All mine. The insomniac's privilege.

I reach in the pocket of my hoodie, pull a cigarette from the pack, click my lighter. Empty. I hesitate, then use the one provided by the hotel for the gas fireplace.

First puff. A gust of wind teases the hem of my shorts, lifts it at the edge of the three white stripes.

*I'm not alone.*

The thought cuts through my mind in a red slash.

Two voices disrupt the night's quiet.

I know these voices. I've heard them intermittently over the past four days, rippling in hushed tones near the spa, in clipped sentences over the dinner table.

The young wife and her old husband.

I recognized them by the pool on our first day, from a *60 Minutes* segment I watched last year. Most of what I know about the world, I learned on TV.

"Look," I told Gabriel, my elbow digging into his ribs. "That's William Brenner."

When he didn't respond, I explained: "He's a big tabloid guy. Wealthy. I think that's his . . . third wife?"

What a pairing they make. Sabrina Brenner, not yet thirty, her skin already tightened by injectables. Her long hair, shimmery platinum. Everything about her delicate and airy, a cloud of sweet perfume enveloping her, something evoking a state fair, the wholesome aromas of sugar and vanilla.

Trailing her, the blunt shape of her husband. William Brenner radiates a bullish kind of confidence, from the shiny top of his balding skull to his professionally polished loafers. He's got that smile, too—the sly grin of a man who has never wanted for the company of ladies. Who knows himself to be not handsome, but charming, and who understands that *charming* is enough to get what he wants.

The *60 Minutes* segment was about the tabloid culture of the early 2000s, specifically the ways in which it ruined people's lives. "People like good stories," William Brenner had said, his bulk perched on an ornate armchair in his Upper East Side apartment. "And we are here to give them exactly that."

What's he saying now?

My cigarette hisses softly as I stub it out on the sole of my sandal. The concept of tobacco does not exist at the Ara hotel, nor do ashtrays. Back inside, in the bathroom, I hold the cigarette butt under a thin stream of water, wrap it in toilet paper, and bury it in the trash can.

Gabriel is still sleeping, curled in a fetal position. Like when we were kids: limbs tangled at his front, a knot of a boy shielding himself from the world.

I grab my key card and slip away.

The voices lead me close to the edge of the compound, to the last patch of sandstone before the hotel ends and the desert begins.

Here they are. The Brenners.

Sabrina paces away from her husband, still in the outfit she wore to dinner, the white satin, the high heels. She's almost fluorescent in the moonlight, a glowing fish darting across the bottom of an aquarium, the sleek folds of her dress rippling like fins.

William staggers after her. He, too, is still in his dinner clothes, white button-down and a suit, the fabric a little too thick for the desert.

Standing about twenty feet from them, I keep my shoulders hunched, hoping for invisibility.

"I'm sorry," Sabrina says, in the voice of a woman who has been sorry for a long time—always in vain.

Has anyone else noticed?

How Sabrina keeps herself out of her husband's reach? How her gaze rises whenever he stands up? How she tracks his movements, no doubt the same way she monitors his moods?

"Oh," William growls. "Now you're fucking sorry?"

He snatches at his wife's arm, misses, stumbles forward.

"Stop lying to me."

Sabrina raises her palms in front of her.

"I'm sorry," she says again. "I'm not lying to you. Let's just go back to the—"

William grabs her young wrists. A phantom pain buzzes through my right side: a pull at my shoulder years ago, my arm hanging limp afterward.

William slurs: "You stupid whore."

I realize I'm holding my breath.

*Get away from her. Leave her the fuck alone.*

Sabrina whips around to face her husband.

"I'm not stupid," she says.

All trace of apology has left her voice. This version of Sabrina is strong, willful, outraged on her own behalf.

William goes still.

"What did you just say?"

"I said, I'm not stu—"

As Sabrina moves to step past her husband, her gaze travels above him.

She spots me.

I think I see her shoulders tense.

She must have assumed they were alone. Our fellow guests are safely tucked in their suites, asleep behind thick stone walls and triple-pane windows.

Within the compound, the Ara has created discrete, hushed bubbles for each set of guests. Our suites are standalone buildings, nestled at the end of individual walkways. Tables in the dining room are distanced, other people's conversations reduced to a low hum. It's a trick the hotel has been playing on us: assuring us that we don't need to concern ourselves with the other guests, that we are safe from one another.

For half a second, Sabrina considers me. Then she gives the faintest shake of the head.

*Don't.*

I understand. Back when I was a kid, the mothers grew irate if we called for help. Their voices rose, indignant: *What the hell do you think you're doing?* If they were in a hitting mood, they hit harder. They made sure we regretted looking for a lifeline, every single time.

William follows his wife's gaze.

*Shit.*

I duck behind a large planter. There are dozens around the hotel: oval-shaped, each the size of a small bathtub and housing a lone tree. The soil is hidden beneath a layer of decorative rocks. "A lot of trees in the desert manage to grow through cracks in the stone," Catalina, the hotel's manager, explained when she gave us a tour on the first day, her sleek, dark ponytail gleaming in the sunlight. "Our architect was very inspired by them."

These rocks aren't ordinary, though. Nothing at the hotel is. "White marble chunks from Italy," Catalina said. "You won't find them anywhere else in the region."

I crouch as low as I can behind the planter and its expensive rocks. My heartbeat pulses in my ears.

"What are you looking at?" William asks, imperious.

Is the sound of his voice closer, or am I imagining it?

"Nothing. I'm not looking at anything."

Still crouched, I inch behind a nearby wall.

*Like a coward.*

No.

Sabrina doesn't want me to get involved.

"Leave me alone," she tells her husband.

"And what would you do, if I left you alone?"

Her answer is muffled as I sidestep back toward the suite. There are words I can't make out, then: "I would thrive."

Her tone is clear and self-righteous. The tone of a woman who knows she contains limitless worlds, and who is sick of reining them in.

Tomorrow, I'll talk to her.

I won't say anything about her husband. I'm not an idiot. But I'll do what I've avoided for the past four days: I'll introduce myself, ask her how her stay is going. I'll make a comment about the weather.

I'll let her know that someone's here for her, that she has a friend if she wants one.

Tomorrow. In a few hours.

Everything's easier in the daylight. We're all braver in the morning.

## 2  ESCALANTE, UTAH

THE FOURTH NIGHT

A decade ago, a developer looked at this flat patch of the Escalante Desert and thought, *I will build a hotel here.* This became the Ara. Hidden from the highway, accessible only via an unmarked dirt road. There's a gym, a spa, a boutique. Of course, the pool. An open-air entrance lounge leads to the lobby, which itself leads to the dining room. The hotel's sleek lines melt into the desertscape. There are no barriers around us, no fences.

A cold splash of water on my face. The moon shines directly into our bathroom, the ivory belly of our soaking tub glowing beneath the arched window. When I return to the room, it's quiet.

Too quiet.

I peer at the two queen-size beds. Mine is on the right, the million-thread-count Italian cotton sheets folded back. On Gabriel's side, a blur of linens where his resting body should be, pillows still punched with the outline of his head. The alpaca wool blanket he plucked from the sofa lies abandoned on the floor.

"Gabriel?"

I switch on the ceiling light.

He's not here.

I pick up my phone from my nightstand, find our most recent text (yesterday afternoon, when Gabriel messaged me from the pool bar asking if I wanted a smoothie), and press the call button.

A buzz breaks the silence. My gaze falls on Gabriel's phone, vibrating on his own nightstand.

*Shit.*

Where is he? At this hour, there's nothing to do at the Ara but sleep. We're a thirty-minute drive from the nearest town. Even if Gabriel had a reason to head there in the middle of the night, we don't have a car. A driver picked us up from the airport in one of the hotel's gleaming vans, an air-conditioned capsule around which the desert materialized like another planet.

"Gabriel?"

I check the patio. Empty. He must have left while I was still outside.

*Stay calm. You're not the person you were fifteen years ago.* A girl with a life like a blank page, everything to figure out from scratch. Delivered to a world that allowed her to be safe only with a man at her side.

The door handle rattles.

There's a sliding sound, the mechanism unlocking at the touch of a key card on the other side.

Gabriel starts when he sees me.

"There you are," he says.

"I— What?"

"Where did you go?"

Without waiting for my answer, Gabriel shuts the door behind him. He squints at the ceiling light.

"Mind if I switch this off?"

I tell him to go ahead.

Even in shadows, I can make out his silhouette. Here, his bare arms, there, the white words on his T-shirt: TIBERIUS & DOMITIAN & NERO & CALIGULA. (Four Roman emperors, four brands of insanity. I learned about them when I picked the names three Christmases ago, before mailing Gabriel the T-shirt as a present. Those four, in order: tyrannical; paranoid; burned people alive; demanded to be worshipped as a god.)

"*I* was looking for *you*," I say. "Just now."

Gabriel disappears inside the bathroom. There's the trickle of water, the sluicing sound of soap lathering against skin.

"I don't know what to tell you," he says from the other side of the door. "I woke up and you weren't here."

He walks back into the room, wiping his hands on his sweatpants. There is a brief ray of moonlight, then the bathroom door shuts, and we're in the dark again.

"Where did you disappear to?" he asks.

"I was . . . outside. Smoking."

I can't make out his face, but I think he's shaking his head.

"If you get us kicked out before the end of the stay, remember you're the one on the hook for the bill."

His voice is light, teasing. I try to laugh, but all I can produce is a small cough.

A whoosh of sheets and blankets. Gabriel folding himself into his bed. I don't need to see him to know his legs are slightly bent. The curse of the tall man: always compressing his body, hunching his way through doors and train cars.

"Are you going to try to sleep," he asks, "or . . . ?"

"I saw something."

It comes out as a whisper.

"What?" he asks. "What did you see?"

My throat tightens. I don't want to talk about any of it with Gabriel: Sabrina and William Brenner; husbands and the things they do to their wives.

It's what kicked him out of my life almost nine years ago.

We've been finding our way back to each other. Still, in our four days at the Ara, there have been moments when he's slipped away. Retreating to our suite in the middle of an afternoon by the pool. Untethering from our dinner conversation and gazing into the distance.

Just yesterday, he skipped a morning hike, invoking a migraine. I believed him. Gabriel has had migraines since we were both fifteen. But I also remember something he told me years ago, once he'd found the right treatment: "Now I only get the migraines that my body wants me to have."

Which meant the timing of his migraines was no longer random. He got them when he worked too hard, or when he was depressed. They became his body's way of forcing him to rest, of bailing him out of moments he wanted to avoid.

Like yesterday's hike.

We came here to talk. But we haven't discussed it yet—the documentary, the thing that brought us here. I've tried to bring it up a couple of times, but Gabriel wriggled out of the conversation. He had a phone call to make, a question to ask at the front desk.

There are layers between us. Things unsaid, embraces that were never given.

But I'm trying.

"Our neighbors," I say. "The Brenners. The old guy and his wife."

"What about them?"

Gabriel's voice is warm, patient.

"They were arguing," I tell him. "Fighting."

"It happens."

I shake my head, even though he can't see me. "This was different. Bad. It reminded me of—"

My voice disappears at the back of my throat.

There are things I can't say. Not even to my brother, not even in the dark.

"Come over here," he says.

A mental picture from our childhood: me on the top bunk, Gabriel on the bottom one. Back when I was the brave one.

I slide down to the floor and feel my way toward him. There, I sit, the wood of his bed frame digging between my shoulders.

"Everything's fine," he says.

"Sabrina Brenner," I tell him. "There's something wrong with her husband."

"There's something wrong with most husbands."

Before I can ask him what he means, before I can insist,

*No, really, Gabriel, I'm not kidding,* my brother shifts under his blanket.

"We're okay," he says, his last word swallowed by a yawn. "It's all going to be okay."

Just like that, he's asleep again.

I stay seated by his bed. In other circumstances, I'd fall asleep right here, the regular pattern of Gabriel's breath like a lullaby.

Not tonight.

I sit, eyes open. Listening. Standing guard.

It's nothing I haven't done before.

## 3 *THE ONLY TOWN WE KNEW, HUDSON VALLEY*

In the beginning, there was Émile.

Émile knew everything. His head was full of ideas, stories, music. He'd built a whole world for us using his thoughts as bricks.

In Émile's world, birthdays were acknowledged but not celebrated. There was no cake, no song. We nodded to the passage of time, and then we moved on.

On the day I turned eight, Edwina, a tall twelve-year-old girl who had started leading our woodworking workshops, came to find me.

I was outside, drawing a figure eight in a patch of dirt with a stick. It was almost time for lunch, almost time to head to the cafeteria. But Edwina had other plans.

"Come," she said.

I followed her. She took me across the old schoolyard, past the communal showers, the cafeteria, the dorms, the reclaimed chapel.

My stomach tightened. "Where are you—"

"Shhh."

"But—"

Edwina whipped around. "No questions."

Impossibly, she led me all the way to Émile's building.

This forbidden land, the only part of the compound in pristine condition. I'd never been inside. Émile's office, we all knew, was on the first floor; his living quarters, equally off-limits, upstairs. He lived there alone, and—for the most part—worked there alone.

Edwina's skirt swished across a small foyer. She nudged me in front of a closed wooden door.

"Stand here."

She knocked and, before I could ask her what she was doing, skittered away.

I braced myself. Misbehaving came at a cost, always. We had learned to be afraid of hands that grabbed, of feet that kicked.

There were rumors, too. Of starvation. Of dehydration. Of a dark and secret place where disobedient children were sent.

On the other side of the door, Émile's voice rose.

"Come in."

He sounded calm, as if he'd been expecting me.

I pushed the door open.

To a child's eyes, Émile's office was enormous. There was a desk. A bookshelf to house his writings, as tall as three kids standing on one another's shoulders. A globe on a console.

At the center of it all, Émile. His eyes, a grayish blue, glinting behind reading glasses. He gestured to one of the two chairs in front of his desk.

"Sit."

I sat.

"Do you know why you're here?"

I shook my head.

"I'm going to ask you a question," he said. "I want you to answer it in the way that feels the most truthful to you."

Truth was a concept he spoke of often. Émile was big on looking inward, on not lying to yourself about who you were.

"This is a test," he said. "Everyone here has taken it. Your answer will tell us a lot about you as a person."

Émile got up from behind his desk. He seemed ancient to me. It would be a shock when, years later, the papers printed his age. He was in his late thirties on the day of this test, in his late forties when the world ended.

The question was insultingly simple. I realized, much later, that he had borrowed it from the most mundane setting imaginable.

In hindsight, it was clear he'd heard it on a plane.

We didn't know, then. We didn't fly. Émile did. Not frequently, but he had to. He was an important man. He went to meet dignitaries, people with their fingers on the pulse of the world.

(Well, that's what he said. When everything came out, we learned that Émile was usually visiting family. Not in his native France—for a variety of reasons, Émile couldn't cross international borders—but in Florida, where he had an uncle and a few cousins. Improbably, he did meet the prime minister of Canada, at the very northern tip of the state of New York, once. He kept a framed photo on his desk of the two of them shaking hands. Later on, it made all the papers.)

"Chicken or fish?"

The question made no sense to a child of Émile's world. We didn't eat animals. They were poison, Émile said. His was a world of plants, beans, pulses. The mothers cooked together, in large batches. Stews were easy to share, one large pot and a ladle. In the mornings, oatmeal, steel-cut, gritty against the roofs of our mouths.

Émile must have sensed the need for visual aids. He switched on a small television against the back wall and fed it a black VHS tape.

"Chicken," he pronounced.

Images flashed up on the screen. Pillowy hunks of white meat, drizzled with brown gravy. A platter of darker cuts, a family joining hands around the table. Smaller pieces, rolled in breadcrumbs, then plunged into hot oil until they emerged, hardened and—Émile adjusted the volume on the television—crispy.

There was incomplete dialogue, a cacophony of music that started and stopped haphazardly. The videos must have been spliced together from TV ads, some of them from series or movies. I didn't realize any of that at the time. All I knew was that I was hungry.

I stood there, stomach roiling, my mouth filling with saliva. "Or fish?"

More delights—baked underneath a golden crust, grilled on hot stones and served with dripping tomatoes. Tender pink slabs fanning out under a tilted fork. Chunks of white flesh in paper-thin batter, stacked against French fries in a paper cone.

A whole world out there—of treasures, of appetites.

Chicken or fish?

It was the most important question of my short life, and I had no idea how to answer it.

Émile weeded out bad people. They were plucked from our lives and disappeared forever. We had no idea what happened to them. In this black hole of knowledge lived every imaginable nightmare.

Émile tapped his foot.

I had to say something. Anything.

"Chicken?"

Émile's eyes flashed. He inhaled.

The exhale was a sigh.

Émile ejected the VHS tape, inserted another one into the VCR.

"These," he said, "are the consequences of your choice."

The new tape did not make sense, either. Chicks on a conveyor belt did not make sense. It was not a thing nature would let happen. Hands, gloved in plastic, shot into the frame, grabbing at the chicks like boiled tomatoes to be squished into sauce. Unbearable sights: chicks fed to a metallic machine, trapped between its jaws. Soft little lives ending in a splatter of blood.

There were chickens on the compound. We didn't eat them—just their eggs, taken as respectfully as possible, our hands wrapped delicately around the shells, careful not to break them, grateful for our bounty.

My heart raced. The massacred chicks were anathema to Émile. Anyone associated with such evil had no place in his world.

Émile switched off the television. We sat in silence for what must have been a full minute.

"What do you think I should do?" he said finally.

Another impossible question. Only Émile knew what anyone should do.

"I'm sorry."

Émile sat back behind his desk and crossed his hands over his abdomen.

"You say you're sorry. Do you know how you can show it?"

No more words. Only my hopeful gaze rising to almost meet his. Only my heart, open, should he want to help himself to it.

"Remember this. Remember the consequences of your actions. Remember that you have this force inside you, and you do not know how to wield it."

I nodded.

Émile leaned over the desk.

"That's why you must listen. Learn. Remember you do not know anything. You need to be guided. If you listen, you have a chance."

I nodded some more, twisting my fingers, palms rising, prayerlike. But no. Émile did not want to be worshipped. He didn't want anyone to call him a guru or a savant.

With a flick of his wrist, he dismissed me.

"You can go now."

The door to his office shut behind me with barely a sound.

What I didn't know, what I wouldn't learn until much later: There was another tape for fish. That one was a mix of big-game and deep-water fishing—hundreds of creatures caught in nets, thrashing, eyes swelling and stomachs popping out of their mouths as they were brought to the surface too fast, the change of pressure too great to survive. Bigger animals with hooks puncturing their mouths. Majestic predators reduced to nothing by the folly of men.

The question was *Chicken or fish?* The only correct answer was *Neither.*

Why had no one warned me?

Everyone took the test, according to Émile—yet no one

talked about it. I'd never heard a word of caution, not a whisper, not a rumor.

Of course.

Everyone took the test, and everyone failed it.

And so we stayed quiet. Every last one of us.

Émile didn't have to ask us not to tell. He didn't need to rely on our loyalty.

Shame kept us silent all on its own.

I certainly didn't feel like telling anyone about my experience.

Later, after everything unraveled, people kept asking the same question. *How did he look so legit to so many people for so long?*

They didn't understand. For the kids, it started when we were eight. The lesson of the test settled around our shoulders like chain mail: There were hurricanes within us, devastation in our bodies. Without Émile to teach us, to save us from ourselves, we would destroy it all. Our dark hearts would end the world.

When Gabriel moved to Seattle—after the disappearance and the body and the police interrogations—we were so good at keeping in touch. We emailed every other day; I visited him in person three times a year. Sometimes we traveled. We met up in Yosemite, in Portland, even in Vancouver. But time does its thing. Our emails got shorter, lighter on the details. Soon, they landed just once a month. In-person visits faded from our calendars. We saw each other twice a year, then only at Christmas, and then—*how did that happen?*—pretty much never.

But then, the documentary. The producers were planning something for the tenth anniversary of Annie's death. I forwarded their message to Gabriel a month ago.

FROM: fridanilsen126@gmail.com
TO: millerg61290@gmail.com
*Did you get this one?*

FROM: millerg61290@gmail.com
TO: fridanilsen126@gmail.com
*Yep.*

I expected a sarcastic comment next, or at least an acknowledgment that he'd trashed the email. But then:

FROM: millerg61290@gmail.com
TO: fridanilsen126@gmail.com
*I think I'm going to do it.*

FROM: fridanilsen126@gmail.com
TO: millerg61290@gmail.com
*Really??*

We never do the documentaries. But Gabriel, apparently, was ready for a change.

FROM: millerg61290@gmail.com
TO: fridanilsen126@gmail.com
*It's been almost nine years. Everyone has said their piece but me.*

FROM: millerg61290@gmail.com
TO: fridanilsen126@gmail.com
*I'm ready. I think.*

FROM: millerg61290@gmail.com
TO: fridanilsen126@gmail.com
*There are things I need to say.*

FROM: fridanilsen126@gmail.com
TO: millerg61290@gmail.com
*If you do it, I'll do it, too.*

That was always our dynamic, *You jump, I jump.*
By then, we hadn't seen each other in five years.

FROM: fridanilsen126@gmail.com
TO: millerg61290@gmail.com
*I'd like to see you. Before the shoot. I think it'd be nice to speak without cameras around.*

That was hard to type: *I'd like to see you.* Gabriel was the one who'd moved away. He was the one who'd stopped writing. But I had to try.

It stunned me that he wanted to do the documentary. Gabriel relocated two thousand miles from home for a chance at anonymity. Even then, he could never fully evade scrutiny. And now he was ready to show himself to the world again?

Not just that—he had *things . . . to say?*

What things?

I needed to talk to him. In person, and freely. Not over the phone or by email. Not in any way that could be traced.

Gabriel came. He boarded the flight out of Seattle while I traveled from New York. We met at the municipal airport. He materialized almost too easily. One second, I hadn't seen him in half a decade, and the next, there he was: tall, mismatched eyes, one brown, one blue, his hands solid around mine.

Sure, some things have changed. It's been five years. His hair is a slightly darker shade of blond. There are new lines on his forehead. He even got a tattoo, his birth year—which is also mine—etched in small Roman numerals on the inside of his left wrist.

This is what time does. It warps people, turns them into half strangers.

---

The first rays of daylight frame our blackout curtains. Outside, the mountains will be turning a glowing shade of amber. Critters will skitter back to their hiding spaces. Catalina warned us on our first day: "At night, you might see a coyote." This is the desert: one world in the dark, a different one in the daytime.

For a moment, I can bring myself to believe in *today.*

*Today,* I will talk to Sabrina Brenner.

*Today,* small acts of kindness will yield impossible results.

I feel it before I hear it.

It's all around us, a vibration in the ground. In a few seconds, it will shake birds out of tree branches, pull hotel guests from their beds, quicken their heartbeats, sharpen their senses.

This *thing.*

This sound.

This scream, fevered and high-pitched, like a hammer to the desert's dome of sacred silence.

THE FIFTH DAY

Gabriel sits up with a panicked inhale.

"What was that?" he whispers, his voice brittle with sleep.

Before I can answer, he leaps out of bed. I struggle to a standing position, my legs numb from my night on the floor.

Gabriel is holding the bedside lamp from his nightstand. He raises it, fingers clutching its iron base, ready to strike—what? Whom?

"Put that down," I say.

Outside the suite, hurried footsteps approach, then fade away. I reach for the door handle.

"Wait!"

Gabriel holds me back with a hand on my arm.

"We have no idea what's going on out there," he says.

But I do.

The images are right here in my head.

"Come on," I say.

Before he can protest again, I unlock the door.

*Fuck fuck fuck fuck fuck.*

I know where to go.

Three hotel employees have already gathered at the spot. Two standing, one on her knees.

We stand at the border between two worlds, where the hotel fades into the desert. Just a few feet from where the Brenners argued last night.

The three hotel employees are looking downward.

Gabriel moves closer. I move with him. I don't want to look, but I have to. I don't get to skip this part.

Sabrina Brenner lies on the ground.

Her body in the shape of a lightning bolt. Her head like Pandora's box, her skull its cracked lid. Blood—so much blood—on the Ara's precious sandstone.

My knees give.

Gabriel clasps my arm and steadies me.

More guests rush over in pajamas, robes, baggy sweaters. They gather in a half circle, faces puffy with sleep, eyelids crinkling in the morning sun. Mouths drop open. Faces turn away from the scene.

One of the standing hotel employees—whom I now recognize as Catalina—leans over her kneeling colleague. The one who evidently found the body, whose scream tore us from our suites. Catalina wraps her arms around the other woman's shoulders and holds her tight.

"Stand back, please!"

Two EMTs burst through the crowd, boots clattering on the tiled path. The guests shift to let them approach. One kneels by Sabrina. The other lifts a radio to his lips: "Unit one-three-four to base. We need paramedics and law enforcement."

"Let me through."

*That voice.*

William Brenner nudges his way to the paramedics. His bathrobe, half-tied, reveals an expanse of pale stomach. This man we have only known to dress carefully, who wore a suit to dinner and kept a polo shirt on even by the pool. Now he's exposed: his white chest hair, his skin dappled with liver spots, his torso already glistening in the morning heat. His legs poking out of a pair of faded blue boxer shorts.

William looks at Sabrina and doubles over.

"My wife," he says with the breathy, disbelieving start of a heaving sob. "My wife," he repeats, this time through tears. "Oh, god," he implores. "My love. My sweet, sweet love." He brings his hands to his head. His shoulders quiver as he takes deep, gulping breaths. "My poor sweetheart."

He falls to his knees. His hands reach for her.

"Sir, please stand back for now," the kneeling EMT says. She's young, moving with a focused competence, pressing two fingers to Sabrina's neck.

"Don't tell me what to do," William cries, and grabs his wife's hand.

The EMT glances up at her male colleague. Softly, he approaches William, sets a hand on his robed shoulder.

"Sir, please," he says. "You have to let us work. It's better for—"

"I said," William snarls, "do not tell me what to do."

He extends an arm, and the young man tumbles back. For a few suspended seconds, no one moves or speaks.

William's sobs resume, his torso quaking.

I feel the small crowd shifting to my left.

Gabriel.

He's stepping forward, his gaze fixed on Sabrina's body. His arms dangle at his sides.

"Hey," I whisper.

With the disembodied movements of a sleepwalker, Gabriel lowers himself to the ground.

William lifts his head. When his eyes land on Gabriel, his face contorts in anger.

"What the fuck do you want?"

Gabriel doesn't move.

"You," William says as he stands up. "What's your problem? Why are you looking at her like that?"

He stomps toward Gabriel.

"Get up," I say, raising my voice this time. I pull Gabriel to his feet.

Something seems to switch back on in my brother's head. He blinks, looks at William as if seeing him for the first time, and takes a step back.

"I'm sorry," he says. "I wasn't trying to—"

William isn't listening. He brings his face half an inch from Gabriel's, grabs fistfuls of my brother's T-shirt.

"That's my wife," William says.

Gabriel squeezes his eyes shut. His hands raise, useless against William's rage. An image straight from our childhood: my brother in trouble, bracing himself for a strike, a mother's hand clasped around his wrist.

"That's my dead wife," William continues. He's screaming now, his face a deepening shade of scarlet. "You like looking at her like that?" With each word, William gives my brother a shake. "You get off on it, you sick pervert?"

*He was in shock*, people will say later. *He didn't know what he was saying.*

I insert my body between William and Gabriel.

"Leave him alone."

I reach for William's fists, try to unclench them from Gabriel's T-shirt. William shoves me back. He's strong, his strike precise and painful against my collarbones. I grab on to his robe, which threatens to come undone.

"Stop," someone says faintly.

William searches for the speaker, then returns his gaze to me.

"Stay out of this, you cunt."

I open my mouth to yell—what? Before I can decide, Gabriel cuts in: "All right."

With a burst of strength, he wrestles out of William's grasp. He takes a few steps back, palm out in front of him, creating space between William and the two of us.

"I'm sorry," Gabriel says, slightly out of breath. "I didn't mean to offend you. I'm sorry."

He smooths the front of his T-shirt. William considers him, seemingly confused, like it has never occurred to him to back down from a fight.

"Don't apologize to him," I say. "He attacked—"

"It's okay," Gabriel cuts me off. "I was in the wrong. I'm sorry. I'm very sorry."

My brother looks at the crowd. "I apologize, everyone. I didn't mean to start anything."

I shake my head.

Gabriel wraps an arm around my shoulders and directs me away from the scene.

"It's fine," he mutters, but I can feel him folding into himself. His hand shakes above my arm; his heart pounds against my ribs.

Gabriel keeps walking. Soon, he's no longer guiding my steps, but holding on to me for support.

I place an arm around his back.

Something travels between us. Memories pulsing with anxiety, a dark hole that nearly swallowed Gabriel's life almost a decade ago. What happens to husbands when their wives are found dead.

THE FIFTH DAY

Most people are handed one true-crime story, at most. Gabriel got two.

First, there was Émile. Then, there was Annie.

Gabriel was twenty-one when they met. Their romance unfolded rapidly, like a montage in a Hollywood movie: dates, drinks, dinners. After six months of dating, a ring. A house in New Jersey.

It was fast, but their love was in a hurry. Maybe they could sense they didn't have much time.

After just two years of marriage, Gabriel returned one evening to an empty home. He waited. Tried to get in touch with Annie. Nothing. Gabriel dialed 911 and reported his wife missing. Then he called me. By the time I arrived, police had taken over the house and told him to wait outside while they searched it. They took Gabriel to the police station for an interview.

Two weeks later, they found Annie's body in the water, a few miles from a waterfall on one of her favorite running trails.

Gabriel spoke to the cops two more times in the following month. They let him go. All three times, they let him go. Gabriel was never charged.

But people couldn't move on. The headlines blared for months. It didn't help that the police declined to name a new suspect, or to charge anyone at all. The focus was forever on Gabriel. There wasn't a cable news channel or newspaper that didn't pick up the story. Annie's murder was, in their telling, a domestic tragedy that belonged to the nation. "Anonymous sources" were happy, even eager, to discuss the time they'd overheard an argument coming from Annie and Gabriel's house. Maybe someone crying. Maybe Annie complaining about their finances.

I did what I could. When people whispered, I raised my voice. When they shot Gabriel withering stares, I stared right back.

It wasn't enough. Gabriel went to unlock his car one morning and found the side mirrors smashed. Later that day, he went to park it and was greeted by furious letters across his garage door, *KILLER* spray-painted in dripping red cursive.

Who could have lived like that? Not Gabriel. He moved to the West Coast and started over in Seattle.

I understood the need to move. But *Seattle*—really? We'd never been there.

"Exactly," he said when I questioned his choice.

"What about Florida?" I asked. "What about Texas? Illinois?"

*What about anywhere that's not in the Tri-State Area but remains reasonably accessible to me?*

But he wouldn't budge. Gabriel was determined to put as much distance as he could between himself and the state of New Jersey.

And for what?

The case has stuck to him like a second skin. For nearly nine years now, a faction of the internet has feasted on it, coming up with flamboyant theories, filing requests for various documents.

I tried to hold on to him. In the end, I lost him in every possible way.

I won't let that happen again.

Gabriel cracks open a bottle of water from our minibar. After a couple of gulps, he hands it to me.

I could have my own. The minibar is complimentary. Anytime we step out, it refills as if by magic. But there are habits you can't rewrite. We didn't have enough to eat, for so many years. And so we live like this. We clear our plates. We rewrap half-eaten granola bars. We tilt back bags of chips over our faces and hoover up the last remaining crumbs. At home, on the rare occasion Charlie declines to eat his breakfast, I pour his kibble back into the bag.

I drink from the same bottle as my brother and return it to the minifridge.

Gabriel sits at the edge of his bed. I do the same thing on my side, facing him, and bury my face in my hands.

"I need to talk to the cops," I say through my cupped palms.

"What?"

He's looking at me.

"About what I saw last night," I say. "Sabrina and William. The police should know."

"Oh. Yes."

Something occurs to me. I look up from my hands.

"Hey. You didn't see them? The Brenners?"

Gabriel frowns.

"Last night," I say. "When I came back and you weren't here. You were outside, right? Did you hear them at all?"

Something in Gabriel dims, and I know what he's going to say next.

"Yeah," he says. "I heard . . . something. Parts of it. I could tell people were fighting." *But.* "I went in the opposite direction. Toward the lobby."

Gabriel stares at his feet. A pink flush creeps up his cheeks.

"I didn't want to get involved. I couldn't. I try to avoid confrontation." Gabriel runs a hand over the wrinkles in his T-shirt, where William Brenner's fists clenched. "Well, when I can."

I picture him: Gabriel, hazy with sleep, in sweatpants under the night sky. Voices rising from the darkness. His resolve fading. This is the Gabriel I know: always a little too scared to go it alone. Capable of big things, brave things, but only with someone at his side.

He looks up and bites the inside of his mouth. "I wish I'd paid more attention. Maybe I could have . . . I don't know."

His breath catches.

"We—" he starts. "Sabrina, we—"

His eyes glisten. He looks toward the window, away from me.

*Sabrina, we* what?

*Sabrina, we could have done something?*

*Sabrina, we could have saved her?*

Or does he mean "we," as in "Sabrina and I"?

I remember them interacting only once. It was on our first day at the hotel. Gabriel and I were walking from the pool to our suite. He bumped into Sabrina, or maybe she bumped into him. They stopped. They both apologized. There was no anger, no tension. In fact, they seemed friendly. I can still picture her, bringing her hand to the side of her head, brushing her hair clip with the tip of her fingers. How she traced the outline of the butterfly shape as she smiled at Gabriel, urging him not to apologize. *No, no it was me, I wasn't looking.*

Gabriel pinches the bridge of his nose.

"What do you think happened to her?" he asks.

I shrug.

"They fought. He pushed her. Or he attacked her with something."

We sit in silence.

Even I almost drank the Brenners' Kool-Aid, the first time I saw them together. That was before I recognized William, before I realized who they were. All I saw then was the image they were trying to project, like the opening sequence in a film: the roar of the car when William pulled up to the hotel, the kinetic energy that circulated through the crowd, drawing our eyes to the vehicle. It was an elegant model, a coupe, slightly sporty. How it glistened under the sun, red, a bold, bright quality that evoked the body of an electric guitar.

William in a white linen suit, handing the key to the valet.

Sabrina extracting herself from the passenger seat, eyes hidden behind emerald-green sunglasses, the lenses as black and opaque as a dormant movie-theater screen.

It took only a few hours of observing them for me to become less optimistic about their prospects. But a violent death? Really?

There is, of course, another possibility. It could have been an accident. Technically, it's possible.

But I know what I saw. Sabrina Brenner lying lifeless on her stomach, the back of her skull fractured open.

Gabriel massages his temples. Maybe he, too, is running through the list of possibilities, eliminating them one by one.

If what happened to Sabrina had been an accident—if she had fallen—then the injury would most likely be at the front of her head, or on whichever side she fell on. But either way, she would still have been resting on that side by the time someone found her.

Unless . . . there is yet another scenario. One where Sabrina falls, or bangs her head or something, and then moves. Could she have crawled a few feet to try to get help, and then lost consciousness?

*No.*

Why am I so sure?

There's something about the scene, an element my mind hasn't consciously processed yet.

*The blood.*

If Sabrina had moved after injuring herself, then there would have been blood all over. She would have brought her hands to the wound at some point. There would be handprints, or some sort of trail.

But there wasn't.

That, I'm sure of. When a woman shows up dead hours after you spied on her in the night, you pay attention.

Which leaves me with only one theory: She was attacked. Struck with some kind of heavy object, or shoved against a hard surface.

A tingle travels down my spine. The police will have arrived by now. Detectives, officers, whatever.

I stand.

"You're going right now?" Gabriel asks.

"I can't wait."

It's true. I can't.

Here's one thing I learned when everything happened with Gabriel and Annie: Once people hear one version of a story, it's almost impossible to rewrite it, even if that version turns out to be wrong. People knew Annie had had dinner and breakfast. They knew that when police found her body, her hyoid bone—a small bone found in the neck, at the base of the tongue—was broken, something that can happen as a result of strangulation. The story became: Gabriel woke up one morning, strangled his wife to death, and dumped her body in the water in a national park about eight miles from where they lived. By the time the police let Gabriel go—because they had nothing on him—it was too late. The narrative had taken root.

"I should change first," I say.

Gabriel glances at my polyester shorts. He teased me when I wore them on our first night here.

"Going to Satriale's?" he asked.

That was a reference to the mob show. I love the mob show. We laughed. For a second, everything was light, easy.

That was four days ago. In another life.

———

The soles of my sandals catch on the Ara's pathway. My ankle twists.

"Shit."

I right myself just before my palm hits the ground and I turn around.

There it is, the spot that made me trip. A thin crack, almost invisible, but enough to make me lose my balance. Like those memories that resurface at the most unexpected moments, that embarrassing thing you said six months ago grabbing you by the throat in the supermarket checkout line. Gabriel, almost nine years ago, sitting at the kitchen table in his empty house.

Annie was missing. In the period that followed her disappearance—and, eventually, the discovery of her body—I came by every day. In my memories, the lights are on only in whatever room Gabriel and I happen to be in. The rest of the world is in shadow.

"I'm sorry," I said, "that they're doing this to you."

He sighed.

By then, "they" didn't just mean the police. Neighbors had started crossing the street to avoid sharing a sidewalk with him. When we'd gone to get cash at the ATM, two women had exchanged knowing looks behind his back.

Gabriel didn't rebel against the police's efforts until after the third interview. Before that, he was open, cooperative.

"It's okay," he said. "They're right to be doing this."

He took a small sip of the chamomile tea I'd made, the only time he lifted the mug to his lips.

"They should be looking at me," he said, and put down his tea. "They always look at the husband."

His hand fluttered like he was searching the air around him for the right words. "I just hope . . ."

I waited for the rest.

Hope for what?

But that was it. My brother's wife was missing, and he found it in himself to *just hope*.

It seemed too passive, like Gabriel had become too familiar with tragedy. Like what had happened to Annie fell within the category of things he'd come to expect.

I hated that we spoke it so fluently, the language of violence, of crime. But it was what we'd been given to work with from birth.

## 7  *THE ONLY TOWN WE KNEW, HUDSON VALLEY*

—

Gabriel burst into my life with the wrong words.

It was almost two years after the test.

Émile was a busy man. He had books to write, seminars to teach. But every morning, he took time to address us.

This was called Assembly. Everyone had to attend, except for the mothers who were in charge of the current crop of babies. Assembly took place after breakfast, in what looked like a Gothic lecture hall but turned out to be, when I conjured up its image in my adult mind, an old, repurposed Catholic chapel.

Émile's world, which he insisted he had created for us, had, in fact, once been a boarding school. A small establishment, two hundred students at most. After the stock market crash of 1987, when enrollment and alumni donations dropped irreparably, the school's lender seized the buildings and the land. Émile, who had been in the U.S. for five years by then, lived nearby in Pough-keepsie. He ran what he called a start-up and what the govern-ment called a multilevel marketing company, selling computer equipment. He took over the school's lease and—well, I sup-pose one thing led to another.

By the time I was born in 1990, Émile had renounced com-puters and modernity as a concept, but kept the buildings. He had also, as it turned out, stopped paying rent, but he'd taken care to register his organization as a church—and after Waco happened, that made the optics of kicking us out almost trickier than the logistics.

And so, there it was. The paradise in which I was born. A heaven in which every morning began with a lecture.

One morning, before Émile started speaking, this boy settled one seat away from me, to my right. We'd barely ever spoken— nothing of significance, just the necessities of life in a commune. I didn't know him. We weren't friends. I'd only noticed him because of his eyes, one brown, one blue.

The brown one was on my side that day. Aside from that, all I could see of the boy was his silhouette, a blur of blond hair, and one of those patchy, hand-knit sweaters we all wore.

Between us was Edwina. Edwina: fourteen, strong, devout. A flame in her, the unflinching focus of a true believer. A wall of seriousness between me and this boy.

Émile stood at a lectern at the front of the room, talking about the importance of self-reflection. There were no robes or anything like that; Émile favored khakis and V-neck sweaters. The only sign that he was part of a better world was the braided bracelet on his left wrist. We all had one, the colors brighter and the band wider as our minds progressed. His was the brightest of all, sunflower yellow, broader than a watchband. Mine, like all the kids', was thin and a grimy white.

"You have to face the truth of what's inside you and act in consequence. It might not be comfortable," Émile said, peering over the top of his reading glasses, "but it is necessary. Other- wise, you're like a . . ."

I perked up. A what?

"A . . ."

Émile cleared his throat. He looked at his hands, probably wishing they were holding cue cards.

This was new. Émile's sentences never trailed off. He always knew what to say and how to say it.

Something moved to my right. The boy was fidgeting.

Behind the lectern, Émile was still hesitating. It felt wrong to stare at him in this situation, lost in the middle of a sentence. I lowered my head and slowly turned it to the side.

The boy sat, gaze down, lips pinched.

Just as I understood he was holding in a laugh, Émile spoke at last.

"If you don't look inward, you're like a chicken," he said, "running around without a head."

A chicken! Running around without a head!

It lit up something in our young minds.

The boy pressed a hand to his mouth. He let out a laugh—brief but full-throated, echoing across the room.

Émile, who had been in the middle of a new sentence ("So be intentional. Look at a person and ask yourself wheth—"), stopped. His head snapped up like he'd been slapped.

Laughing at Émile—what an obscene thought.

But the boy could not be tamed. He rested his hands on the back of the chair in front of him, shoulders quaking.

His laugh traveled to me. It started deep in my belly, worked its way up my throat. My brain sent out warnings: *Do not laugh do not laugh do not laugh, whatever you do, just please do not—*

I started with a giggle, close-mouthed, almost discreet. Then, a bright cackle. The seal was broken. My laugh freed itself and cascaded through the air.

To my right, the boy relinquished any pretense of fighting for his composure. For a few absurd moments, we encouraged each other.

It was hubris. It was bliss.

It was self-destruction.

The boy knew the risks as well as I did. My memories of this time in our lives are all superimposed with a layer of bruises, cuts, injuries at various stages of healing. Wounds that were so routine I stopped noticing them.

A hand clasped my arm and tugged me from my chair. There was a pop. A bright pain surged in my right shoulder. Somewhere off to the side, the boy was wrenched from his spot, too.

Émile stood behind his lectern. The sun caught in his blond curls. I swear there was a halo around him.

The hands dragged us across the schoolyard, past the dorms and the communal showers, to the cafeteria. We staggered to the back of the service area. A door opened. We tumbled into darkness.

Later, with adult eyes, I would see the Secret Place for what it was: a fucking broom closet. But to a child, it was a cave. We were pushed inside, and it sealed around us like a coffin.

We stood, backs to a wall. There was no light. No air.

Just us.

We felt around. A hand brushed against my nose. The boy, already, was all limbs.

"Sorry," he said.

"It's okay."

In the dark, a hand grabbed mine. Wrong side. I squeaked.

"Sorry," the boy said again. "Did I hurt you?"

"It's not you. It's my arm. Something's . . . wrong with it."

He tried my other hand.

"This one's fine."

We searched for a resting position. You couldn't sit in the Secret Place. There was no room. All you could do was crouch and feel your muscles pulling at your bones, your joints calcifying into place.

My shoulder pulsed. The pain was so bad I was shaking. When I tried to move my arm, it didn't respond.

"I'm Frida," I said through chattering teeth.

"Gabriel," the boy said.

I nodded, then realized he couldn't see me.

"Did he choose it?"

No need to specify who "he" was.

"Yep," the boy muttered.

This wasn't a surprise. It meant that the boy, like me—like all the kids I knew—had been born here. Only adults without children ever seemed to join. It was like it was too late for the others—once you'd built yourself a life with a house and a job and all those things people thought they needed, there was no more room left in your heart for Émile.

"First time?" the boy asked.

He meant first time here, in the Secret Place.

"Yeah," I said. "You?"

"Same."

The door opened.

"Please," I said. "My arm—"

"I don't want to hear it," a mother said.

She thrust a hand inside the Secret Place. Something wet hit me, sending a fresh wave of pain down my right side. I grabbed my shoulder with a yelp and regretted it immediately.

"What the—"

The flashlight revealed the scene: two cups and a puddle of water on the floor.

"Look what you did!" the mother yelled.

She let out a sigh and shook her head, the flashlight casting shadows over her face.

"Seems like you need more time to reflect," she said. Her tone was calmer then, almost sweet. "I'll give you two some space."

The light moved, hitting me in the eyes. "And you," the mother said. "You're in pain? Look inward. You caused this. You did this to yourself."

Before we could try to apologize or beg for more water, the door slammed shut.

We waited for the mother's footsteps to fade away. Then, with my intact arm, I pushed against the door. Gabriel helped, presumably with both hands. When that didn't work, we felt the four walls around us, looking for—what?

A window. A hole we could widen. A spoon to dig a tunnel. Anything.

The urge to scream rose in my throat, and, I assumed, in Gabriel's.

But we didn't scream.

Help wasn't coming. We knew that.

Gabriel and I bent toward each other.

"I'm sorry," I whispered.

"Not your fault."

We waited. And waited. And waited.

Time was lost to me.

Finally, my arm went numb.

My ears buzzed. My skin was sticky, the inside of my mouth woolly.

And yet.

After a while, I did not hate it.

Being there, with this boy.

The darkness was ours. It was, in its own way, welcome. For the first time in ten years—a lifetime of too many words, of speeches, of rules, of Émile overexplaining everything to us, of mouths opening in castigation, of lips buzzing with sermons—words were not needed.

Gabriel's rib cage shook against mine. Was he crying?

No.

Laughing again.

"Sorry," he said, but he wasn't. "It's just—"

"The chicken?"

He couldn't reply, but I felt the prickle of his hair on my shoulder as he nodded.

Incredible. I laughed, too. Not at the chicken thing. I was over that. But at this boy. This *boy*. In the darkness of the Secret Place, in this temple of fear, this boy found it in himself to laugh.

There was something unknown there. A lightness, a defiance. A part of himself he hadn't surrendered to anyone. Something I needed in my life.

We waited some more.

In my head, I recited incantations. I sang silent songs. I repeated them over and over and over, until the words stopped making sense.

There was a groan. I didn't understand immediately that the door was finally opening, that our time in the Secret Place was over.

The mother stood there. She was waiting for us to scamper.

We didn't move.

"Come on, stupid kids."

Nothing.

The mother had to pry us apart before she could pull us out.

It was a severance. The brutal white light of childbirth, the two of us torn from a womb.

Finally, our backs straightened, the knots in our muscles unfurled. My right arm hung limply at my side.

The boy's gaze met mine. For the first time that day, I saw him clearly: Taller than I was, already, by three inches. Long limbs. Freckles on his nose. One eye like the sky, the other like a rain puddle.

We walked back to the classrooms together, realized they were empty, and made our way to the cafeteria. I tried to pick up a tray, but it was impossible with only one arm.

"Got you," Gabriel said, and he carried my tray for me.

We sat down. He gulped down the day's stew (root vegetables) in frantic, greedy spoonfuls. I was hungry; he was starving. I reached across the table and placed my piece of bread by his bowl.

In the outside world, later, I'd say "brother," he'd say "sister." But we hadn't been taught to think that way. We hadn't grown up with the words of family, of infatuation, of marriage, of reproduction.

In Émile's world, we were just us. Something that mattered more than any of the concepts that tied our universe together. Brighter than everything else.

## 8 ESCALANTE, UTAH

### THE FIFTH DAY

I do not want to see Sabrina Brenner's body again.

But I owe her at least that much.

When I get back to the edge of the compound, the hotel guests are gone. Three new figures have materialized, wearing the same uniform: khakis, long-sleeved shirts, and ties, badges gleaming above their left breast pockets, weapons hanging at their waists.

One is crouched next to Sabrina's body, looking up every ten seconds or so at her colleague, who jots down notes. The third is holding a roll of yellow crime scene tape.

After the police found Annie's body, they spoke to me, too. Just once. They wanted to know about Gabriel, his marriage. It was a brief conversation. There had been a condescension about it, a hint of *What would you know?* I was an unmarried, childless woman. What could I understand of marriage, of domesticity, of *family*?

Still, that interview taught me the basics: With the police, say only what you need to say. If the question is *Do you have the time*, then the answer is *Yes* or *No*, not *Ten-thirty*.

The policeman with the crime scene tape—young, brown hair, and the squint of someone who wishes he'd remembered his sunglasses—wraps one end of the roll around a nearby tree, then unfurls it toward one of the large lanterns that line the Ara's pathways.

"Excuse me, Officer?"

The young cop turns around.

"Deputy," he says. Then, in a weary voice: "Only deputies out here."

*Right.*

I watched a documentary, once—a missing wife and their two children, a husband who may or may not have killed them. It happened in a small town in Arizona, not too far from here.

"They could have caught him," the missing wife's sister told someone off camera. But the local police force did too little, and what little they did, they didn't do fast enough. The husband vanished. "For all we know, he's living the good life in Brazil or something," the sister said, rolling her eyes.

This world of small-town crime, of sheriff's offices stretched too thin, of deputies moonlighting as prison guards—it was new to me. The cases in my own life were big enough, one handled by the feds, the other by a robust police department. Which doesn't mean that everything went swimmingly. Obviously. Annie's murder was never solved. As for Émile, well. It was—still is—complicated.

"Could I speak to you?" I ask the young deputy.

He raises an eyebrow.

"We're still working on the scene," he says. "Stand by. We'll get to you."

"It's important."

The deputy looks over his shoulder at his colleagues, who are still busy examining Sabrina's body. Does he feel excluded? Those two doing important police work, and this guy over here on tape duty. What will he tell his partner, his friends, his mom, when he comes home tonight? *Someone died and I took care of the tape?*

"Go ahead," he says.

Something moves behind him. One of the two deputies is leaning over Sabrina's body.

I'm nauseous.

"Actually, could we speak somewhere else?"

The cop opens his mouth.

"Please," I say, "Deputy . . ."

"Harris," he says. "Fine."

He lifts the crime scene tape and steps over to my side. With a wave of his hand, he leads me to the entrance lounge. An expanse of sandstone dotted with cream-colored benches, on top of which employees have fluffed embroidered pillows in earth tones. Linen drapes separate the space from the lobby. Sail canopies, tented above us, shield us from the sun.

"So," Harris says, wiping his forehead. "What did you want to tell me?"

"Last night," I say. "Sabrina Brenner and her husband had a fight."

I establish the basics, the where and when, the *around three in the morning* and *at the edge of the compound* of it all.

"I saw them," I say. "He grabbed her, and—"

"You were following them?" Harris asks.

"No. Or . . . I guess I was. I couldn't sleep, so I was up. I heard voices. I wanted to know what was going on."

"Continue."

"It wasn't just an argument," I say. "It got physical. William grabbed Sabrina's wrists. And he insulted her. Called her a whore."

Harris stands there, one hand in his pocket, the other scratching the back of his neck.

"So you heard them having a dispute," he says.

"Saw. I saw it happen."

This time, he removes a notepad from his pocket and scribbles a few words.

"You witnessed an argument," Harris says. "Did you see anything else? Did Mr. Brenner strike his wife? Did things get physical beyond him grabbing her arm?"

"Wrists."

Harris nods.

"I went back to my suite," I say. "But there's something else."

"You witnessed something else?"

I shake my head.

"Just . . . little things. They always looked tense. You could tell she was on edge around him."

"How so?"

"It was a . . ."

*A feeling I had?*

"A collection of details," I say, and wince internally. *A collection of details.* That'll look nice on the police report.

Harris scribbles some more.

"Okay," he says. "I'll let my colleagues know."

It's not enough, but it's all I have.

I thank the deputy for his time and head back to our suite. As I'm about to press my key card to the reader, my phone dings.

It's a text from Gabriel.

*There's food in the dining room. Where are you?*

I'm not hungry, but Gabriel needs to eat. It's the whole migraine thing: He should eat regularly, sleep enough, not work too hard. Which is hilarious, because for most of our lives, all three of those were complete impossibilities.

As long as my phone's out, I check on my dog: He's at one of those fancy doggy day cares right now, the kind that sends you updates every day and lets you watch a live feed of your pet. Its app informs me that Charlie is "doing very well" and has "eaten most of his food."

I text Gabriel back: *Be right there.*

———

The Ara's lobby was designed for relaxation. You can tell someone looked at the space and thought, *This is where people will go to chill.* It's furnished with custom-built banquettes and plump ottomans. At the center of the room is an enormous vase filled with dried flowers ("globe amaranths," per Catalina), fluffy white puffs raised to the ceiling. For the duration of our stay, a gas fireplace has burned at the back of the room, oblivious to the desert and its heat.

Today, the peace has been disrupted. Guests are milling all

around. There's the youngish couple and their two kids. Next to them, the divorcée who was having words with her lawyer over the phone the other day. A few feet from them, an actor I recognize from the most recent season of *Law & Order: SVU*.

The divorcée is scribbling on a piece of hotel stationery. The actor scrolls on his device. The couple is in a tense conversation. I catch snippets: "flights," "stay," "worried about nothing."

There are things people can't say. Things they must all be thinking.

*This was not a cheap trip.*

*We won't be able to get a refund now. Not unless the hotel kicks us out.*

*We don't even know what happened.*

*Would it really be so bad, staying?*

———

Gabriel waves me over to a table in the dining room. He has changed into shorts and a fresh T-shirt. At a nearby table sit the three young women I've seen throughout our stay posing for various photos, Instagram tiles come to life, one leg forward, the other back, or crouching by the pool, tongue out. A seemingly endless parade of outfits, neon shorts, matching sets in stretchy fabrics, crocheted halter tops.

Now the three influencers are human again, swallowed by cotton hoodies in neutral tones. Flamingos painted gray.

Gabriel slides a plate toward me. "I grabbed you some stuff," he says. A hard-boiled egg, a banana. "But go see what's left, too."

At the front of the room, someone has unfolded a table and covered it with a tablecloth that doesn't quite match its contours. There are coffee and hot-water dispensers, tea bags, sliced bread, containers of yogurt on a bowl of ice.

This isn't how the hotel does breakfast. There is—usually—no *buffet* at the Ara. Until today, we've sat and studied the same set menu every morning. In the soft, dimmed glow of the dining room, we've sampled the American, the Continental, the Wellness. Silky scrambled eggs, delicate croissants, artful muesli parfaits with slices of melon fanned out on the side.

It sat so unnaturally with me. Luxury, always unnecessary, forever unearned.

At the buffet, people are lining up, reaching around one another in search of sugar and jelly. Their voices are hushed, their gestures nervous. A vision from the world Gabriel and I left behind: kids lined up inside a cafeteria, a meager bread pile, a self-styled prophet sipping coffee at the back of the room.

I return to our table.

"Nothing?" Gabriel asks.

I shake my head.

"Not hungry."

He plucks a pastry from his plate—a small Danish with a red puddle of jam at its center—and deposits it on a napkin in front of me, along with an unopened container of yogurt.

"In case you get hungry later," he says. "Not sure when we'll next get the chance."

"It's okay. I really don't think I'll—"

I'm interrupted by a yelp. Somewhere at the back of the dining room, furniture clatters against the floor.

"Get off me!"

Guests look up from their tables. Our gazes follow the sound to its origin: the lobby.

More outraged exclamations make their way across the room like storm clouds: "I have rights!" and "I want to speak to my attorney!" Each word more strained than the last.

I spring up from my chair. Gabriel does, too. We're not the only ones. The influencers rush to the lobby. Around us, a constellation of semi-strangers: the *SVU* actor, the divorcée, and behind those two, Lazlo and Fabio, who are staying three suites away from us and flew in from Miami.

We reach a collective halt.

"You have the right to remain silent. Anything you say can and will be used against you . . ."

At the center of the lobby, William Brenner struggles against Deputy Harris, both wrists pinned to his back. Harris unhooks a pair of handcuffs from his waist. They zip shut.

"This is ridiculous!"

"You have the right to an attorney," Harris continues. His colleagues hover next to him, their earlier dynamic reversed: Harris is at the center of the action now, and they are the supporting cast. "If you cannot afford an attorney . . ."

The suggestion that William can't afford his own lawyer is required by law, but laughable. *Of course* he can afford his own attorney. He probably has him on speed dial.

How many domestic violence complaints has he made disappear?

How many payments, how much hush money, how many women silenced by a check?

This rich man. This violent husband.

William squeals and protests and strains against the handcuffs. Harris, unflappable now, steers him toward the door to the lobby.

On the threshold, William turns and looks right at me. I swear he does.

Or maybe it's happening inside my head. Maybe I can't believe he'd go down like this, William Brenner, without one last jab.

## 9 *THE ONLY TOWN WE KNEW, HUDSON VALLEY*

EIGHTEEN YEARS AGO

Gabriel and I pawed blindly at what it meant, the possibility of the two of us.

All we knew, in the beginning, was that it felt good. Good to have a someone.

Good to make a common decision: *You take the top bunk, I'll take the bottom one.* Good to trade whispers in the dark. Good to find out we were the same age. His birthday was June 12, mine December 6. We loved our intertwined numbers, his 6/12 to my 12/6. It seemed like a sign. Of what?

We couldn't wait to find out.

Here's how life worked, in Émile's world: You were born. Children were cared for collectively by the women. You never belonged to your mother, or to your father. Émile demanded total detachment. "The family unit is a source of great corruption" was one of his refrains. "Rejecting it is the best thing you can do, not only for yourself, but for the children." *The* children. Not *your* children.

Ideally, your parents did such a good job (in Émile's eyes) that you never found out who they were. Some (mine, and, as it turned out, Gabriel's) managed it. It's amazing, the cruelty you can coax out of people if you convince them they're doing the right thing.

Some of the other parents—well, they always seemed to hover over a particular child, or group of children. So there were rumors. Physical resemblances, too. Early in the life of the cult, before I was born, some parents apparently hadn't been able to play by the rules, so Émile had sent them away.

That had done the trick. Your mother, however yearned for, feared, or resented, was forced into a corner of your mind. And your father—well, the fathers didn't matter. Only one man mattered: Émile.

From three to eighteen, you learned Émile's philosophies, some history, grammar, math, and some science. Survival skills: how to plant vegetables, how to light and put out fires, how to tie a tourniquet. From six to eighteen, you had chores on top of classes. Cleaning, gardening, meal preparation, clerical tasks.

The goal was self-sufficiency. To never have to rely on the outside world.

Before you knew it, you were eighteen.

You were expected to keep working on behalf of Émile: caring for the facilities if you were a man, for the children if you were a woman. Vetting and evangelizing new recruits. Selling Émile's books and—once they became a thing—his online seminars. Even as an adult, you had to keep taking classes. If you were successful, you'd start teaching them, too, first to kids, and then to other adults.

We never left. That was the most important rule. Émile had gifted us a perfect world. It would provide everything we would ever need, if only we allowed ourselves to be molded by it.

Émile had a car—an old, perpetually muddy 4x4 when I was a kid, and later, a shiny sedan he said ran on electricity—but he never took anyone on his drives. He could be trusted with the outside world; we couldn't.

And that was it. That was your life.

You wanted it.

Worse: Like every cherished thing, you were afraid to lose it.

Gabriel and I sat together at meals and during class. (Never at Assembly. No one had to tell us; we knew.) We made up little games, the rules too childish, too embarrassing, to explain to other kids, but between us, there was no shame. We coached each other through chores. We made up chore-specific songs. Within weeks, we had a window-washing song. A cleaning-the-cafeteria song. A sorting-through-paperwork song.

A year passed, then two, then five. Gabriel towered over me. For a while, he was horrifyingly skinny, and then he filled out again. Me, I stopped growing at five feet five. I was slight, but tough, my body making muscle out of our meager meals.

On the day I turned fifteen, Gabriel brought me a little *F* carved out of wood.

"From woodworking," he said.

I turned it over in my hand. The shape was blunt—the bottom bar tilted at an odd angle—but it was the first birthday present I'd ever received.

"Thank you."

By which I meant: *This means the world to me.*

One evening, Gabriel and I stood in an empty classroom, sorting pamphlets into stacks.

"Simon was talking yesterday," Gabriel said.

He meant in the boys' dorm. From fourteen to twenty, boys and girls slept in separate quarters. The only part of Émile's world that wasn't coed.

It was unlike him, this concern with propriety. But we didn't question it too much. Émile had his ways.

"What was Simon saying?" I asked.

Gabriel knocked a stack of pamphlets against the table to smooth its edges.

"That he and a couple of other guys went outside."

"Outside? Like sneaking out of the dorm?"

This happened on my side, too. Girls waited for the rest of the compound to fall asleep. There was the pitter-patter of their bare feet on the dusty tile, the swoosh of the sheets they wrapped around their shoulders. If you pressed your face against a window, you'd see them, clandestine ghosts glowing against the night sky.

I never joined. Once I was in bed, I liked to stay there.

"No," Gabriel said. "Outside-outside."

The elastic band I was wrapping around a pile of pamphlets snapped against my fingers. I ignored the pain and stretched it back into place.

"What do you mean," I said, eyes still on the rubber band, "'outside-outside'?"

Gabriel put down his stack. He placed a hand on my pamphlets and left it there until I looked up.

"I mean," he whispered, "outside. Of here."

*Here we go*, I thought.

Gabriel and I craved the same things, always.

Well. We had until that point.

But this time I would have to say no. I would have to tear myself away from him.

I couldn't imagine tearing myself away from him.

"Cool," I said.

I picked up an empty cardboard box. Gabriel snatched it from my hands.

"Hey!"

"Just listen to me."

Gabriel liked to flirt with the idea of mischief, but he'd never taken it past the talking stage. *Imagine grabbing two pieces of bread instead of one. Imagine getting up during Assembly and just leaving. Imagine a mother tells you to clean all the windows and you just say no. Imagine just saying no. Imagine, imagine, imagine.*

It seemed to excite him, this flicker of rebellion trapped in his obedient body. The memory of the day he had laughed at Assembly like a flash of something else, a glimpse into a new world he couldn't bring himself to explore.

I tried to reason with him: "We shouldn't—"

"Let me talk."

A mother appeared in the doorway.

"What's all this chatter in here?"

I took the box back from Gabriel and placed it on the table with the requisite reverence. "Sorry," I said.

The mother—nameless, beige clothing, hair in a bun—glared at us for a couple of seconds.

"I'd better not hear anything else," she said.

I nodded vigorously.

The mother walked away.

Once the sound of her steps had retreated into the distance, Gabriel pulled me to a corner of the room.

"Come here."

More pamphlets were waiting. They needed to be unwrapped and checked for typos, one by one (Émile insisted), then organized in stacks of twenty.

Gabriel and I knelt and pretended to work.

"We wouldn't have to stay out long," he whispered.

I considered him. His eyes were shiny, his skin blotchy. Did he have a fever?

"Gabriel," I said, my voice a string tethering a helium balloon to earth. "We can't."

He rubbed his eyes.

"Don't you ever wonder," he said, "what it's like out there?"

I shrugged.

"I do," he said. His gaze bounced to the door and back to me. "I don't want to leave forever or anything like that. I would never."

I believed him.

"It's just—I wonder sometimes," he added, his voice a crackling whisper. "I wish I didn't. Sometimes I worry that if I don't—"

He stopped.

Something inhabited my brother.

Something I couldn't rescue him from.

"We can't," I told him. "I can't."

We had been in each other's lives for five years. I saw his pain, felt his restlessness.

I saw it all, and I chose myself over him.

For a time.

———

Guests head back to the dining room in a slow march.

"What the fuck," one of the influencers mutters.

Gabriel and I stand there.

He's got to be picturing it, too. The Miranda warnings, the handcuffs, the charges. It's exactly what almost happened to him nine years ago.

"Hey."

Gabriel has snapped out of his trance. He's nudging me. I follow him back to our table. There's adrenaline in the air, an uneasy mix of excitement and relief.

Catalina walks across the dining room and stands in view of the tables. She clears her throat.

"Good morning," she starts hesitantly. "On behalf of everyone at the Ara, I wanted to say that we appreciate your cooperation. Of course, we understand that these are . . . unique circumstances."

She gives the crowd a pained smile.

"I wanted to let you know that we are . . . open. As usual. That includes our spa and the swimming pool. Guest services are operating, so please let us know if you'd like to book a guided hike, or if you need help figuring out the trails."

She winces slightly.

"So, that's it," she says, clasping her hands. "That's the update. We're available if you have questions."

Catalina waits a beat, then flees back to the lobby.

*Well. That was quick.*

I've heard of this happening. Murder suspects arrested within hours of a kill. Damning crime scenes, veritable buffets of hard evidence. Or: Cops acting on a hunch, counting on the arrest to trigger *something*—a confession, a signed search warrant from a judge, maybe both. It's a risk, of course. But sometimes, it pays off.

Other people might have spoken, too. Guests who noticed the same things I did—the tension between the Brenners, his mood like piano wire strung too tight. Maybe someone else overheard last night's argument, after all. I got to Harris as fast as I could this morning, but one or two guests could have beat me to it, while I was talking to Gabriel in our suite.

And there was William's readiness to fight Gabriel this morning—the insults, his fists clinging to Gabriel's T-shirt. Those things don't prove anything on their own, but they don't look *good.*

There could be more. Who knows what housekeeping found in his room? Who could imagine what the staff knows that we don't?

Gabriel and I look at each other.

*Is this really what we're supposed to do? Go to the pool right after a guy . . . killed his wife?*

"I'm not saying it will be great, but if you would let me speak—"

I turn my head in the direction of the family I spotted in the lobby earlier, the couple and their two young children. Mom is talking to Dad, who is trying to contain a squirming toddler on his lap. Next to them, their little girl clutches her face between her hands, elbows on the table.

"What else do you want to do with them?" the woman stage-whispers to the man. "And I mean—"

She nudges her chin in the direction of the lobby.

*He's been arrested,* she seems to say. *We can move on now.*

Dad shrugs, like, *I guess. This vacation's already such a disaster anyway.*

He gets up, toddler on his hip. The woman leads them out of the dining room, holding the girl's hand.

Other guests follow. Fabio and Lazlo. The influencers. No one looks thrilled, but there are talks of bathing suits and sunscreen.

"Should we . . . go to the pool, too?" Gabriel asks.

I bite my lip.

What's the alternative? The hiking trails? Did those yesterday—not in the mood to risk dying of dehydration again. A spa treatment? What kind of psycho gets a facial the day after a death?

"Let's do it," I say.

Gabriel nods.

"I'll bring a book."

For twelve years, Gabriel has worked as the assistant to Howard Auster, America's foremost chronicler of the Roman Empire. If Gabriel brings a book, then he won't really be *going to the pool.* He'll be at work.

And he'll be with the Romans. His darling Romans, a fascination that started in his early adulthood.

I asked him, back when he got his job: What *was* it about the Romans?

He shrugged. At first, I thought he wouldn't be able to explain—that it hadn't occurred to him that anyone could hear about the Romans and not want to devote their entire intellectual life to them.

"It's the stories," he said finally.

"You mean the drama?"

He shook his head.

"The gods. The emperors. They all had families."

I didn't understand.

"We never did," Gabriel added. "We didn't have any of that."

It didn't have to be the Romans. The Russian czars would have been good contenders. And let's not even get into the British monarchs. France, too, had a couple of viable options. But the Romans got to Gabriel's psyche first, and once they did, they never let go.

I didn't point out that the families he found so fascinating included sons who killed their fathers, and fathers who ate their sons.

Gabriel didn't see the horrors. Or if he did, they didn't give him pause.

Most of all, he loved Romulus and Remus, the orphaned twin brothers who were suckled by a wolf, then taken in by a shepherd, and went on to build the city that became Rome. Except, here's the story: Romulus and Remus couldn't agree on a location. They tried to resolve their disagreement with a bird-watching contest, but that didn't work. Things escalated. In the end, Romulus killed Remus by throwing a spear at his head.

Gabriel didn't seem to mind the fratricide part. It was like it didn't exist. All he saw was the rest of the story: the two abandoned kids, raised by a wolf, who started an empire.

—

EIGHTEEN YEARS AGO

Two weeks after our first conversation about outside-outside, Gabriel wilted. It happened in the morning, during class. We were sitting next to each other, listening to a mother drone on about the cosmos. Émile's foundational tome *(The Book of the Universe)* lay open on the desk in front of her.

"Ow," Gabriel mumbled.

He was rubbing his forehead.

"You okay?"

Before he could reply, the mother shot us a look. We lowered our heads.

Gabriel fell behind as we walked to the cafeteria.

"What's going on?"

"My head," he said, clutching the right side of his face.

"You have a headache?"

He shuddered.

"It's . . . like someone's banging a hammer on my skull. A hammer on fire."

*Yikes.*

We hurt, sometimes. Kids fell. The little ones were always slicing themselves open, spraining their ankles. Most ailments had to be waited out. Wounds scarred; joints healed; bad teeth fell out.

In the lunch line, Gabriel had trouble standing. Every time the line moved, he rearranged his posture to hold on to something new: the rusty rails on which our trays slid lazily, the glass case that might have housed dessert once, but which was now used to keep bread away from our greedy hands. The skin on his face was a shade of pale I had never seen before. Even his lips were white.

I surveyed the cafeteria. Simon was sitting at a table we liked, by the window. I didn't trust Gabriel to make it that far without dropping his tray and the bowl of lentil stew on it.

Mealtimes were supposed to be calm, a time for self-reflection and gratitude. There was a rhythm to them: We waited in line, we sat, we ate, we cleaned up. If we had to, we spoke—but only in low voices, and only if we were certain that what we had to say was worth disrupting the quiet.

"Let's just sit here," I whispered, and pulled out a chair for Gabriel at the nearest table. It was empty except for a small kid at the other end.

Gabriel sat and pushed his lentils to the side. He held his head with both hands like it was too heavy for his neck.

At the back of the cafeteria, Émile sat at his usual table, surrounded by the small group of mothers he favored at the time. He was telling a story between mouthfuls of stew. (Émile was allowed to speak freely at mealtimes.)

"Maybe we should tell someone," I said softly. "Maybe one of them"—I nudged my chin in the direction of the mothers, who were all looking rapturously at Émile—"could tell him."

Gabriel grunted. I knew what he meant. *And then what?*

Whenever one of us got sick—really, really sick—or when a mother gave birth, there were special meditations, perhaps an herbal tea brewed by Émile himself. But he wasn't a healer, he insisted. Only the power of positive thinking could make us better.

Gabriel was moaning. The skin on his face had turned green. His eyes didn't seem to be able to open all the way.

Suddenly, he looked up.

"I don't feel—"

He sprang to his feet. His chair clattered to the floor behind him. Gabriel didn't notice. He was too busy running toward the door.

"What the hell do you think you're doing?"

A mother darted over, grabbed his arm, pulled him to a stop. At fifteen, Gabriel was taller than most women on the compound, but he was weak that day. His body crumpled like a sheet falling from the clothesline.

"Please," he said. "I don't—"

There was a gurgle, and the sour smell of vomit. The mother released his arm. Gabriel fell to the ground. His rib cage quivered. He dry-heaved between eruptions of yellow bile.

Two mothers grabbed him, a hand under each arm, and headed for the exit. He was only half-conscious by that point. His eyes rolled in their sockets; his head lolled like a newborn's.

I got up and ran toward the scene.

"Silence!"

There was a loud bang. The mothers who had been dragging Gabriel stopped. The cafeteria went completely quiet. There was not a chair scraping against the floor, not a spoon knocking against the bottom of a bowl.

Émile had gotten up. His right hand rested in a closed fist on the table, where—I realized—he had slammed it.

"Sit. Back. Down," he said. His gaze swept across the room from Gabriel to me. "Now."

It was demeaning, somehow—being spoken to directly by him, in front of a crowd.

I scuttled back to my table.

Émile considered the mothers, who were still holding Gabriel.

"Take him away," he said.

The mothers didn't point out that they'd been doing just that. They walked Gabriel out of the cafeteria.

Émile leaned forward, gripping the table in front of him.

"Now," he said. His voice simmered with something. *Rage,*

I thought. *Barely contained rage.* "Return to your meal. Think good thoughts. By which I don't mean kind thoughts. Think about what needs to happen for this community to remain in good health. That's all you can do. Do not seek to control anything else."

I wanted to scream, *What are you even talking about? What does any of this mean?* I would have yelled until my throat was raw, if I'd been braver. *You just saw how sick he is. Do something. Please.*

*You're Émile. You have a car. Get him help.*

*You love us. You love us so much.*

But there were no doctors in Émile's world. No medications, either. He had told us how it worked, outside. How Big Pharma pushed poisons on people, how crooked companies told lies for profit. It sounded so wretched.

I ate my lentils.

———

That night, when the girls in my dorm snuck out, I followed them.

Gabriel hadn't shown up for class that afternoon. He'd missed dinner, too. When I'd gone to pack some orders of Émile's books, a task Gabriel and I had both signed up for that evening, I'd ended up alone.

Maybe his brain had broken irreparably. Maybe he had died. No one had any information. Anything was possible.

It was a whole new world outside, the night air on my shoulders, the glimmer of the moon on our faces.

I left the girls under a birch tree and kept going. It wasn't easy, making myself walk all the way to the boys' dorm. Five years after the Secret Place, my shoulder still didn't feel right. There was always a pull, a discomfort down my arm to remind me of the consequences if I was caught disobeying.

But I needed to see him.

I opened a door, then another. The boys' dorm, like the girls', was a dark, musky place with bunk beds against the walls and rows of twin beds at its center.

I crossed this sea of sleeping boys. There was something tender there, a feeling that would find me again, years later, when I watched a horror movie about haunted dolls. The innocent protagonist walked into a warehouse filled with toys, unaware of their dark powers. That the dolls would wake up was a given. But what would they do, then? Exactly what were they capable of?

Gabriel had told me that his bed was a bottom bunk at the far end of the room, underneath a window. I eliminated one sleepy face after the other until I spotted his.

He was awake.

Barely.

Gabriel lifted his head when he saw me, just an inch off the pillow. Above his bed, a thin curtain let in the moonlight. The skin on Gabriel's face was gray, filmy, his lips so dry they had started to crack.

Maybe he *had* died, then clumsily come back to life.

"What . . . doing here?" he muttered, his voice muffled by one of those scratchy blankets we all had.

"Are you okay?"

He shook his head. On the mattress, poking out from under the blanket, his hand was shaking.

Gabriel was in agony. Had been for hours.

And there was absolutely nothing I could do about it.

I sat on the floor, by his side.

"I'm sorry," I said. "I'm so sorry."

If any other boys saw or heard me, they didn't say anything. I stayed for what felt like a long time. Then, once I could convince myself that Gabriel had fallen asleep, I returned to my dorm.

The next morning, Gabriel resurfaced in the breakfast line. His eyelids were puffy, his movements rigid.

"But look," he said, and rolled his neck.

He could stand. He could move.

That evening, while we were filling shipping boxes with Émile's books, I told him.

"I think we should go."

Gabriel looked up from a recalcitrant roll of packing tape.
"Go where?"
"Outside."
His eyes widened. Before he could answer, there was a loud clatter. The two of us looked around, wild rabbits checking for dogs.
Just a window banging shut.
"For real?" he asked.
"For real."
"I thought you said—"
"Forget what I said."
I saw Émile's warnings about the pharmaceutical industry in a new light: There were pills out there, and people who dispensed them.
"You need . . . medication or something," I said. "For when it happens again."
"You think it's going to happen again?"
The horror on his face. Sweet Gabriel.
Three years earlier, one evening before dinner, my body had conjured up an unfamiliar kind of pain. I was bleeding. Gruffly, a mother had told me two things: that this was normal, and that this little stunt would recur every month.
The lesson: Once a body taught itself to do something unpleasant, it didn't stop. It performed the trick again, and again, and again.
"Shit," I said. "Money."
We'd never handled money. Émile had explained about capitalism, about the cruelties of outside-outside. Only he had a wallet. We saw it in photos taken during his travels. Émile in airports, Émile handing cash to a stranger on the street.
Gabriel pinched his lips.
"You know we can't," he said.
*Sure we can.*
"I'll figure it out," I said. "Don't worry about it."
Something limitless had opened within me. I was fearless, drunk with my own determination.
People made so much of it, later on, after we became adults.

Journalists, documentarians, people on the internet. Trying to read into our past like in tea leaves. *Even when they were fifteen, her brother did whatever the fuck he wanted,* someone wrote in an online forum. *It was his temperament. There's just something about him that doesn't understand boundaries.*

Bullshit. All of it.

My brother was in pain. I had to make it stop.

It was that simple.

## 12  ESCALANTE, UTAH

—

### THE FIFTH DAY

Gabriel and I find two chaises next to each other. Up until today, it's been easy to look at the pool and see an oasis. This big rectangle of turquoise water in the desert, the large magnolia tree mysteriously kept alive in this murderous climate: It's not subtle. But now, only children venture in for a swim. Adults sit around the pool in palpable discomfort. Most of them scroll on their phones; some resort to newspapers and books.

I keep my T-shirt on, even though it's past noon and the sun is beating down on us. Usually, an employee would set up an umbrella, but—despite Catalina's assurances—the hotel isn't back to normal yet.

Gabriel lies down and pulls his hat over his face, his book abandoned at his side. He's in dark green swim trunks—the same pair he's been rinsing and hanging to dry over the windowsill every night. Under my clothes, I'm wearing a navy one-piece, one of two options I brought for this nine-day stay. (*Nine days*, I thought when I made our reservation: one for each year since he moved away.)

Our time at the hotel has been peppered with small awkwardnesses. Every detail (like the fact that I can afford a spare bathing suit and Gabriel can't) is an obnoxious reminder of the ways we each live: he, with just enough money to get by; me, comfortably.

I had a job, once. For about a year. It was the closest thing I'd ever witnessed to a miracle: me, receiving an offer of employment from a bank. Becoming a *financial analyst*—the junior kind, plucked right out of college.

The work was so busy, so intense. I loved everything about it. Loved waking up at five and checking the news to see what disasters would upend the markets. (Already, I had an anxious mind, and nothing pleased me more than being given an actual reason to worry.) Loved having an office, a desk, a chair. Morning meetings? After a childhood of Émile's assemblies, morning meetings were *riveting*.

When the shit hit the fan and we all got caught up in a manic swirl of numbers and reports—that's when I felt truly at peace. When we had to work until midnight, which was most days, I didn't feel like I was missing out on life. I was brand-new to the world. I didn't have any real hobbies. My family was Gabriel and Annie. I had just enough time for a family of two people.

And, of course, I didn't mind the money.

After Annie's death, I didn't think anything had to change. I kept going to work. One evening, while Annie was still missing, I made the mistake of speaking to a local TV reporter. I didn't say much—just that we were desperately worried about my sister-in-law.

When I returned to work the next day, there were whispers. Things developed from there. People wouldn't meet my gaze. At meetings, there was never enough time for me to contribute.

After six months of tension, my manager asked me to sit down for a chat. "I feel," he informed me in a frigid conference room, "that you've been distracted lately. Personal issues, maybe."

It wasn't a question. He'd made up his mind.

A couple of hours after that meeting, my manager clicked out of a window right as I walked past his desk. Not fast enough. I had time to glimpse the blurry photo, Gabriel on the receiving end of a paparazzo's long lens, the headline: HUNGRY FOR

JUSTICE . . . AND A SUB: SHADY HUBBY GRABS LUNCH AS SUSPICION MOUNTS.

It wasn't even a new article. Gabriel had made the ill-fated trip to a sandwich shop just days after the discovery of Annie's body. He hadn't shopped for groceries, and in his dazed state didn't think of the optics.

I kept walking. My legs were shaking.

My boss. My *boss*. Reading up on the case, looking up shitty little articles from his work computer.

I quit.

Not even my beloved job was worth another judgmental stare, another meeting with this asshole.

In fact, I was done with bosses altogether. After a childhood of being belittled and blamed by the mothers, I didn't need anyone looking over my shoulder, searching for mistakes.

I became self-employed.

Day-trading is such a weird job. There's no service rendered. I still check the news at dawn, make some early trades on the round-the-clock markets. By the time the rest open at nine-thirty, I'm ready.

What does it take to be a day trader? Well, it requires observation. It means understanding what people value, and what they don't. I don't have to agree; I just have to *know*.

Every morning, I look for opportunities; I pounce. In the afternoon, I go back for another round. The dance stops at 4 p.m., when the markets close. One last go on the round-the-clock markets, then I update my trading journal (yes, keeping a log helps) and read more news.

You can be a day trader and spend two hours a day at your computer. I choose to be the kind who puts in fifteen-hour days, because work makes me feel good. It's the only activity during which I enjoy taking risks.

Not everyone can make a living day-trading, but I've pulled it off. And so I make a very healthy, very comfortable amount of money.

I've tried to share with Gabriel. It's the natural thing to do. But he has always resisted me, in ways big and small. When I booked the hotel, I was going to get him his own suite, but that went too far for him.

So I agreed to split one. I worried it would be awkward, sharing space again after so many years, but it's not. It remains the most normal thing in the world.

———

I open my book, an Italian novel in translation.

My eyes bounce around the pages. Sentences travel through my brain with the elusiveness of water streaming through a strainer.

I could be wealthier, by the way. But I choose not to. What I do—I enjoy it, but I'm not *proud* of it. It doesn't add value to anything but my own brokerage accounts.

So I keep myself in check. I'm careful not to give myself everything I want. In New York, I live in one of those horrific new buildings, the walls a blinding white, the same gray floors in every unit, chrome parts glistening smugly in the kitchen and bathroom. I'd much prefer one of those creaky prewar buildings with a view of Central Park or the Hudson River. But I'm wary of letting myself get too comfortable, too *content*.

Around us, the guests begin to relax. They remove their T-shirts and lie in the sun with something resembling abandon. Adults wander into the water. An employee checks on the various groups, returns with glasses of water and the occasional cocktail and lunch items.

Just the thought of food makes me want to throw up. I'm finding it hard to breathe.

Maybe if I shift my position a bit. I sit at a ninety-degree angle, drop my head.

Is it working?

*No.*

There's a bright pinch between my ribs. I try for a deep inhalation that never comes.

When I close my eyes, a nightmare awaits at the back of my eyelids: Gabriel with his hands behind his back, head bowed, the red and blue lights of a police car flashing on his face. Gabriel in a courtroom. Gabriel in an orange jumpsuit. Gabriel behind bars.

The pain travels from my rib cage to the back of my throat. There's a weight on my shoulders, on my chest.

*Think soothing thoughts.*

*Think about—*

Charlie. My dog, my perfect good boy. The smell of his paws, of his belly after a long walk in the heat. This goofy creature, eighty-percent German shepherd, twenty-percent whatever else. He settled into my life with a disconcerting ease, curling up on my couch the minute I brought him home three years ago. *Duh*, he seemed to say. *I've been waiting for you.*

I. Can't. Breathe.

Can't swallow, either. My throat has seized.

Gabriel remains oblivious, his face buried under his hat.

*Get a grip.*

For years now, I've worked to domesticate the wild beast that is my anxiety. My social life used to consist entirely of Gabriel (and, once upon a time, Gabriel and Annie). After they both departed, I looked for ways to give shape to my days outside of trading hours. Most activities, I have found, bump against the sharp contours of my mind. So every day I have two options: do things that scare me or die of boredom.

I started rock climbing. A couple of ladies at the gym—Cara and Jessie—became my belay partners. Cara meets me there on Tuesdays, Jessie on Fridays. Every session is a fight against my intrusive thoughts—*what if I drop her what if she drops me what if I didn't tie my knot correctly*. It's a workout for my mind, even more than for my body.

The sounds of children splashing in the pool reach me from a great distance. I squeeze my eyes shut. When I open them, I'm looking at the world through a deep, dark tunnel.

Maybe I'm having a heart attack.

*No. Keep trying.*

Twice a week, I go to a pottery workshop. I sit and shape clay and place it in a kiln. Pottery is the opposite of rock climbing in that it puts my mind to sleep. No thoughts there—just the whirl of the wheel and the dozens of beautiful, breakable things I've made. When the workshop ends, I wash up and go to the Irish bar around the corner for a beer with two or three of my fellow potters.

I get up. There's the ground underneath my feet, the gritty tile. Something real, finally. I wait for a loosening in my chest. Nothing.

Maybe I'm dying.

Is this what it feels like to die?

I can't die. I've got things to come home to.

Charlie, Cara, Jessie, the potters. And my car.

I bought it—an old convertible Fiat 500—once I resigned myself to the fact that I would no longer be flying out to Seattle. On weekends, especially during the spring and fall, I drive on country roads, with the top down. Aside from one cursed area I dutifully avoid, the Empire State is my oyster. There are so many things to look at. I take pictures of foliage. I listen to birds. I stop at diners. I've yet to run out of roads. Or birds. Or diners.

Gabriel must have felt me move next to him. He takes his hat off his face and sits up.

"What's wrong?"

"I can't breathe," I say, except I don't, because you can't speak when you can't breathe.

"Sit down," he says.

Gabriel lowers me back to my chaise.

"Put your head between your knees."

*Does that really work?*

"Is she okay?"

I think I recognize Lazlo's voice. My arms are numb. In fact, I can't feel my body. My eyes are shut. When I open my mouth to speak, all that comes out is a series of increasingly desperate gasps for air.

Gabriel's hand tightens around my shoulder.

"Hey," he says. His voice, reassuring just a few seconds ago, is tense. "You okay? Did you eat something?"

I shake my head.

"Excuse me," Lazlo says. I raise my head but can't see who

he's talking to. "Is there a doctor here? Someone's not feeling well."

"No . . . doctor," I manage to mumble.

The sound of my own voice gives me hope. Can I breathe? Maybe. My head spins.

"You're okay," Gabriel says.

His hands, I realize, are clutched on either side of my head, holding me steady.

I open my eyes. It should comfort me, looking at Gabriel's face. I know it so well. The scar on his chin, from a slippery floor and an ill-positioned table twenty-two years ago. The mole on his temple, which he didn't get checked until we were both twenty-one, because that's how long it took for us to get access to doctors. This face I defined in opposition to mine: Both my eyes the same brown, my hair darker than his, my nose more upturned. His normal jawline versus my very slight underbite. We're not carbon copies, but we look alike enough—similar hair color, similar complexions, and, more convincingly, all the mannerisms that people who grew up together tend to share. The elocution, the way of standing, the gait.

For so many years, Gabriel's face anchored me to the world, to myself. But I look into his eyes—one brown, one blue—and I'm falling.

That's what it feels like. Like there's no more chaise under me, no more ground beneath my feet. No more hotel, no more desert, no more world. Just a great big void, and me hurtling down it, body and mind.

"Lie down," Gabriel says.

He guides me, lifts my feet onto the chaise. I raise my arms on each side of my face to open up my rib cage, but someone guides them back down. Something about blood circulation.

A crowd has gathered around us. Somewhere at the back of my mind, I'm embarrassed.

Lying down helps. The whooshing in my ears recedes. My chest rises and falls, up and down, a little too fast, but it's doing its job. I smooth my T-shirt over my stomach. It's drenched in sweat and my fingers are shaking, but at least I can move.

"Thank you," I say.

I raise a hand to appease our worried onlookers.

"It's just the heat," I lie.

Through a half-open eye, I see Lazlo nod, then walk away. The crowd dissipates.

I sit up.

"You good?" Gabriel asks, still kneeling at my side.

"I'll be fine."

My breath has settled. Gabriel waits a couple of seconds before standing and returning to his own chaise.

I swallow. My heartbeat slows.

Something tugs at the corner of my consciousness, but I can't figure out what it is. There's Gabriel next to me, children in the pool, adults settling back into their activities. Nothing to report.

Unless—

I crane my neck.

There he is. Deputy Harris, standing at the edge of the pool area, gun hanging at his waist. Evidently, he didn't miss a moment of my little scene.

When he sees that I've noticed him, he glances away.

———

EIGHTEEN YEARS AGO

É mile had a trip the following weekend.

That was my chance.

In the dorm, I waited for the right moment. We'd been in bed for a while. Everything was silent; no one was sneaking out. There was no time to second-guess myself. I sloughed off my blanket and stepped out of bed. Outside, I made my way to the main building, the one where Émile lived and worked.

All day, I'd run through the itinerary in my head: dorm, outside, office. It had seemed to me an impossible journey, full of peril, doomed to fail. But in reality, it all happened so quickly. There I stood, at Émile's door.

I was prepared for it to be locked. I thought I'd have to search for a key, break in somehow. But I turned the knob, and the door opened. It just did.

Émile hadn't locked it.

My initial shock gave way to shame.

Émile trusted us. He counted on us to respect his rules, his space.

From the first floor, his office drew me in like a force field.

I stood in the foyer, listening for the pitter-patter of some-one else's steps, for the rustling of clothes.

Nothing.

And so, I went in.

It was the weirdest thing, being alone in his office. I took it in, a strange tenderness in my heart. Naïve Émile.

He was the most brilliant man in the world, and he was an idiot. Thinking himself safe among his women, among the mothers he had trained to stand guard.

I ran my hands over his desk. Thinking: *If I had money, where would I keep it?*

No idea. I didn't have money. I didn't have *things*.

I dipped my fingers into his pencil holder, brushed the cover of a notebook.

*Open it?*

No.

I lifted the lid of a rectangular wooden box.

Small items had been carelessly thrown inside. There were buttons, fallen from Émile's polo shirts, that a mother would sew back on. There were bright pieces of candy. (Strange: We didn't eat candy.) There was a chubby key that I would later realize was for his muddy 4x4. Elastic bands, paper clips, and *yes, yes*—

Coins. Silver and copper-orange.

Pinned underneath them, wrinkled, abandoned like they were worth nothing—bills.

I tugged at a corner of one, the paper thin and breakable. Out slid one, two, three bills. On one of them, a two and a zero. On the other two, a one and a zero. Two tens and a twenty. Forty dollars.

Deeper in the box, a flurry of bills with just a one.

How many should I take? How much did pills cost?

*Think.*

The bills, abandoned in the wooden box, buried between buttons and pieces of candy, were not cared for. Forty dollars and a bunch of dollar bills evidently did not amount to a fortune.

*Do it. You've come this far.*

At the bottom of Émile's box, one of the dollar bills had a shape printed on its surface.

I pulled it out, lifted it up: the imprint of lipstick. Like in the images Émile had shown us from the world outside, women pouting in advertisements, their beautiful faces, their exquisite bodies contorted in absurd positions to sell useless things.

It repelled Émile. He said it did. And still, he had kept the dollar bill in his little box.

I inspected it more closely. The scene materialized in my head like a shape in the fog. A lady—it had to have been a lady— running the lipstick over her lips. Pressing them against the paper. *Kiss kiss.* Then handing the bill to Émile, and Émile taking it. A man accepting a gift. It was an illusion, a fantasy taking place at an unclear location. Somewhere dark, a heavy dampness that stuck to the skin, and Émile radiating light. Good Émile, pure Émile. The dollar bill making contact with his skin like a poisoned dart.

He had to have liked it a little.

A tug in my chest. Captivating, this version of Émile. The best man, torn apart by temptation.

The dollar bill, then, in my pocket. Not to spend. More like a bird I wanted to trap in a cage to better observe it.

Once I'd pocketed the first bill, the rest came easily: two, three more dollar bills, and one of the tens.

The heady thrill of it: stealing from Émile.

I wanted, almost, to protect him. To rescue him from myself.

Once I'd gathered the money, I shut the wooden box, delicious adrenaline rushing up my spine.

I lingered.

I breathed the forbidden air, shut my eyes for a few moments. In my mind, I became Émile, the master of this domain. I played with the idea of it: *my desk, my chair, my world.*

Then it was time to go.

Check: The desk looked undisturbed. I hadn't moved anything except for the box's lid, now back in its place.

There was a sound. Steps.

*Shit.*

The steps crept closer.

There was nowhere to hide. Not under the desk, not behind a curtain. No exit.

*Shit, shit, shit.*

Could I leave through the window?

Yes, in theory, but it was too late. The steps were right outside the door and the knob was turning and someone was about to enter, a mother who would punish me, send me back to the Secret Place, tear out another one of my limbs.

The doorknob turned. Slowly, the door opened to reveal—

Not a mother.

Just a man.

The man I'd just held in my mind like a butterfly trapped under a cup.

Émile.

Back early from his trip.

Émile in the flesh: blond curls, polo shirt, a travel bag in his left hand. Standing at the entrance of his office.

"What are you doing here?"

*Think.*

"I was looking for—"

*What?*

*You?*

*No.*

Émile taught us to observe the world. We could search for knowledge. For goodness. For enlightenment. He urged us to do it. To be curious. Challenge your own mind, always. Look beyond. Look for the truth. Look for more. Look for—

"Answers."

Émile startled. Just the tiniest bit, a quick widening of the eyes. Then, composure.

"At two in the morning?"

The hardest part of a lie, I learned in that moment, was telling it for the first time. I cleared my throat. Straightened my back. Then, with all the aplomb I could muster: "I couldn't sleep. I have so many questions."

My little voice, trying so hard to sound confident.

"What kind of answers?" he asked.

Émile's bills rustled in my pocket. I felt a twinge of panic: He would look inside the box and see the missing cash.

"I'm not sure," I said.

Émile cocked his head.

*Don't break.*

*Look at him.*

He wasn't the tallest man I would ever see—Gabriel would eventually outgrow him by a few generous inches—but he was, or seemed, the strongest, for sure. For one thing, he was the only well-fed human I had ever encountered. He worked out. He traveled. In the world we lived in, his intelligence was unrivaled. And I was a malnourished, thieving fifteen-year-old girl.

But I could love.

I could worship.

He needed that.

"You're always answering questions I didn't even know I had," I said.

Émile dropped his bag to the floor. He walked to his desk.

"Like, for example . . ." I began.

My head was empty. Émile's words made sense when he spoke them, but the second you tried to repeat them, they were like cigarette smoke between your fingers.

The one sermon I remembered: the one, all those years ago, that had gotten me sent to the Secret Place. The one that had brought Gabriel into my life.

"One time you said: 'You have to face the truth of what's inside you and act in consequence.'"

Émile considered me. Unreadable.

I would later understand that he, too, forgot his sermons as soon as he delivered them. They were word salads, utterly meaningless. But in that instant, I figured he was struck upon hearing his own words recited back to him, verbatim, conjured from the past.

"What did you mean by that?" I asked. "How do you face the truth of what's inside you?"

Émile sat behind his desk. I held my breath. After what seemed like an eternity, but could only have been a few seconds, he gestured to the empty chair on the other side of it.

I sat, but stuck to the edge of the seat.

"It's a good question," he said.

*It is?*

"Because, you see . . ."

Émile talked. Talked and talked and talked. About life and how it was meant to be lived. The world and how it was meant to be searched. Words and words and words.

I leaned a bit farther back in the chair, never taking my eyes off him. If I did, a spell would be broken.

There was something else. It was in Émile's thin, tapered fingers, dancing in the air around him, marking the cadence of his words. In his gaze on me, like being knighted.

"I can see that you want to learn more," he said, both elbows on his desk, hands clasped. "I can teach you."

*Me?*

Émile kept a circle of mothers around himself, but he had never chosen a kid.

I swallowed.

He seemed so tall, even in his desk chair. Not a god, maybe, but a man like a star, his brain like galaxies.

And still, so silly. Leaving the door to his office unlocked, his money in a box. Émile craved a world where he didn't have to be careful. Where he could lean across his desk and look into the eyes of a fifteen-year-old girl and see that in this moment, he was everything.

"That would be," I said, "unbelievable."

Émile raised an eyebrow. Amused. Tickled. He liked it, I realized. Having a project. A young mind to shape.

"Yes," I repeated. "Yes."

Émile smiled.

"We'll meet in the mornings," he said, "before Assembly. I will teach you—"

I stopped listening.

Who cared what he planned on teaching me?

I was safe. I had money.

Nothing else mattered.

THE FIFTH DAY

I open one eye.

"Gabriel?"

I'm in our suite. The curtains are drawn; the AC is whooshing softly.

What time is it?

I check my phone: seven in the evening.

"Gabriel?"

He's not here.

*Not again.*

I call him. He picks up on the second ring.

"Where are you?" I ask.

There's ambient noise behind him, people talking over smooth jazz.

"I left you a note," he says.

There it is on my nightstand, in Gabriel's choppy block print: "Went to dinner. Call if need anything."

"I see it now," I tell him over the phone. "Did I really sleep this whole time?"

After I spotted Harris at the pool, I told Gabriel I was tired and would be heading back to the cabin for a nap. It was only half a lie. I *was* tired. I'm always tired. But really, I wanted to get away from Harris and his stare.

"Apparently."

*Guess I'm finally paying off that sleep debt.*

"I'll bring you back a plate," Gabriel says.

"Don't. I'll come over."

I hang up and kick the covers, as if to prove something. My head swims; my eyelids are heavy. But I'm standing up. Quickly, I peel off my pool clothes and my bathing suit. I pull on a linen jumpsuit, gather my hair into a bun.

It's okay. *I'm* okay.

A woman came to the desert and died, and her husband has been arrested.

This is how those things are supposed to go. The justice system will do its thing. William Brenner will be punished.

I search for my key card, slide my feet into my sandals.

*Everyone is moving on already.*

*I can do it, too. It'll be easy.*

---

There's one small thing I need to take care of before I join Gabriel in the dining room.

Catalina didn't lie. There are coyotes around us. I've seen them from our patio, while everyone was asleep and I was smoking secret cigarettes. One of them ventured surprisingly close to me on our first night.

That's how I saw it was injured. One of its front legs had a gash, the skin an angry red. The coyote was limping. It seemed to have been suffering for a while: It was skinny, tired.

The next day, I made some calls. Someone from a wilderness service told me they knew which coyote I was talking about, that there was a den off the main hiking trail, the one closest to the hotel. The person said they'd send someone to look, but it might take a couple of days.

It didn't feel good to wait and do nothing.

There was a coyote on the compound, one summer when we

were kids. It started lurking near the cafeteria, poking around, disturbing our piles of compost.

We were fascinated. A new animal! One we'd never encountered before! The coyote became a subject of hot gossip. Those of us on cafeteria cleanup duty started dropping potato peels, making a trail to our compost piles. Updates were shared in hurried whispers—Delphine from my cooking class had seen it, Simon swore he'd managed to touch it.

We woke up one morning to three missing chickens and a trail of bloody feathers. Émile deputized a group of fathers, ordered them to secure the chicken coop. After meals, the mothers scoured the cafeteria for detritus.

Our coyote went away.

We'd been sad for the slaughtered chickens, but we missed the coyote more. We talked about it for weeks. It got to the point that Émile used one of his assemblies to forbid coyote talk. It wasn't good to dwell, he said. Not good at all to live in nostalgia.

But I never forgot. It was the closest thing we'd had to a pet at that time. And that night at the Ara, it was impossible to look at the injured coyote and not see a shade of my Charlie in it.

So, on our second day at the hotel, when Gabriel said he was getting hot and left me alone by the pool, I went to the bar, asked for a water bottle, a paper cup, and a bag of crackers, then headed for the main hiking trail. A few feet from the main path, I found the coyotes' den.

"My" coyote was nowhere in sight. I poured some water into the cup, set it on the ground, scattered a handful of crackers next to it.

When I turned to look at the den again from the trail, I saw it. My coyote, drinking the water, eating the crackers.

I knew I wasn't supposed to feed it. But the coyote was already in bad shape. I couldn't just watch it suffer.

That night, I spotted the coyote again, hobbling in the distance. Either the helpers hadn't arrived yet, or they hadn't been able to find it. So, on the third day, when Gabriel skipped our hike, I ventured off the trail for a few minutes and replenished my furry friend's snacks.

I know. I know! Wildlife, National Park. But I couldn't help myself.

I didn't get a chance to go yesterday. Gabriel didn't beg off any of our activities, and I didn't feel like explaining. He'd worry about me, my safety. *You went where? You did what? They're wild animals, Frida.*

In our suite, I grab a fresh bottle of water, one of the paper cups stacked by the coffee machine, and a bag of crackers from the selection of complimentary snacks arranged next to the minibar. Then I make my way as swiftly as I can out of the hotel, off the hiking trail, back to the coyotes' den.

I pour the water, shake some crackers from the bag.

When I step back onto the trail, I hear the coyote crunching away.

*Yes.*

I like it, this wordless kindness. It's imperfect, I know. Some people would scold me for it. But in this moment, it feels right.

———

There's a lightness in my step as I approach the main building.

"Thank you," a voice says. "Yes, I'll let you know."

*Are you kidding me?*

There's just no way.

But here he is. Ending his call, sliding a finger across his phone screen. He hasn't noticed me, but I can see him clearly from where I stand: dark circles under his eyes, polo shirt untucked. He's been through it, but he's here, *right here*, in the fucking entrance lounge. No handcuffs. Just a man in a hotel, finishing a phone call, cracking his knuckles.

William Brenner has returned.

Slowly, I take a few steps back. Why are my sandals so loud? But William doesn't notice me. He's focused on his phone, tapping on the screen with his index finger.

Who's he writing to? A friend? A lawyer?

Probably both.

I tiptoe behind him and slither to the dining room.

Where's Gabriel?

A hand waves from a table at the back. Like it did just this morning, moments before William's arrest.

How long was he even at the police station? Seven hours? Eight?

"Hey."

Gabriel gets up, pulls the chair across from his away from the table.

"You want to order something? I'm sure we can get you a menu if—"

"He's back."

Gabriel, who was trying to catch a waiter's attention, goes still.

"Who?"

"William Brenner."

His arm comes down.

"What?"

"I saw him just now. Outside."

"But he was—"

I motion for us to sit. Gabriel looks down at his plate. Saffron risotto, looks like. Next to it, some kind of mixed drink—a mocktail, I assume. Gabriel doesn't drink. Per my count, he's been sober for eight years.

"Are you sure it was him?" Gabriel asks.

"I saw his face."

"But—"

He picks up his fork. As he's about to take a bite, the hum of conversation stops.

I turn in my chair.

There he is.

William Brenner makes his way across the room in complete silence.

Confident, unbothered by our ogling, he takes his usual seat at his usual table. He raises a hand, and a waiter materializes at his side. We're still gawking by the time the sommelier returns with a bottle of red wine.

The popping cork snaps us out of our collective daze.

People turn back to their plates. I untwist and face Gabriel. He's squirming in his seat, trying to look over my shoulder.

"Don't stare," I say through clenched teeth.

"What is he doing?"

Reluctantly, I swivel to take another look. William is holding his phone, raising it with his left hand, tapping at the screen with his right.

The little squint, the faux casual waving of the phone: I know what he's doing. We've all been there. The fake selfies to snap a celebrity three tables away at a restaurant, the secret shot of a stranger's purse to investigate the brand and model.

I picture the dining room sweeping across his screen. He gives the phone a couple more taps before settling on his target.

It's us.

William Brenner is pointing his phone camera at our table. He's probably already taken a couple of shots and is treating himself to a few extras.

I whip around. Gabriel is looking down at the table, one hand on his forehead, trying to hide his face behind his arm.

"Let's get out of here," I whisper, pushing back my chair.

"Don't," he says without looking up. "The photo will be much better if we stand."

He's right.

But it's torture to just sit here.

Gabriel gives my fingers a squeeze. *Hold the line*, he seems to say. *This is what needs to happen. Sit and bear it. There is nothing else to do.*

I've never experienced it with him before. The intrusion, the scrutiny.

We wait it out together.

After a few seconds, Gabriel's hand relaxes around mine.

"Is he done?" I ask.

Gabriel nods.

"Now can we get out of here?"

He doesn't reply. Already, he's folding himself out of his chair. I need to jog to keep up with him. Gabriel, always with his long legs, his six feet, two inches of height, one step for two of my own. I glance at William, who places his phone next to his plate. So smug. So satisfied. He got what he needed.

Gabriel and I move together, out of the dining room, through the hotel, back to the suite.

No need for a discussion. No need to hash out all the possibilities together. I know we're both wondering the same thing: *To be released so quickly—it suggests something went wrong. The cops made a mistake. Overplayed their hand. William didn't seem worried, just now. If anything, he was righteous. The triumphant confidence of a man who considers himself wronged, and who expects the people in charge to make it up to him.*

I take out my laptop.

The equation is simple. Even Gabriel, who's never excelled at math, has already solved it.

He's a tabloid owner + he apparently just wriggled his way out of a murder charge + he's sneaking pictures of us = We're leaving.

"Eleven okay?"

Gabriel doesn't need me to explain I'm looking at flights. He gives me a raised thumb, then plops his big, empty backpack onto his bed.

I wait for the flight confirmation to land in my inbox and fill my own suitcase. We work quickly, silently. *Goodbye, Ara. Goodbye, dream vacation. Goodbye, plans.*

We haven't talked about the documentary. I haven't asked Gabriel what he wants to say, or why he's suddenly decided to sit in front of the cameras.

I'm not even sure what he's going home to. Gabriel's life in Seattle is a mystery I haven't managed to crack. As far as I can tell, he's given shape to his days like I've done to mine. There's the work he does for Howard, always, first and foremost. Back when I still visited in person, he introduced me to the local hiking scene. Even when his emails got terse, he mentioned books he read, movies he saw—even Titus, the stray cat he took in. That last detail made me smile. We were apart, on our way to estrangement. Nevertheless, our lives found ways to mirror each other.

Still, the quieter Gabriel got, the harder it became for me to picture him doing things—sitting in a park, visiting the Space Needle, finally buying a coffee table instead of the upturned laundry hamper that fulfilled that function during my visits.

But maybe we never needed to talk.

There's a sixth sense between us. We grew up together, and then we lived together. Our bodies forever crammed into small worlds, cramped spaces.

Sometimes people ask. Not that many get the opportunity, nowadays. But back when I used to date, it came up. I think Annie came close to raising it, once or twice, but she could never find the words. People online, on the other hand, wonder openly.

It's an expected—if awkward—question, once people realize I spent years of my life pretty much curled up next to a guy to whom I'm not biologically related.

It wouldn't have been illegal, or even wrong, I guess.

But it was never going to happen.

Few of the children on the compound had siblings, but those who did, knew who they were. For years, I couldn't figure out why Émile gave them that information. He took so many pains to erase the idea of family from our minds. Then I read a little book called *Flowers in the Attic*, and I understood: It was better for everyone if people knew.

Years later, when we finally did the paperwork, when we sent away for birth certificates and Social Security cards and all that good stuff, Gabriel and I got official confirmation: His birth parents and mine were different people.

It was something, seeing their names in writing (mine: Susan and Joseph; Gabriel's: Patrick and Moira). Parents. What a strange concept. They didn't seem entirely real, a bit like those very bright frogs whose colors couldn't possibly have occurred naturally. But they did bring the definitive confirmation that Gabriel and I didn't share DNA.

For about three days after we got the news, I didn't know how to move around him; Gabriel didn't know how to look at me.

Technically, anything was allowed.

But.

That thing between us, it was never nascent love. Never a crush. In my teenage years, when I pondered those things, it was Simon I pictured, not Gabriel. Simon, with his broad shoulders and strong hands. Or Simon's friend Isaiah, who had the most wonderfully floppy hair and soulful brown eyes. Or Louisa, a girl from my cooking class whose thin hands wrapped themselves decisively around a whisk or a rolling pin, who could cut a whole bowl of apples into slices of identical thinness.

All I'd craved, back when I met Gabriel, was a sibling. That's what I projected onto him. When all the possibilities opened, that image remained, like the shapes at the back of your eyelids after you stare at the sun.

I wasn't blind to his physical self. His body meant something to me. Often, it existed as an extension of my own. His breathing meant safety; his hands meant a new world. It was chosen, animal, this thing of ours. It was alive.

And then it died.

And now it's alive again.

I go to bed first. About ten minutes later, Gabriel slips into his own.

The day we arrived, seeing the two queen-size beds almost four feet apart, it was impossible not to think of the dorms. Of our bunk beds from the ages of ten to fourteen, Gabriel at the bottom, me at the top.

There's a rustling on Gabriel's side. Our suite glows faintly with LEDs, a tiny red eye on our dormant TV, green buttons on our AC control panel. In the darkness, I squint to see the white shape of his arm extracting itself from the sheets, reaching across the space between us.

That was our thing.

In the bunk beds.

If I reached down and he reached up, our index fingers

met for a few seconds. Our knuckles interlocked. We held our breaths; we waited.

Just long enough to think, not even say, *Good night.*

We never talked about it. That little gesture was not spoken of in the daytime. It was childish and pure and sincere, a quiet acknowledgment of all the ways we needed each other.

For five days, I've remembered this detail. For five days, I've wondered if Gabriel remembers, too.

I reach out my arm.

Time compresses. We're ten years old again. My shoulder feels strange; the bone was wrenched out of its socket not too long ago. I'm learning about pain at the same time as I'm learning about love. We are eleven, twelve, thirteen. Soon we'll learn how to get away with things. But for now, we are good. We do our chores. We obey. We share everything with everyone else. The one thing that belongs to us, our one secret, is the linking of our fingers at night. Later, I will look back on it and think, *Maybe that was the first step. Maybe that's how we realized that some things were allowed to exist, as long as we were the only two people to know about them.*

But for now, I am thirteen. I am thirty-two. Gabriel's hand is surprisingly soft—moisturized, cared for. It used to be calloused, back in Émile's world, what with all the manual labor. But we've changed. Gabriel has changed. Maybe there isn't a cell in his body left over from the boy he once was.

At the border between our two beds, my brother loops his index finger around mine.

———

THE SIXTH DAY

Gabriel's phone alarm goes off. He doesn't snooze. We never formed the habit: Back in Émile's world, when it was time to get up, we got up. Ditto in our early adulthood. There *were* those six months when Gabriel didn't get out of bed, but that wasn't snoozing; that was depression.

When I come out of the bathroom, he's looking out the window, sipping an orange juice from the minibar. He lines up his migraine meds on the desk, tilts his head back to swallow them.

"Ready?" he asks.

I am.

He shoulders his backpack; I wheel out my suitcase.

*Fuck, I'm going to miss him.*

I haven't allowed myself to feel his absence too much over the past five years. That's always been the deal: Sometimes in life you have to shed the people you love, the world you know.

We stop by the front desk. Catalina's forehead wrinkles when she spots our bags.

"Are you leaving us?"

"We are," Gabriel says. "We've had a lovely stay. It's just . . . an emergency. At home."

Catalina nods. She clearly doesn't buy it, but she pecks diligently at her keyboard.

"I see your reservation was prepaid," she says. "That means that, unfortunately, we won't be able to refund you for the unused part of your stay."

"That's fine," I say.

*Forget about the money, Catalina. I'll make more. Just let us out of here.*

"Would you like a printed copy of your receipt?"

*Jesus.*

"That's okay," I say. "But we're going to need a car to the airport."

"Of course. Let me call one of our drivers."

"Before you do that . . ."

Gabriel and I turn around.

Deputy Harris is standing in the lobby, by the big vase of dried flowers.

"We're about to make an announcement," he says. "To all the guests."

"We have a flight to catch," I say. "Sorry."

He continues like he doesn't even hear me.

"We're asking everyone to gather in the dining room. It won't take more than ten minutes. Everyone's been very cooperative." He waits a beat, then: "It's heartwarming, really, to see the community rally around an investigation."

*Very subtle.*

I hold back a sigh.

No choice, then. I want to get out of here, but I'd rather do it without "asshole" written next to my name in Harris's notebook.

We follow him to the dining room. Most guests are already there—Fabio and Lazlo, the divorcée, the couple with their two kids. Harris goes to stand next to his two colleagues. They exchange a few sentences; Harris checks his watch. He looks around the room, searching for someone who's evidently not here yet.

The influencers join us. The *SVU* actor. Most tables in the dining room are full, but the cops keep waiting.

William walks in. Harris's face lights up. He gestures to the front of the room.

Was he . . . saving him a fucking seat?

William sits, holding a cup of coffee and a pair of sunglasses. Relaxed. Righteous.

*Didn't your wife just die?*

Harris clears his throat.

There's a special language cops speak when they find themselves tangled up in a mystery. A person is an *individual*. A woman is a *female*. You're not dead; you're *deceased*. Time turns into a series of dates. Random activities become alibis. The adrenaline of fear, numbed by the tedium of bureaucracy.

"Good morning," Harris says.

He looks down at his notes. For an actual press conference, they'd be typed, but for us—this huddle of anxious tourists—he's jotted down a few lines, his chicken scratch visible through the lined paper.

"As all of you know, we were called to this hotel on the morning of July fourteenth to reports of an unresponsive individual. This person, a female, was deceased. We were able to identify her quickly as Mrs. Sabrina Brenner, twenty-four years old."

My god, she *was* young.

At the mention of his wife's name, William brings a hand to his face. It's like he's just remembered the role he's supposed to play: the grieving husband, a man whose life was just upended by tragedy.

Harris glances up from his piece of paper. He avoids William's gaze as he delivers this next part:

"Mrs. Brenner's death is currently the subject of a murder investigation. We need all the information we can gather. We are determined to get to the bottom of this."

He reads from his notes again.

"To this end, we will be looking to speak to all of you. We can't compel anyone to stay, but I do want to say this: We would greatly appreciate it if no one left at this stage."

Harris's gaze sweeps over the crowd and—I swear I'm not imagining it—settles on me and Gabriel. He lowers his notes.

"Allow me to be candid. Our life will be much, much easier if all our witnesses stay in one place. Most of you are booked at least through tomorrow, and we will do our best to be done quickly. But we will not look favorably on anyone who decides to leave now. The Ara is working with us to accommodate everyone until we've made enough progress."

People exchange looks.

*Is he . . . threatening us?*

"However," Harris continues, "should you decide to leave anyway, we'll work around that. We were able to collect your names and addresses from the hotel. We can reach you at home. We'd rather not have to do that. It's more work for us. But if we have to, then we will."

He gives the crowd a quick smile. One of the influencers raises her hand.

"No questions," Harris says. "That's it from me."

———

Gabriel and I walk back to our suite.

Another decision we don't need to discuss. Except, this time, it's not because we agree. We just don't have a choice.

What I do have is a headache.

We unpack our bags.

*What the fuck just happened?*

William Brenner, in his front-row seat.

The police arrested him. It was a gamble, arresting William that quickly—and, clearly, it didn't pay off. William didn't talk. The judge didn't sign the warrant. The evidence wasn't as conclusive as it seemed at first.

Whatever it was, William's back.

The cops must have thought it was a measured risk, that arrest. Here's a thing I learned on TV: You can't try someone for the same offense twice, but you can certainly arrest them more than once. It's not like the cops were using their one and only chance.

That might have worked with a regular guy. But William's not a regular guy. He's wealthy, powerful, and angry. Meaning: He's a problem.

He probably threatened to sue them. For what? Who knows. He's a rich man. Rich people can usually think of three lawsuits they might want to file at any given time.

And Harris. This young police deputy, cutting his teeth in this tiny department.

He'd be easy to scare, if you were a wealthy, vindictive man.

Gabriel sits on his bed, his half-empty backpack at his side. He sighs.

I sit next to him, wrap an arm around his shoulders.

*Hey,* I want to say. *We're going to figure it out.*

But I don't. I don't like to make promises I can't keep.

I dig my phone out of my pocket and google William Brenner. Some biographical details ring a vague bell: New York native, promising baseball player in his youth until a shoulder injury ended his career before it could begin.

So: journalism. William earned his stripes at a tabloid in the city, covering the courthouse beat. When his father died, he used his inheritance to buy a local paper in the Hudson Valley. Now he owns a smattering of tabloids in the Tri-State Area.

I skim through the list of his publications on Wikipedia. One of them, like a dagger: After Annie's body was found, that rag called Gabriel a murderer in every way it could without risking a lawsuit.

It was the paper that gave Gabriel his tabloid nickname, "Shady Hubby." Always in a question, a sub-headline providing an implicit answer. DID SHADY HUBBY PUSH WIFE OFF BRIDGE? NEIGHBORS SAY THEY HEARD "SCREAMS" NIGHT BEFORE SHE WENT MISSING; DID SHADY HUBBY KILL WIFE FOR LIFE INSURANCE? COUPLE HAD "EYE-WATERING DEBT," SAYS FRIEND.

A few years before that, the same paper had given Émile his own nickname: "Sicko Svengali." The man we'd worshipped for the better part of our lives, squeezed into one cartoonish alliteration.

William's an owner, not an editor in chief. But presumably he reads his own publications. This old-school newspaper man, with his jackets and his polo shirts and his ire—it's hard to imagine him doing anything else.

Did he recognize us? More likely, he recognized Gabriel and has a hunch about who I might be.

That photo William took at dinner—did he send it to a team of reporters somewhere? Did he ask them to have a look around, see if they could confirm my identity?

"Just when I thought I was out," Gabriel says. "They pull me back in."

I look up from my phone, eyebrow cocked.

It's a reference to the mob show. Except it's not a quote from the mob show; it's a quote from the third *Godfather* movie that a gangster in the mob show references in season one.

In other circumstances, it would be funny. But evidently I lack Gabriel's gallows humor.

I get up and walk to the door.

"Where are you going?" Gabriel asks.

"I need some air."

"Then go on the patio," he says.

"I need a walk."

He opens his mouth, but I ignore him. I push down the handle, unlock the door, open it, and—

Walk straight into Harris.

"Wow," I say, a reflex. "Deputy."

His hand is raised, balled into a fist. Evidently, he was about to knock on our door, but I just spared him the trouble.

"Hello," he says.

His voice is confident, his posture resolute. This cop arrested the wrong man at the wrong time, and he's not prepared to let it rattle him.

Gabriel has gotten up, too, and stands next to me. Harris extends a hand toward him.

"I'm Deputy Harris."

Gabriel nods and shakes his hand.

"I'm the one your sister spoke to yesterday," Harris says.

This time, his tone is acerbic, his bonhomie clearly forced.

I gave him a solid reason to look at William. Shortly after that, he was twisting handcuffs around Brenner's wrists. And a few hours after *that*, he let William go and returned to the Ara with his tail between his legs.

It can't have been just me. There must have been more to William's arrest than my meager testimony—*it's always the husband*, after all. But if Harris needs a scapegoat, someone to blame for his bruised ego and reputation, then I'm the perfect candidate.

And clearly, Harris has done his homework about us.

Just now, he referred to me as *your sister.*

Except: There isn't a document in the world that states Gabriel and I are related. We don't share a last name. And when I spoke to Harris, I didn't say anything about our relationship.

That means he's looked us up and come across—what? Probably one of the magazine pieces that ran after Annie was found dead. The kind that explained about Émile, about Gabriel and me. The kind that spun all sorts of theories.

"Mind if I come in?" Harris asks.

He's talking to Gabriel, not me. I open my mouth, but he cuts in: "Like I said, we're going to want to talk to everyone. A lot of guests have already volunteered to speak to us."

I try to catch Gabriel's gaze. *Don't do it*, I yell at him mentally. *Not like this. Not without a lawyer. Maybe not ever.*

"It's fine," Gabriel says.

He puts a hand on my shoulder. It does nothing to reassure me. I don't trust it, this part of us, childlike, raised to believe in compliance.

"I'll ping you when we're done," Gabriel tells me.

It took me years after Annie's death to grasp the boldness of Gabriel's decision to talk to the police—by himself—three different times. It was reckless. We didn't know it at the time, but it was. He did everything he wasn't supposed to do, and he got lucky.

Maybe he learned all the wrong lessons from those three interrogations. Maybe he emerged with an unearned, dangerous confidence.

Through the closed door, I hear him—or maybe it's Harris—dragging our desk chair across the floor. I picture the two of them sitting down, one on the chair, the other at the end of a bed. Harris looking at Gabriel. My brother's face like a puzzle he's trying to solve. In his eyes, a million possibilities.

## 16 THE ONLY TOWN WE KNEW, PLUS A THREE-MILE RADIUS AROUND IT, HUDSON VALLEY

---

Twenty minutes. That's how long Gabriel said we could stay out the first time.

"But how do we do it?" I asked. "How do we leave?"

Gabriel hid his mouth behind a pamphlet. We were back in the packing room, where he had first brought up the possibility of outside-outside.

"We just . . . go," he said.

I didn't understand. His expression was patient, like he had experienced the same confusion and was prepared to walk me through it.

"There's no fence," he explained. "No locks or anything. We can just . . . go."

The only thing was timing. You had to wait for the weekend, after lunch. The mothers did laundry then. Émile retreated to his office or had meetings with the three or four women he kept as his entourage. There was a lull, an opportunity.

The possibility was right there. It had always been.

We met up the next day behind the communal showers. No one ventured there in the middle of the day.

Gabriel raised his eyebrows at me. *Ready?*

I nodded. While all the girls were busy with chores, I'd retrieved Émile's cash from the hole I'd torn in my mattress.

"Let's go," Gabriel said.

We walked. That was what leaving looked like: walking, and walking some more. No running. It had to look natural. Easy. We had to look innocent.

First there was the edge of Émile's world. Then a small stretch of road—no sidewalk, just two lanes of asphalt, untamed brush and trees on each side.

Soon enough, we came to a fork in the road.

"Simon said turn left, then right," Gabriel said.

So we did.

Émile's shadow lurked in every corner. Whenever I looked up, I expected to find him there, staring at us, a look of irreparable betrayal on his face. Every gust of wind was his hand trying to bring us back, every blade of grass the punishing fingers of a mother around our ankles.

How much time had elapsed?

I'd expected we'd know what twenty minutes felt like. Our days were so regimented. There was an assigned duration to each of our tasks: thirty minutes to package those pamphlets, forty to clean the entire cafeteria. But time outside-outside moved differently.

My breath quickened. How would we keep track? What if we stayed out too long? Fuck, what if we got lost?

"Hey," I said, trying to look calm in front of Gabriel. "How long do you think it's been?"

He didn't panic. Just paused and pulled something out of his pocket.

A stopwatch.

"Where did you get that?"

He shrugged. "P.E."

Émile kept stopwatches for fitness classes. For drills, too. He trained us. One day, maybe, men in uniforms would descend upon us, he'd explained. If that happened, we'd all have jobs. Mothers had to shred documents. Fathers had to hide supplies.

And the children—well, we mainly had to make sure our rooms and bodies were clean. We had to look healthy, well-fed. Stand close to the mothers. We were to be near them, as if they were a normal part of our lives. Like we had grown up close to them, loved by them.

Of course, the stopwatches were not for us to keep. They were expensive pieces of equipment, to be returned after each use, safely tucked away in a cardboard box.

"You took it?"

Gabriel clicked his tongue. He'd resumed walking, faster than before, and I had to jog to keep up with him.

"You have another idea?" he said.

Point taken. He had shouldered a risk for both of us, and here I was, making him feel bad about it.

"We're here," he said. "I think."

There, in front of us, was something we'd never seen before. A small town center. Buildings for which we didn't have words: a coffee shop, a convenience store, a bagel shop, a library.

We stood on a sidewalk, two kids in graying shirts that had been cream-colored once, Émile's fraying bracelets dangling from our wrists.

The coffee shop was so small we could see inside of it from the sidewalk: baked goods on the counter, black-and-white tile on the floor, a lone table with two chairs. Inside, a woman—tall, long black hair, green leather purse hanging from her shoulder— lifted a paper cup from the counter. When she stepped out, a whiff of something hit us—coffee beans, and then sweet smells like when the mothers baked, and an array of flavors and aromas we had never experienced.

Outside-outside pulsed all around us.

This *world*. We had no idea how to begin exploring it. We didn't know these trees. These streets. These leaves. These patches of grass. These people didn't know about Émile, or they chose not to live in his orbit.

Either way, we could not understand them.

"Now what?" I asked.

Gabriel took the stopwatch out of his pocket again.

"Now we go back," he said.

The world, right there, and yet so remote. A flash of possibilities, green leaves and a new sky—blue, open. A few dizzying breaths, standing on a sidewalk next to my brother, the most anodyne situation, and also the biggest taboo.

"Come on," Gabriel said.

He stuffed the stopwatch back in his pocket.

"How much time do we have left?"

"Let's just go."

He grabbed my arm and pulled me forward.

"Just tell me!"

Gabriel started jogging.

"Wait!"

I ran after him. Clearly, we'd messed up—taken too long to find the town center, lingered a few too many minutes on the sidewalk.

Soon I was running so fast I couldn't feel my legs. My chest burned. I kept pumping my arms, launching myself forward. My feet were as heavy as rocks; my calves were on fire.

Once Émile's world was in view again, Gabriel slowed.

"Time?" I asked between choppy breaths.

He looked at the stopwatch. His shoulders relaxed.

"One minute," he said, then let out a long exhale.

We were back, two furtive animals having outrun a pack of wild wolves, two kids and their fear nipping at their feet.

———

Every day at dawn, I met Émile in his office. We sat together at his desk. It was just big enough for two people to fit there side by side.

The memory of those times: golden, warm, bright. Sacred.

He always had work waiting for me.

It wasn't very difficult work, but it demanded all my attention. There were documents to print, pamphlets to sort into piles. Émile pulled books from a shelf and asked me to read passages out loud for him. After a couple of weeks, he asked me to proofread his own writing.

"You want me," I said, "to proofread . . . you?"

"Yes. I want to know what you think."

No one had ever wanted to know what I thought.

The first time I found a typo, my neck stiffened.

It wasn't a pleasant task, having to tell Émile he had made a mistake.

Maybe it was another test. Maybe I was supposed to pretend I hadn't seen the typo.

Or maybe he had made it on purpose. Maybe he wanted to see if I was ready to be honest with him.

"Here," I said, my pointer finger on the extra *n* in *plannet.* "I don't think that's right?"

Émile leaned over my shoulder to look. He frowned.

*Oh, no.*

"Good catch," he said. "Thank you."

The sweetness, then, of this powerful man, was so moving.

The next day, he plopped a binder on my side of the desk.

"Open it," he said.

The binder was full of numbers. There were tables and spreadsheets.

"Accounting," Émile said. "Can you check the numbers for me?"

I said yes, even though I wasn't sure what *checking the numbers* meant.

It didn't take me too long to figure it out. The numbers themselves showed me the way. It wasn't rocket science: For each line, for each column, I had to follow a pattern (usually addition or subtraction) and make sure the numbers added up. When they didn't, I affixed a small sticky label next to the problem area (this was called a flag, Émile said) and suggested a solution.

This became my favorite task. Numbers didn't care about complicated moral codes. They didn't expect you to *reflect*, to practice *radical self-honesty*. They were correct or they weren't. That was a level of clarity I had never experienced before.

While we worked—what a thrill, being a *we*—Émile spoke. He told me about his trips, about the people he'd met. He told me all he understood of the human mind.

Émile didn't ask much of his audience of one. Just listening. Just nodding. He, the sun, and me, the sunflower.

"Look at this," he'd tell me, and he'd pull out a book, skim to a specific passage.

Sometimes, when he was especially animated, it wasn't enough to let me read by myself. He cleared his throat and spoke the sentences for me. He would reach for something behind me. He would put his hand on my shoulder.

He wasn't a mystic. Not a healer. He never pretended his hands had powers.

But I felt it, the crackle of energy. A force not of our world.

———

Every morning, Émile and I worked until it was time for breakfast. "Walk with me there," he said, and that became a thing we did, walking to the cafeteria together.

People noticed.

Suddenly I was special. In class, I always had somewhere to sit. Other kids moved aside to let me through. Even the mothers cut me a break. They stopped telling me to work harder, to walk faster, to hold my back straighter.

I stopped fearing their hands.

There was jealousy, too. Loud whispers in the dark of the girls' dorm. *She thinks she's so special.* One night, my ratty blanket, stolen, and a line of girls swearing they had no idea what had happened to it. When the adults couldn't see, and even at times when they could, feet jutting out into my path to trip me. A splatter of blue ink at the back of my sweater.

Edwina was their ringleader, the blaze of faith in her eyes. She had burned hotter and brighter than any of us. She had tried so hard, but Émile had chosen me. Not her.

Me.

There was a darkness to Edwina. Her step was heavy, her shoulders hunched. She was nineteen years old. Past her prime. Too late for her to ever rise to my rank. In a few years, she'd be one in a sea of mothers.

I had been jealous of her, once. Jealous of her faith. Of the belief that seemed to animate every part of her—her proud posture, her confident gaze, her head always held high.

Now I pitied her.

I didn't mind it too much, the pettiness. It came with the territory. For the first time in my life, I had something worth being jealous of.

I wore the girls' envy like a heavy crown, a burden fit for Émile's little soldier.

———

For a while, Émile didn't say anything about his missing money. Not to me, and not, as far as I knew, to anyone else.

One evening a few weeks after our morning meetings began, I was walking behind Edwina and her friends from the bathrooms to our dorm. A commotion cut through the silence. We startled, girls like a herd of deer.

Émile had his hand around a mother's arm. The collar of her dress was yanked down, the top of her shoulder exposed.

"It wasn't me," she said.

"Don't lie."

He shook the mother's arm.

"Stealing," he said. "Really?"

She let out a small whimper. He brought his face closer to hers.

"What were you going to do with it?" he seethed. "What could you possibly have thought would come of this?"

"It wasn't me," the mother said through tears. "I swear. I told you. I don't know where it is. I have no idea."

Émile shook his head, the world's disappointment dripping down his shoulders. His voice was almost a whisper then, and still so clear, each word a stab wound: "You. Disgust. Me."

Words like spit on the mother's face.

A punishment that had been meant for me.

The mother shifted. Our eyes met.

I stood, legs bare in the evening breeze. A blizzard in my rib cage, ice caps melting in my brain. That's how I felt: a natural disaster of a girl.

Émile followed the mother's gaze. It landed on me, on us. Girls in nightgowns, hair down, the skin on our faces still shimmering with sink water.

My face burned as Émile's eyes met mine.

He squinted, then straightened his back. Nothing to apologize for. This was a complex situation, and we were just girls.

The next day, the mother showed up at breakfast. She kept her head bowed above her tray, brought spoons of gruel to her dry lips. Only when she went to collect the other mothers' bowls did I see them: bright-purple blotches on her arm, where Émile had gripped.

In the foggy light of the morning, her skin was thin and wrinkled, like tissue paper after it's been balled up. Her right eye was partly obscured by a puffy eyelid. There was an angry, bloated red stain underneath her eyebrow.

Émile didn't ask for our silence. He never, ever needed to.

Whatever we had seen, we didn't want to talk about it. Didn't even want to think of it.

## 17  ESCALANTE, UTAH

—————

### THE SIXTH DAY

There is no world in which I allow Gabriel to speak to Harris without my supervision.

I walk around our suite to the edge of our private patio.

If our sliding door were cracked open, I'd be able to hear Gabriel and Harris's conversation from here, but it's closed. Of course it is. I'm the one who locked it last night. Who checked, checked, and checked again.

I even pulled the thick blackout curtains behind me, tugged them all the way shut.

Which means that as long as the curtains remain in this position, these two can't see me, and I can't see them. But I can *hear* if I get close.

I give Gabriel and Harris a minute.

The curtains don't move.

I tiptoe onto the patio. Walk up to the sliding door, press my palms against the glass. Slowly, I lean forward, turn my head to the side, and bring my ear to the panel.

There it is. Gabriel's voice, muffled but unmistakable.

"What can I do for you, Deputy?"

"Can you tell me where you were two nights ago?"

The deputy's tone, as best as I can make it out through the glass door, is casual, almost breezy.

"Here," Gabriel says. "In this hotel."

Harris asks Gabriel who he was with. Gabriel names me. He doesn't say "my sister" or "my friend." Just my name: "Frida Nilsen."

Smart man. Sticking to the question. Maybe he can handle this, after all.

"And what did you do that night?"

"Well," Gabriel tells him, "we went to dinner, and then we went to bed."

"At any point during dinner, did you see Mrs. Brenner?"

"She was in the dining room," Gabriel says.

*Yes.* Sabrina, beautiful and alive, dipping a piece of pita into hummus, wiping the corner of her mouth with a quick flick of her thumb, her pink acrylics shimmering even in the dimmed lighting.

"Did you notice anything unusual?"

I hold my position against the sliding door. The sun is already beating down on the hotel, dappling my shirt with sweat. Every surface around me so white, so bright.

Another silence. Gabriel must be gazing at the ceiling, biting his lip the way he sometimes does when trying to focus.

"Actually, yes," he says. "She and her husband—they had a quick dinner. Just appetizers, I think. Everyone else was still eating when they left."

"Do you know why that was?"

"No idea."

"At any point in the evening," Harris continues, "did you lose sight of Frida?"

Gabriel's answer rings from the other side of the glass pane, clear and immediate: "No."

My hand almost slips from the door. I flex the muscles in my arm and try to still myself.

Images from that night come back to me. Indisputable.

During our meal, between our appetizers and mains, Gabriel got up from his chair.

"I'm just going to grab a sweater."

He said it, and then I lost him for a few minutes. I sipped my chamomile-infused water and waited.

Gabriel reappeared a short while later, clutching a sweater I'd never seen before this vacation, a sleek cream knit that looked impossible to fold.

"What did I miss?" he said.

It was all so innocent, so completely innocuous. The hotel was still full of people milling about. All this little interlude did was delay the arrival of our entrées by fifteen minutes.

Gabriel said he was going to get a sweater, and he came back with a sweater.

Why not tell the truth?

Does he not remember?

Maybe his memories are jumbled.

Or—maybe he's panicking. That's how it all began, with Annie: a woman's dead body, police asking questions. Enough to unsettle the steadiest person. Gabriel's most painful memories unlocked, the stitches of his trauma coming undone.

"What time did you go to bed?" Harris asks.

"A little before midnight."

"Did you hear anything unusual?"

"Not until the morning, when we heard a scream."

That's not exactly true, either. Gabriel heard Sabrina and William arguing during the night; he told me as much. But if Gabriel were to disclose that, then he would have to tell Harris that he had stepped out of the suite to look for me. And evidently he's not prepared to do that.

"Thanks for being forthcoming," Deputy Harris says.

Gabriel tells him of course.

The sounds of their voices shift. Harris must be walking toward the door, tucking away his notepad. Gabriel must be accompanying him, grabbing the door handle, preparing to let him out.

"One last thing," Harris says, his voice more distant than it was a moment ago. "Did you interact with Sabrina Brenner? At any point during your stay?"

Gabriel is quiet for a couple of seconds. Then: "No. I don't think I ever spoke to her."

"Nothing at all? Not even a few words?"

"No."

*No?*

I remember differently.

Day one of our vacation. The only interaction I recall between Gabriel and Sabrina. A vague memory, nothing I paid attention to at the time. But under the magnifying glass of Gabriel's omission, the image comes into sharper focus.

We were at the pool. We'd just checked in at the Ara and were still working out our vacation routine. I forgot my book; Gabriel forgot his hat. I offered to get it for him, but he said no, that he would come with me to retrieve it.

On the way to the room, my phone chirped. I checked it and fell behind a few feet.

When I looked back up, Gabriel was talking to Sabrina.

He had just bumped into her, or she had just bumped into him. Either way, she was laughing. Smiling in a way that meant either *Don't worry about it* or *I'm so sorry*. She brought her hand to Gabriel's arm.

He smiled back. Eyes crinkling, a brightness in his facial expression that I could recognize even from a slight distance.

I hadn't seen him smile like this in years. Not since he'd had a wife.

Sabrina patted Gabriel's arm.

"I'm sorry," she said.

He put his hand on top of hers.

"No," he said. "I think it was me."

And then—maybe I imagined it, but I replay the scene in my head, and here it unfolds with the same blinding clarity— Gabriel gave Sabrina's fingers a squeeze.

She didn't startle. Didn't jerk her arm back.

She raised her gaze to meet his. Her hand stayed on Gabriel's arm, just his arm, but—the intimacy of it.

Sabrina waited until Gabriel's grasp loosened, then slowly lowered her hand.

It was nothing. Two adults bumping into each other, a discreet apology.

But it feels memorable to me now. It feels, certainly, like *interacting with Sabrina Brenner.* Like exchanging *a few words.*

"Okay," Harris says.

There's the sound of a door opening. When Harris speaks again, his voice is no longer traveling through the glass pane, but from the other side of the suite.

"Twenty-nine, right?" he asks, and I can picture him pointing to the number engraved at the entrance.

Gabriel confirms.

"Good," Harris says. "You'll see me around. And if anything else comes up—I know where to find you."

## 18 *THE ONLY TOWN WE KNEW, HUDSON VALLEY, AND OUTSIDE-OUTSIDE*

We learned to optimize our trips. As soon as Émile's world was out of sight, we ran. I taught Gabriel how to look at the bend in the road and find the tangent, that invisible line at the top of the curve that meant you ran the most efficient course.

I retrieved Émile's money from my mattress before every trip and put it back when we returned. Except the dollar bill with the kissy lips. That one stayed hidden, always.

Our initial twenty minutes stretched into thirty. The first time we reached that duration, we found a pharmacy, a couple of side streets off the main road.

The store was an explosion of colors and letters, a treasure trove of unfamiliar items. For the first time ever, we felt the artificial breath of AC, an unnatural cold snaking up our sleeves, down our collars.

My eyes landed on a sign marked PAIN RELIEF. Gabriel and I spent ten minutes trying to decipher brand names and dosages.

"Can I help you?"

An employee, "Max," according to his badge, appeared next to us. He was probably—I realized years later—trying to figure out why two kids wanted to shoplift a bunch of ibuprofen, and how we could be so bad at it.

"No, thank y—" Gabriel started.

I cut him off.

"He gets headaches," I told Max.

"Okayyy," Max said slowly. "What . . . kind of headaches?"

Gabriel shrugged.

I answered for him: "The . . . bad kind, I guess."

I told him how Gabriel had collapsed, how he'd thrown up. I repeated what Gabriel had said about feeling like a hammer was beating against his skull, a hammer on fire.

"For migraines, you'll need the prescription stuff," Max said. I had no idea what he was talking about. "But in the meantime, you could try these. Take them as soon as you start getting symptoms."

Max picked up a bottle of vermilion pills. He went to hand it to me, then took his hand back.

"You two aren't from that . . . cult, are you?"

Émile had warned us about people saying stuff like that. They were to be avoided. But we wouldn't encounter them, Émile assured us, as long as we stayed where we were supposed to be.

Max was one of them.

And he held the pills.

"We're not," I said too fast, my cheeks burning.

Max studied us for a couple more seconds, then shrugged.

"Cool," he said. "Heard the guy who runs it is a real freak."

Gabriel opened his mouth. I spoke first.

"Total freak," I said, blocking the word from my brain as I repeated it.

Max handed me the pills.

I forced myself to walk, not run, to the register. The lady behind the counter announced that I owed her twelve dollars and ninety-six cents. I reached into my pocket and handed her Émile's ten and three singles.

The lady took the cash like it was nothing. She counted my

change and waited for me to extend my palm so she could drop coins onto it.

"Bye," she said.

"Bye."

As Gabriel followed me outside, I turned my head away from him.

He put a hand on my shoulder. I shrugged it off.

"Hey!" he said.

I shoved the paper bag against his chest.

"Just take them."

But he didn't. He kept his hands at his side, left it to me to carry our contraband.

We walked in silence.

"That guy didn't know what he was saying," Gabriel said after a while.

He meant Max.

"He was an idiot," Gabriel continued. "You can't talk to people when they're that dumb."

I knew what he was doing: rewriting history, pretending I hadn't said what I'd said. Gifting me a world in which I hadn't referred to Émile as a *total freak*.

"Just the stupidest guy in the world," I said.

Gabriel giggled. I did what I always did when I heard him laugh. I joined him.

It almost scared me, how much I needed him in that moment.

I pulled the pills from the paper bag and stuffed the bottle in my pocket. It rattled the whole way back. As we reentered Émile's world, I placed my hand over it. The pills went silent.

———

THE SIXTH DAY

M y phone buzzes in my pocket.
*Done.*

Gabriel, texting me, as promised, to let me know his interview has ended.

I step off the patio as quietly as possible.

When I return to the suite, Gabriel is standing by the desk,
leafing through a book—not actually reading it, just flipping
through the pages. We're not the type to scroll on our phones.
Another habit we never formed. This is what Gabriel does instead to put his mind on pause.

He looks up when I come in.

"How did it go?" I ask.

For a second, I hope he'll give me a brief grimace. *It was
going okay*, he might say, *until I freaked out, and—*

That would make his lie acceptable. If he confessed. We'd
figure out a solution together. We always do.

"Fine," he says.

*Come on.*

I could insist.

*I overheard*, I should say. *Why didn't you tell him about that time
you bumped into Sabrina? Or when you went to get a sweater?*

That's how we used to be, back in Émile's world: our minds superimposed to the point of transparency, nothing we wouldn't talk about.

Right?

Well.

Almost.

There was a place inside of Gabriel that remained out of reach, even to me. A mother would pull him away from a chore, and he'd return quiet, eyes down, shoulders sagging. The same thing happened sometimes when he came back from class.

Years later, I asked him about it. "When we were kids," I said, "sometimes you'd get all . . . weird."

"Weird?" he said.

"Yes. Suddenly, I couldn't talk to you anymore. What was that about?"

Gabriel frowned. We were sitting in a McDonald's, eating Quarter Pounders and fries. For a few months, after Émile and before Annie, we spent what little money and spare time we had trying out everything Émile had kept from us. Junk food. Meat. Candy. Movies, when we could afford tickets. Music, when it played for free.

"I got in trouble," Gabriel said.

"What do you mean?"

He tsked.

"What do you think? We were always getting in trouble. All the time. It was the only thing that ever happened to us."

I chewed a fry. That part, I understood. Émile needed us bad so that he could make us good.

Most of us had accepted it. But Gabriel, I realized the night of the Quarter Pounders, had woken up every morning of our childhood yearning to be perfect. Every time, he had made a promise to himself—that this would be the day when he made it to bedtime without messing up even once.

All Gabriel had ever wanted was to be blameless. Pure.

When he failed, he retreated into himself.

Early on, I'd tried to pull him out of his funk. I'd cracked jokes, thrown topics of conversation at him. Nothing had worked.

In time, I learned: All I could do was wait for him to come back to me.

Gabriel's mind like a Houdini trick: Struggle too hard against your restraints, and you'll get nowhere. Relax into it instead. Let the knots be knots, and watch them come undone.

———

"There's a group hike."

"Huh?"

Gabriel has put down his book and is looking at a hotel pamphlet. There's a picture of the Ara on the cover. Gabriel tilts it in my direction to show me a page. "Guided group hikes depart every Saturday at ten-thirty," it says.

I check the time on my phone. That's in twenty minutes.

*A hike? Really?*

Then again, what's the alternative?

I can't leave.

I don't want to stay in the hotel with William Brenner.

And as of ten minutes ago, I don't feel like being barricaded in a suite with Gabriel, either.

"I'll put on some running shorts," I say.

## 20 THE ONLY TOWN WE KNEW, HUDSON VALLEY, AND OUTSIDE-OUTSIDE

EIGHTEEN YEARS AGO

Gabriel and I expanded our perimeter. We explored outside-outside.

One scorching August afternoon, we walked around, parched, in search of water. We'd had a dehydrating lunch: One of the mothers had accidentally knocked a saltshaker into the stew.

"I'm so thirsty," Gabriel complained for the third time since we'd arrived on Main Street.

We turned a corner and stood outside a place we didn't have a word for yet—a *sports bar.* To our eyes, a place of impossible wonder. The glow of TV screens through the windows, the secret dances of sports we didn't play.

"Let's just ask here," I said, and pulled Gabriel by the wrist before he could protest.

The bar was cool and dark, with tall wooden tables and barstools. Mostly empty, except for a woman behind a counter.

"Hi-i?"

What had begun as a greeting ended in a question. What did she see? Two scrawny kids in weird, handwoven beige clothing. Dirt on our knees. Eternity behind our eyes, the arrogance of faith straightening our spines.

"H . . . hi," I said.

I tried to swallow, but I had no saliva left.

"Would it be possible . . ." I cleared my throat. "To have some water?"

The woman tilted her head. I waited for her to quiz us like Max had. *You two aren't from that . . . cult, are you?*

She shrugged.

"Sure."

I walked up to the counter. Gabriel followed me. Behind the bar, the woman filled two glasses.

"Here."

The glasses waited on the counter, beads of condensation rolling like sweat onto the varnished wood. Something held us back.

The transaction with Max at the pharmacy had been just that, a transaction. This was kindness. It was asking for help and receiving it. From someone who wasn't Émile.

The woman raised her eyebrows.

"Go ahead," she said.

I took one of the glasses. Gabriel shadowed me. We drank without catching our breaths, then returned our empty glasses to the counter.

"Joan," the woman said.

We told her our names.

"You two are welcome anytime," she said. "We're open every day. I'm usually around, but if I'm not, I'll tell my friend Scott to take care of you."

Years later, it occurred to me that, from the moment she'd first seen us, Joan had known where we'd come from. People around town knew about us, the people from the cult. They knew about the mothers in dresses, the children in dirty clothing, the handmade bracelets hanging off our wrists. Some had had their own encounters with Émile and his posse.

People who stood in Émile's way exposed themselves to years of harassment. Émile and his people started rumors, sent cease-and-desist letters, filed frivolous lawsuits. They buried their enemies under mountains of paperwork. Several locals had already gone bankrupt trying to cover their legal fees alone.

But Joan didn't confront us. She never made it our responsibility to explain.

And she was never afraid to help.

———

We came back. The following weekend, and every weekend after that.

Joan gave us our first taste of soda (Sprite, with a lemon slice). One afternoon, she slid a plate in front of us—yellow triangles covered in mashed avocado, cheese, and diced tomatoes.

"You ever had nachos?"

I shook my head. Gabriel leaned back on his stool, away from the food.

"We can't pay for this," he said.

Joan smiled. She seemed venerably old to us, but looking back, she couldn't have been more than twenty-three.

"On the house," she said.

Every bite of food, every sip of soda, was heaven and hell. Fleeting pleasure, then guilt like a heavy blanket.

One afternoon, pointing to the bar's TV, Joan taught us about baseball. We were Yankees fans, she informed us. She explained the rules multiple times, in vain.

"Maybe it's like foreign languages," she said. "Maybe it's harder to learn when you're not a little kid."

Regularly, she tried to give us things—better clothes, extra food to take with us.

"I know," she said. "I know you can't bring anything back. I just can't help asking."

Years later, I would read Joan's name in an online tabloid article. In her early thirties, she had moved to another small town in the Hudson Valley. There, she worked at a convenience store by day and played in a Rolling Stones tribute band by night. According to the article, Joan had been identified as one of the victims of a local serial killer, newly arrested.

An obituary mentioned Joan's love of music, her work ethic, her generosity. I wished I could have added to it. Wished I could have told the world that, in her younger years, Joan gave two children their first experience of kindness.

Joan taught us, gently, one glass of soda at a time, that the outside world didn't have to be scary. That there were wonders awaiting us.

## 21 ESCALANTE, UTAH

---

### THE SIXTH DAY

We meet our fellow hikers in the lobby.

"Let's head out as soon as possible," our guide, a young man with long legs and a straw hat, says in a good-natured voice. "We don't want to give the sun more of a head start than it already has."

Gabriel and I have each grabbed a bottle of water from the minibar, a small preventative measure against the desert's heat.

Our guide, who introduces himself as "I'm Ethan, by the way," leads us to the hotel's exit. We follow him onto the flatland that surrounds the compound: dirt and bitterbrush, mountains in the distance.

Fabio and Lazlo have joined the hike. Ditto the influencers and the *SVU* actor. The dad is here, too, though his wife and kids appear to have stayed at the pool.

"One day, this could be automated," the dad tells Ethan as we head toward the mountains.

"What? The hike?"

"Well, not the hiking part. But the guiding. All you'll have to do is think about where you want to go, and the algorithm will show you the best itinerary. If you get into trouble, your phone will call 911 right away. It'll be so much more efficient."

*Oh, shut up.*

It's so hot that my thoughts melt before I can fully form them. I focus on the hypnotic pace of our collective steps, left, right, left, right, sweat trickling down my back, my calves straining as we start up our first hill.

"It's not just hikes," the dad tells Ethan once we've reached the main hiking trail. "Most processes could benefit from automation. Even"—he glances back in the direction of the hotel—"murder investigations. Just imagine what AI could do if you put all the evidence into a computer. It could come up with a list of theories, rank them by likelihood. Imagine how much more efficient the court system would be."

I need to get away from this guy. From all of them.

How can I possibly think with all these people around me?

My coyote. I could go check on it. I don't have snacks, but I could share my water. Maybe.

At the very least, I won't have to listen to this dude tell Ethan how exciting it is that robots will take away his job in a mere few years.

"What are you doing?"

Gabriel's looking at me. I'm standing, sagebrush up to my ankles, three feet from the rest of the group.

"I just—"

Behind Gabriel, something rustles.

My coyote. It found me before I could even look for it.

From its hideout, it peeks at us.

"I just need a break," I tell Gabriel.

"I'll wait with you."

As if on cue, the coyote stills, ears raised. Gabriel hasn't seen it. I don't want to point it out.

"Go ahead," I tell Gabriel. "I'll catch up."

He sighs.

"Don't get lost," he says.

"I won't."

"I'm serious."

"I know."

Really, I do know. People die hiking. It happens all the time.

Finally, Gabriel steps away.

The coyote darts from the hiking trail, toward the den. I follow it. When I look back toward the footpath, I can't see the group.

*Good.*

The coyote stops at the short hill under which the den is located. I stay about ten feet away. It sniffs the base of a small dry bush, huffs, and lets out a bark.

There's a second of tension. Wordless communication, but clear: The coyote wants something from me.

*Oh.*

My little friend knows I have access to water and snacks. It saw me on the hiking trail but didn't wait for me to deliver the goods over there. Instead, it led me here, back to the den.

Suddenly, I'd bet money that my coyote's a mom and there are pups inside. Babies she hasn't been able to feed as much as she needs to due to her injury—which is why she led me here.

"Oh. Um—"

I pat the sides of my running shorts, as if a snack is going to materialize by magic.

"I'll come back," I tell the coyote, because that's something I do now. Talk to animals. "I'll . . . figure something out."

Before I turn around, I lean forward, hoping to catch a glimpse of the den, see if I can confirm my theory about the pups.

Something glints in the small dry bush.

I squint.

It's . . . black and shiny?

So out of place in the desert. Inorganic, man-made.

It's a phone.

*Her* phone.

I'd recognize it anywhere, the sleek black metal, and around it, the plastic shape, grimy and beaten up but still recognizable, the white ears and the whiskers, the little red dress, and the realization when I first spotted it that Sabrina Brenner was the only adult in the world who could pull off a Hello Kitty phone case.

Her fucking *phone.*

The cops must have looked for it.

Has William noticed? Did he realize that his wife's phone was missing?

Maybe he took it and chucked it into the wilderness. Maybe he counted on it disappearing forever, swallowed by a canyon, a needle in the desert's three-thousand-square-mile haystack.

Sabrina's *phone.*

There could be so many things in there. Things her husband doesn't want the police to see.

I'm dizzy just thinking of the possibilities. Notes about William Brenner's violence—verbal and physical. Audio recordings. Videos. Calls to a divorce lawyer. Maybe she was going to leave him, and he found out.

I need to know.

First things first. When I get to the phone, I won't touch it with my bare hand. There might still be fingerprints on it. I won't mess with those, and I'm certainly not going to put mine in their place.

Slowly, I bend and untie my left shoe. I remove my sock, push my foot back inside my sneaker, curl my toes against the bare insole.

I slide the sock onto my right hand. It's not perfect, but it's the best I can do.

I take a couple more steps in the direction of the den. The coyote bares its teeth, raises its hackles. It doesn't trust me near its babies. No wild animal would.

*Am I really going to risk rabies for this phone?*

*Oh, yes.*

I raise my hands in a gesture that I hope communicates appeasement, but all it does is rile up the coyote. It lets out a string of tense, pissed-off barks.

I leap forward. There's no other way. I'm about five steps from the phone when the coyote pounces, four steps when it reaches me, three steps when its snout brushes against my ankle.

The phone is in my line of vision. I bring my knee to the ground, feel my fingers close around the metal—it's hot to the touch, almost too hot to hold, after being in the sun for

so long, and I think about internal damage, about metal melting, about a woman's secrets forever trapped in a faulty piece of
technology—and spring back up.

I keep running. Or rather, I try, but my left foot won't work,
because—of course—there's a coyote attached to it.

Its teeth have sunk into my sneaker. I shake my foot. The
coyote presses harder around my shoe. I anticipated a bite—a
puncture wound, the sharp, burning pain of skin torn open—
but not this: the squeeze, the brute force, the coyote's jaws like
a vise.

I squeal. Despite my best efforts, I fall forward.

*Shit.*

I ignore the sting in my elbows.

The impact loosens the coyote's grip around my shoe. I free
my foot, push against the ground, and hoist myself up. Clutching the phone in my right hand, I sprint away.

———

At the top of the trail, the group comes into view. I slip the
phone into the side pocket of my running shorts, put my sock
back on, and catch up with the others.

"What happened to you?" Gabriel asks.

I look down: my outfit is covered in dust; my right elbow is
bleeding.

"I fell," I tell him. "It looks worse than it feels."

I nudge my chin forward.

"What's going on here?"

People are standing in a circle. Ethan is at the center, backpack at his feet, a vague air of panic on his face. Two of the three
influencers have their hands on their hips; the third is yelling at
the *SVU* actor.

"Why don't you tell us where *you* were, you creep?"

Fabio gasps.

"I'm not sure how it started," Gabriel whispers in my ear,
"but this guy"—he nudges his chin toward the *SVU* actor—
"got into it with those three"—the influencers. "About alibis
and stuff."

"Ah."

"She"—he tilts his head in the direction of the influencer presently yelling at the actor—"was saying she overheard Harris talking about the investigation. Something about how Sabrina died after three in the morning."

"Okay."

"One thing led to another," Gabriel continues. "I think the *Law and Order* guy started talking about direct evidence versus circumstantial? And then she"—our influencer in chief, again— "asked him if he knew all that from his little show. He did *not* like that."

"I'm sure."

The *SVU* guy gestures at the sky.

"I was on a call with my agent!"

"In the middle of the night?" the influencer sneers.

"Madison," one of her two friends says, but Madison doesn't seem to hear her.

"He's a Hollywood agent!" the *SVU* guy squeaks, waving his hands around wildly. "You have no idea how these things work!"

The *SVU* guy is holding up a finger, telling Madison to wait, wait, reaching inside of his pocket, hopefully for his phone.

"Look at my call log," he spits out.

I can't see his screen from here, but Madison leans forward, squints, then leans back with a resigned smirk.

"I hope that makes you feel really good," she says. "I hope that makes you feel like a big man."

The actor drops his head in exasperation.

"Why me?" he asks. "Why not anyone else?"

Madison considers the rest of the hikers, apparently waiting for us to proffer our own alibis.

*Jesus.*

No way am I telling Madison that I left my suite that night. That I was one of the last people to see Sabrina Brenner alive.

That Gabriel was out there, too.

"Ethan," I say while Madison and the actor keep bickering. "Should we maybe go back to the hotel?"

Ethan gives me a resigned nod.

"Folks," he says, and extends his arms to herd us back into a tidy line. "Let's head back. We've lost a fair amount of time, and it's only going to get hotter from here on out."

Defeated, he leads us down the trail. Madison and her friends walk directly behind him; the actor sulks at the back.

Gabriel and I stay quiet.

I'll tell him about the phone when we're back.

Maybe.

Or maybe I don't have to.

That's how it works between us.

*You run, I follow. No questions asked.*

So many times throughout our lives, it's been vital, this unspoken agreement. We have each other's back. Always. Even if there are things we don't know. Especially when there are things we don't understand.

## 22 *THE ONLY TOWN WE KNEW, HUDSON VALLEY*

Word of our expeditions spread. Not to the adults, but to the other kids.

No one would have dared tell on us. Émile had chosen me. People knew that. They resented it, but they weren't foolish enough to try to turn him against me.

Gabriel and I enjoyed our newfound clout. We turned sixteen. We turned seventeen. People wanted to be around us. And so, they dealt the only currency they had.

They told us secrets.

It began with small things. There were dozens of tiny transgressions, hundreds of micro scandals waiting to be whispered into our ears.

A secret crate where stale bread was stored. The mothers didn't count the pieces. If you took one or two, no one would notice.

The mothers' stash of forbidden books. Well, we assumed it was the mothers'. The men on the covers like an alien species, with their long hair and unbuttoned shirts, muscled torsos and pants that hung low on their hips. Illicit materials, hidden in shifting piles of unwashed laundry. We did not imagine the fathers capable of such cleverness or agency. The clandestine library was women's work.

And then, there was the secret I refused to hear.

Gabriel and I had gotten into the habit of meeting with the others at night. Everyone was always slipping out, all the time. Edwina herself did it with her own friends. Even after she turned twenty and moved away from the girls' quarters into the adults' coed dorms. She kept coming by, meeting with the younger members of her posse, outside or in the dorm, sometimes walking out with one girl, sometimes with a small group.

It had been a turbulent day. Two people had been sent to the Secret Place for breaking dishes—somewhat intentionally, according to most versions of the story. Émile had been spotted whispering feverishly to a mother outside of his office. Kids weren't paying attention in class.

We were growing older. It was almost summer, and there were wild birds inside of us.

"I'll leave," Simon announced. "When I'm eighteen or whatever. I'll just go."

A group of us—me, Gabriel, Louisa, Simon, his friend Isaiah—had been whispering under a tree, an old elm whose trunk had recently become covered in invasive black spikes.

Everyone went silent.

"What?" Simon said. "People do it."

Louisa shook her head. "They don't choose to leave," she said. "Émile makes them."

Simon rolled his eyes. "Émile," he said. In a falsetto voice, he repeated: "Émile, Émile, Émile." He turned to stare at Louisa. "What's Émile going to do when I go? Come and get me?"

Louisa shrugged, but Simon couldn't let it go. He was the gossiper in chief, the original keeper of outside-outside. And, over the past couple of years—it occurred to me as I watched him nudge Louisa with his elbow—his status had been threatened. By Gabriel and me and our repeated journeys beyond the center of our shared universe.

"You should care more than anyone," Simon added. "You and all the girls."

Louisa frowned. I pretended to ignore what Simon had just said, but I kept listening.

Thankfully, Louisa took the bait.

"What are you talking about?"

Simon looked at her in mock incredulity. He was pleased, really—so pleased to know something she clearly didn't.

"You have no idea, do you?" he asked.

Louisa clicked her tongue.

"Shut up."

Simon shook his head.

I don't know what I pictured then. I couldn't have spelled it out. There was something dark and cutting at the center of Émile's world, something of which I had only a remote sense. The knowledge was in the soil under our feet, in the vegetables we grew and ate.

Something I didn't want to confront.

"Seriously, Simon," I said. "Shut up."

Simon turned his gaze to me.

*Come on*, he seemed to say. *You of all people should know.*

———

I n the lobby, our group disbands. The actor speed-walks away from the influencers.

Gabriel's phone rings.

"Hey," he says, then mouths "Howard" in my direction. "No, that's fine. I can talk."

He steps away, presumably heading back to our suite.

Where *is* Harris?

I spot his colleague, the young woman who examined Sabrina's body two days ago, speaking to Catalina in a corner of the lobby.

"Excuse me," I say. "Deputy . . ."

The police deputy turns around.

"Calhoun," she says.

Her hair is in a bun at the nape of her neck, though some strands have become loose and frame her face. She swipes them back.

"I'm Frida," I say. "I spoke to your colleague yesterday. I've been—"

"I know who you are."

*Fantastic.*

Catalina scuttles away. Deputy Calhoun eyes me up and down.

I become aware of my dirt-streaked shorts, my half-undone ponytail.

"I was in the desert," I say. "Walking."

She folds her arms across her chest.

"There was a coyote," I blurt out. "I followed it because . . . That doesn't matter. The point is, I found this."

I wrap my right hand in the folds of my T-shirt and extract Sabrina's phone from my pocket.

The deputy's eyes widen.

"It was Sabrina Brenner's," I say.

"How do you know that?"

"I recognize it."

Calhoun considers me.

"It's the case," I say. "It's pretty—I don't know—eye-catching."

"Indeed."

She raises a hand.

"Hold on one second."

Calhoun disappears behind a side door marked STAFF ONLY. A minute later, she returns with a latex glove on her right hand.

"Here," I say, and drop the phone onto her palm.

"Where did you say you found it?"

"In the desert. Near the main hiking trail? It was slightly off the path. Well, it was at the entrance of a coyote den."

She eyes me.

"We've searched that area multiple times," she says flatly.

The rest of her sentence hovers between us unsaid: *And we didn't see a phone.*

Well, I don't know. *Maybe you missed it, Deputy Calhoun. Maybe the coyotes moved it. I'm just the messenger.*

"I'm going to ask you again," she says. "Where did you find this?"

*Okay. I see we've stopped playing nice.*

But I force a smile.

"I'd be happy to show you, if that helps. It was partially hidden behind a bush."

Calhoun raises an eyebrow.

"But if you don't need me for now, I'm going to go back to my suite," I say.

A key thing, when dealing with the police: understand when to give up, and remember that you're free to go.

Just one last thing.

"There's an injured coyote in the desert," I say. "Right off the main hiking trail. I reported it, but it looks like no one has come. Can you get animal control out there, or something?"

I leave before she can say no.

---

Gabriel's call has evidently wrapped up. He's sitting cross-legged on the bed, typing on his laptop.

"We need to talk," I say.

He raises his head.

"We do?"

I've tried to avoid this conversation, but there's no way around it. Deputy Calhoun didn't address me like an innocent party just now. She spoke to me like I was a suspect.

And so I need to know why Gabriel lied.

"Listen."

Do I even know how to talk to him anymore?

We haven't had a real conversation in so long.

"I know Harris asked you about the night Sabrina died."

"Huh?"

I sit next to him.

"When he spoke to you earlier. I know you said you didn't lose sight of me. But that's not true, right? You left the table."

"What?"

"And I know he asked you if you'd ever interacted with Sabrina."

Something shifts in Gabriel. He sets his laptop on his night-stand and swivels so that his back is to me, his feet on the floor.

"And I don't know," I say. "I don't know why you said those things. It's complicated. But . . ."

I can't say it. Not completely. Can't look at Gabriel and

form the words: *Why on earth would you do something so stupid? So sloppy?*

"Help me out?" I ask instead.

Gabriel mutters something I can't hear.

"What?"

"How do you even know about that?" he asks, overenunciating.

"I overheard."

He lets out a bitter little laugh.

"Overheard?"

"Fine. I was listening."

"I can't believe you."

He plants his palms on the bedspread to push himself up. I grab his left wrist, the one closest to me, and stop him.

"I'm sorry," I say. "I got scared."

He snaps his wrist from my hand.

"Gabriel," I say. "Please. We need to talk about—"

"I don't want to talk."

He's not yelling. In fact, he's almost too calm, adjusting his position, rubbing a hand over his face.

Gabriel. Always pushing things down. Swallowing back his anger, his hurt pride, his shame. Yearning, always, to be not just better than the rest of us, but better than himself.

"Come on," I say. "Lying? To a cop?" It's a relief, of sorts, to speak this absurdity out loud, to dump Gabriel's poor choices at his feet. "People probably saw you! They'll remember you leaving the dining room, and they'll remember you speaking to Sabrina. They'll tell Harris, if they haven't told him already. And then what?"

Gabriel glances at me over his shoulder.

"You have no idea," he says.

"Then tell me."

"What?"

"Tell me what's going on. Gabriel, we've been here for six days, and sometimes I feel like—"

*Sometimes I feel like there's no limit to the things you're holding back from me.*

"Take a guess," he says.

"What?"

He stands.

"I don't know," I say, and get up, too. "Maybe you panicked. Maybe you didn't want to . . ."

He opens his mouth.

"Maybe you didn't want to get into the details with Harris," I try again. "Maybe you figured it would be easier that way, after everything . . . else that happened."

Gabriel steps toward the sliding door.

"Not that I think you have anything to—"

When he turns around, every muscle in his face is tensed up. He's outraged.

I've never had to spell it out. Never had to say anything to the effect of: *I don't think you had anything to do with it; I don't think for a second that you killed your wife.*

Gabriel's innocence has always gone without saying. That was the case when he reported Annie missing and when the cops searched his house and all three times Gabriel spoke to them. It stayed that way when the neighbors turned on him and when he packed two suitcases and boarded a one-way flight to Seattle.

And now I've just made it look like his innocence does, in fact, need to be stated.

"I'm sorry. I didn't mean—"

"See, that's the problem." There's a simmering quality to Gabriel's voice, somehow worse than if he were yelling. "I never know, with you. I can't ever tell for sure what you believe."

I want to walk up to him, put a hand on his shoulder, calm us both down, but his words have pinned me to my spot.

*What do you mean, you can't ever know what I believe?*

*Have you doubted me all these years? Is that why you stopped visiting me? Why you stopped writing?*

*Because you'd convinced yourself that I thought—?*

"That's not fair," I say.

He shrugs. "Isn't that why you ghosted me?"

"What?"

Gabriel shakes his head, like, *That's not even the point.* But he continues: "You never visit anymore. You never call. You never write. What else am I supposed to think?"

*You're the one who pulled away.*

*Aren't you?*

*I tried. I waited for you.*

*I'm sure I did.*

"I'm sorry," I say.

"I can't do this right now."

He walks toward the bathroom.

"You've got to talk to me."

I rarely speak like this, in the imperative, but in this moment it feels good—so good—to tell Gabriel what to do.

"I don't need to explain anything."

"I'm not asking you to. But, Gabriel . . ." I try to compose myself, but there's a shiver in my arms and legs that has nothing to do with the cool draft of our AC. "We have to deal with this together. No matter what I do next, it affects us both. If I match your story, I'm lying. But if I tell the truth? Harris won't care who's lying and who isn't. All he'll see are two stories that don't match. We'll both look like liars."

When Gabriel turns around to look at me, he's rolling his eyes.

"You know I'm right," I say.

"Well, I'm sorry," he says. His voice escalates until he's yelling, really yelling, this time, on the "sorry," and it occurs to me that Gabriel and I have never—not once in twenty-three years—had an argument. Not even in our darkest moments. "I'm sorry that I didn't handle everything perfectly. I'm sorry that I made even more trouble for you," he continues. "Seriously, Frida, sometimes I wish—"

He catches himself.

"What?" I say. "You wish what?"

"Forget it."

He moves to shut the bathroom door. I should let him go. Hope that he'll cool down, try again later.

But I can't. My hand shoots out, wedges itself between the door and its frame.

"Please," I say. "Just talk to me."

A bitter smile slashes across his face.

"I feel you watching me. All day long. Like you're waiting for—something. I don't know what. Like you're waiting for me to let something slip."

*Yes, maybe I am watching you. There are things about you I still don't understand. How to talk to you. How to bring up the past. How to talk about that goddamn documentary.*

*We've known each other for most of our lives, and still, you keep me on my toes.*

There's no point in trying to explain any of this. He wouldn't believe me.

I thought it was over, years ago. When the police closed the case. When Gabriel walked free. Even when he decided to start over on the other side of the country. I dropped him off at the airport and waved at him while he joined the TSA line and thought, *Now we'll put all this behind us.*

But it's not behind us. It's in our skin cells, in our hair follicles, under our fingernails.

This case.

It never ends.

"You always treat it like a miracle," Gabriel says, acerbic. "The fact that I wasn't arrested. That I wasn't charged or convicted."

"Mistakes happen. Innocent people get charged all the time."

"Do you think I don't know that? But at the end of the day, I didn't commit a crime, and I wasn't convicted of one. That's not a miracle. It's just fair."

I close my eyes.

It *did* feel like a miracle when Gabriel walked free. Not because I thought he was guilty, but because in the world I know, innocence doesn't bail you out; it just makes you easier to trap.

"I never thought you killed her," I say, my voice low. "I swear. I just . . . have less faith in the system than you do, I guess."

He scoffs.

"Remind me what you do for a living?"

"What does that have to do with anything?"

He shakes his head.

"I just think the system has worked out for you. In some ways."

*Touché.*

Gabriel has never verbalized it before, but I've intuited it for years—his resentment that I took to the real world much more easily than he ever did. That I made it work for me, when he kept bumping into walls.

And there it is. Lurking underneath it all, that poisonous notion—the idea that he would have been better off staying with Émile.

So many things wouldn't have happened, if Gabriel had stayed.

He's given up on closing the bathroom door. Instead, he's standing in front of one of the bathroom sinks—"his" sink, the one on the left—and running the water.

"We can fix this," I try. "If Harris asks me, I'll tell him the same thing you did. I'll say we were never out of each other's sight. I'll say I never saw you and Sabrina—"

"For fuck's sake, Frida!" Gabriel's voice shakes with fury. "I don't need you to lie to the police. Don't do it. Especially not for me."

He reaches for something. I'm not sure what. His hand clips his toothbrush—electric, like mine. In the mess of the past nine years, one thing hasn't changed: Gabriel and I are both obsessive about dental care. We didn't get to see a dentist until we'd both reached the age of twenty-one. By then, our mouths had hatched a litany of problems that would take months (and hundreds of dollars we didn't have) to fix. So now we don't mess around.

Except Gabriel forgot his charger when he packed for this trip. We've been sharing mine. It falls to the floor, along with Gabriel's toothbrush, in a clatter of plastic.

"Fuck!"

Gabriel kneels to pick up the pieces. I go to help him, but he stops me with an extended arm.

"I've got it."

"It's fine."

"I said, I've got it."

"Gabriel, it's okay, it's just a—"

But he really has, in fact, got it. Gabriel has gathered all the plastic pieces. He tries to fit them together. They resist his clumsy attempt, slip out of his hands and back onto the floor.

"Fuck it!"

Before I can try to help again, Gabriel has picked up the base of the charger and hurled it at the wall behind me.

I don't move.

I've never known Gabriel to have a temper. Not with me. Even as kids, we knew how to disagree peacefully.

Well. Clearly, things have changed.

Or maybe they were never what I thought they were.

"I'm going to get some air," Gabriel says through clenched teeth. "Don't follow me."

*I wouldn't dream of it.*

No, seriously.

I let him go.

For the first time in twenty-three years, I truly let him go.

THE SIXTH DAY

turn off the bathroom faucet and sit on my bed.

Gabriel's side of the suite is alive with his absence.

It's too easy, in this moment, to believe that this is it. That he'll never come back. That we'll never make this right.

Too easy to believe that things only get worse from here. That this is the kind of moment my life inevitably serves up. That I am built for loneliness, for loss.

There are things I remember, in my worst moments. Whenever I'm having a bad day, or whenever I feel ashamed or embarrassed, there's a movie my mind likes to play.

It's made of memories. The kind I like to think I shoved into a mental trunk before locking it and throwing away the metaphorical key.

That image sounds healthy to me. A coping mechanism.

But.

My memories are not carefully organized. My mind is not a trunk.

It's something more dangerous. With its nooks and crannies, its hidden labyrinths, my mind is a beehive.

A beehive like any other: Approach at your own risk. Poke your hand in, feel the heat of a thousand stings.

## 25  *THE ONLY TOWN WE KNEW,*
## *HUDSON VALLEY*

———

I didn't realize until years later that this is how the story always ends.

For people like me, who grew up in this kind of world. A world with a man at its center, a universe shaped by his presence, his ideas, his wants.

Another thing I didn't immediately grasp: why he waited until we were eighteen.

There was a lot I didn't know then.

It was December. I'd finished school the previous summer. More than ever, my days belonged to Émile. We worked together in the morning. In the afternoons, I taught class. Made meals. Once a month, people who were thinking of joining came to the compound for introductory sessions. Kids weren't privy to that aspect of things; Émile didn't want them near outsiders. (Didn't want them to talk too candidly, I later realized.) As an almost-adult, I'd discovered the ritual: We entertained them in the reclaimed chapel, served them coffee and home-baked cookies in the cafeteria.

Other girls (I still thought of us as girls) looked after the children, but I was exempt. I didn't have to tell Émile that I didn't want to do it; he sensed it. And I was chosen. I didn't do things I didn't want to do.

That's something I'm still ashamed of. That I taught his classes. That I shared his word. That I left my least favorite tasks up to the other girls.

This is not the person I try to be.

Here's what happened: I turned eighteen, and for a few hours, nothing changed. I met Émile in his office. I proofread a blog post for his website, which was up and running by then. I had lunch. I taught class. We roasted parsnips for dinner. I went to bed.

I woke to someone shaking my shoulder.

Edwina.

"Follow me," she said.

Just like ten years earlier.

She led me back to Émile's building.

I knew Émile's kingdom; I had its metaphorical keys. In his office, I knew which window was easy to open and which one got stuck every time. I could have recited the titles of his books in the order in which they were stacked on his shelves.

Inside the building, I headed toward the office.

Maybe it was the test. Maybe we all had to take it again, once we turned eighteen. A second chance.

It took me a couple of steps to notice that Edwina was no longer in front of me.

"Where are you going?" she whispered.

She was standing at the bottom of the staircase that led to Émile's living quarters.

"Come back here," she said.

I followed her up the steps, down a narrow hallway. I'd never been up there. She stopped in front of a door.

Edwina didn't knock. She opened it, and there it was.

There *he* was.

There's what I know happened, and there's what I remember.

What I remember: The bed was, oddly, in the center of the room. I'd never seen an individual bedroom, only dorms, but even to me, that placement didn't feel right.

The light was off.

Émile didn't speak much. He presented what happened next as a sort of sacrament, except he wouldn't have used that word.

What would he have said?

If I close my eyes, if I deprive all my senses, I can still hear it.

His explanation, the mild vibrato in his voice, almost like he was choking up.

A *culmination*. That's what he called it.

The result of years of devotion.

The sheets were scratchy. Their touch invoked the mothers in the laundry room, bent over vats of soapy water, nails scratching against the washboards, their cheeks glowing red in the steam.

His hands were—well. I don't remember his hands. I remember the whoosh of his skin against fabric. I remember a force pulling me forward, slowly but decisively.

I remember that I understood nothing but somehow knew everything.

Émile was a shape above me, a weight pinning me to the mattress. He was a chaos of movement, grunts, and fingers.

His breath was slow at first, and then something hurt, and everything quickened.

When I tried to get away, the word *wriggle* popped into my brain. I spelled it out for myself, w-r-i-g-g-l-e, like maybe it could save me. Like maybe if I focused on this funny word and its spelling, I might find a way back to myself.

*Wriggle*, I thought, *like a worm*.

I remember that I was cold when I leaped from the bed.

I don't remember what Émile said, if he said anything. Maybe he tried to hold me back; maybe he knew he didn't need to. He had thought of everything.

Edwina stepped into my path. She must have been standing in a corner of the room this whole time. I hadn't noticed. I didn't see her there until her body became a barrier between me and my only exit.

She led me back where I'd come from. That, I haven't forgotten. When things started up again, she was there. Front-row seat.

The next time I tried to do it, the next time I tried to *wriggle*, her hands did not hesitate. They wrapped themselves around my ankles.

What I do remember—what I will never forget—is that she kept me there until it was over.

And here's what I know: That I shed a part of myself just then. That a version of me is trapped in that moment. That in some ways I've never gotten back up, never freed myself from Edwina's grasp.

It ended. Technically, it ended.

There are flashes: The white shape of Émile's back as he sat on one side of the bed. The door shutting behind me. I don't think he met my gaze once. Outside, the ground was frozen; I'd forgotten my shoes on the second floor. I didn't go back for them, made my way back to my dorm in socks.

When I got back into my own bed, I couldn't feel my feet.

I couldn't feel anything.

———

The most insulting part: Life went on.

It went on right outside my window. Owls hooted. Bushes rustled with the furtive steps of deer and raccoons.

The sun rose.

I reported for duty as usual. In the daylight, Émile was back to his usual self. He greeted me, pulled out my chair, handed me the day's work.

I proofread his fucking pamphlets. I organized his fucking books.

The blur of his body next to me, his movements as familiar as an old song.

But that day, my own gestures were imprecise, clumsy. Objects slipped from my hands. My entire body ached. My shoulders. My legs. There were a hundred little pains, a thousand alarm bells all going off at the same time within me.

At dinner, I found Simon.

It felt weird, going to Simon instead of Gabriel. But I needed to know.

"There's something I need to ask you," I said.

Simon looked up from his soup.

"Yes?"

"Not here."

Maybe he understood.

"Under the elm," he said. "As soon as you can."

I nodded.

That night, I slipped out of bed. My feet took me to the spiky old elm as if on autopilot. It was too cold for anyone else to be out. Simon and I had the tree to ourselves.

"The thing," I said. "The thing you wanted to tell us about Émile."

Simon pinched his lips.

"What was it?" I asked.

He sighed and looked in the distance.

"You really want to know?"

*I think I already do,* I wanted to say, but the words wouldn't come out.

Simon took a breath in.

"Émile," he said. "He . . . he sleeps with the girls."

*Yes.*

It had made an intuitive sort of sense, that whatever Émile had done to me, he'd done to others. He had a process. A system. He and Edwina had both moved with such confidence.

"Since when?" I asked.

Simon shrugged.

"Since forever."

*Of course.*

What had happened in Émile's building wasn't an anomaly, something that ran parallel to an otherwise healthy world. It was the point. It was why he'd created this world in the first place.

I thought about them. The other girls. Girls on a conveyor belt, like the slaughtered chicks on the video from the test.

Émile taught us that we were the menace, and the world had to be protected from us. But this whole time, we were the chicks. Soft little beings, raised and groomed with a purpose in mind. Until hands would pluck us from our blind little world and deliver us to our fate.

I had more questions. Simon had answers.

Who knew? Everyone knew. All the adults. All the mothers.

No one did anything about it. Wasn't that wrong? It was. But Émile waited until the girls were eighteen, and apparently that made it less wrong—at least according to Simon's vague understanding. How often did it happen? That was unclear, but Émile rotated through the available girls. Once it started, it happened with some regularity.

There was one question I wasn't sure how to ask.

Did all this mean that Émile was . . . a father? Everyone's father? Some people's father?

Simon shook his head. The fathers were the fathers. Émile was something else.

(It would be years and so many developments until a meticulously reported magazine profile mentioned Émile's vasectomy. It was also, as it happened, the profile that taught me the test was rigged.)

"How do you know all this?" I asked Simon.

He shrugged. I could guess what that meant: *Some girls spoke. Obviously. But I can't tell you which ones.*

I thought about Edwina, slipping into the girls' dorm, extracting a rotating crop of them from their beds. Sometimes a group, sometimes an individual girl. In some instances—when she'd left with multiple girls—she must have, truly, been meeting up with friends. But when she'd made her way out with just one girl—those nights, she'd been on a mission. She was headed to Émile's house. Doing his bidding.

Simon and I went back to our respective dorms. The world had shifted under my feet. I sat on my bed, knees to my chest, arms around my legs.

I knew nothing of this Émile. A man who *slept with the girls.* A man with a system. Who waited until we were of age, until he was off the hook. A man who helped himself to *the girls,* marked us as if with a branding iron. Desire like an assembly line, a thing that had to be done.

I had believed in him.

A man, powerful but sweet; the implicit trust of his unlocked office.

It was a lie, this version of him that I'd trusted my whole life.

Pure Émile, beautiful Émile, the best man accepting a dollar bill marked with lipstick, an angel led astray, giving in to temptation, just once.

He wasn't real.

All he was, all he had ever been, was a story I'd told myself.

———

The next morning, at dawn, I went back to his office.

As long as I lived in his world, there was no other choice. His rules. His desires.

Around seven, he did something.

Ah, yes.

That, I remember.

His fucking hand on my fucking shoulder.

At ease. Unquestioning. Proprietary.

Disgusting.

"Oh," he said. "I almost forgot."

He grabbed my wrist. With a long pair of scissors, he snipped off my white bracelet. It fell to the ground, dirty and worn and abandoned.

"Here."

He reached into his pocket and produced a new bracelet. This one was blue, larger than its predecessor. It wasn't special: Everyone got one when they turned eighteen. Gabriel had received his own six months earlier.

"Hold still," Émile said, and tied it around my wrist with a triple knot.

Later on—much, much later on—I swam in the Atlantic Ocean and felt the creepy swirl of seaweed wrapping itself around my ankles. It brought me back to that moment, Émile's office and his fucking bracelet around my wrist.

Émile held up my arm, admiring his handiwork.

The bracelet was supposed to feel like a big deal. It was a privilege, an achievement.

Émile dropped my wrist and turned his gaze to me. His expression was exalted, expectant. He was waiting for me to say something.

"Thanks," I said.

That's when I knew.

---

Gabriel and I were on cafeteria-cleaning duty that night. On our way out, I whispered to him: "Can you meet tonight?"

"Sure," he said.

Under a bare-limbed red oak, Gabriel sat next to me. Our shoulders were touching. It was well below freezing. I wore my ratty sweater and my thin coat over my nightgown, pants underneath, my blanket wrapped around my shoulders. The night wind didn't care; it reached my skin as easily as if I'd been naked.

Gabriel and I huddled. Our breaths made foggy shapes in the dark. I felt the warmth of my brother's exhale, the soft widening and collapsing of his rib cage.

I told him what had happened. I didn't know the proper words—didn't know there *were* proper words. I described it as best as I could, and when I was done, Gabriel was wincing.

"I can't stay," I said.

Speaking the words out loud made it sound so deliberate. It gave the whole enterprise the illusion of choice.

Gabriel shifted away from me. The cold nipped at the side of my body against which he'd been resting.

"No," he said. "You can't."

He said more things: *I'm so sorry* and *Are you okay* and *Edwina*. I waved his outrage away. There was no time.

"I can't go by myself," I said.

In the silence that followed, I was suspended in the air. I was droplets of condensation. I was a breeze so thin it could barely be felt.

Gabriel swallowed. Ran a hand through his hair. Gazed up at the sky.

"You can't," he said again.

He looked at me then. We were back in the Secret Place, the two of us in the unknowable darkness.

"You don't want to go," I said.

He shook his head.

"It's complicated."

A chasm opened in me.

I was going to lose him, too.

After all this time. After all this love.

"Actually, no," Gabriel said, his voice louder—almost too loud. "Forget what I just said. It's not complicated at all."

The relief.

And the vindication: What Émile had done was unaccept-able to Gabriel, too.

"We can't just go, though," Gabriel said. "It's too easy for him. If we just go. He gets to keep doing it. He gets to keep . . . everything."

*Oh.*

"You mean we should do something?" I asked.

He nodded.

"But what?"

"I don't know yet," he said.

Outside-outside, Gabriel was always the one following me, and I was always the one pulling him in new directions. Our dynamic had shifted: Now I was the one asking questions, and Gabriel was calling the shots.

I didn't like it. It was another thing I'd been robbed of.

"I'll think about it," I said. "I mean, we'll think of something."

It didn't take long.

---

THE SIXTH DAY

I'm not giving up.

Gabriel is gone.

Doing what?

None of my business. Not right now.

Gabriel's in trouble. He's lying to the police, and he won't tell me why. Meaning: He made some kind of mistake, and now he won't let me help.

*Don't you realize how fragile your life is?*

*I can't fix it if you don't tell me.*

And so I'm going to find out.

Our suite is mine, for now.

I have to move swiftly.

*Who did you become, Gabriel, in the years you've spent away from me?*

I open the armoire in which we've now unpacked our clothes twice—mine on the right, his on the left. My piles neat, his forever collapsing. Gabriel is the kind of person who leaves a small trail of mess wherever he goes: a wet towel on our clean beige floor, a worn T-shirt hanging by the soaking tub where a fluffy towel should be, random papers crumpled on his sandalwood nightstand. For six days, Gabriel has made his way around the hotel like a small tornado, and I've done my best to contain it. I've picked up the towel, folded the T-shirt, thrown away the papers.

But even I can't fix everything, and housekeeping hasn't come to lend me the usual assist. The shorts Gabriel wore yesterday are abandoned by the side of his bed. A novel about the Roman emperor Hadrian languishes facedown on the desk. By contrast, my side looks neurotically organized: the two pens in parallel alignment on my nightstand, the espadrilles and clean sneakers carefully tucked against the wall.

Back to the armoire. I riffle through Gabriel's clothes, his very simple T-shirts, his Old Navy shorts. A humble wardrobe, clothes for a man who doesn't want to be recognized or even seen. Next to his bed, a single flip-flop. In the drawer of his nightstand: earplugs, eye drops, a metallic tin of all-purpose moisturizing cream. Toward the back of the drawer, a pen and—

*Hey.*

A notebook. Kind of small, the cover lined with blue fabric.

Has Gabriel been keeping a diary?

For how long?

I shouldn't read it. Obviously.

And I wouldn't, if a woman weren't dead. If Gabriel hadn't lied to a cop, then lied to me about lying to a cop.

I flick open the notebook.

There's Gabriel's name on the first page, and a date from about a year ago, and—

Nothing. The rest of the page is blank.

I flip to the end of the notebook and work my way backward. Here, in an entry from a month ago: "Documentary producers emailed. They want to talk about everything. About A. I think they need to"

Another blank space.

A couple of pages before that: "Went for a walk today. Tried to clear my head. Didn't work. Nothing seems to work. I'm— what? Sad? Angry? Sure. Sometimes I wonder if I could try"

More empty pages, then, from this past Christmas: "Went to the diner. Samantha's meat loaf. She's kind. Something about

having to rely on other people's kindness makes me feel . . . I
don't know. Something like shame. Like I'm broken and she's
just taking pity on me. Like if she knew, then she wouldn't"

I skim through the rest of the notebook. All the entries seem
to end the same way, in the middle of a sentence, interrupted by
a thought he couldn't put into words.

What aren't you telling yourself, Gabriel?

And what aren't you telling *me*?

I drop the notebook back in the drawer.

Nothing in his armoire, nothing in his nightstand, nothing
up his sleeves.

Where else?

Where *is it*, Gabriel? The detail that will solve the mystery
of your life for me?

It could be anything. A small belonging at the bottom of a
pocket. A word scratched on the back of a receipt. Our lives are
full of them, those tiny pieces of ourselves that we let slip.

I step inside the bathroom. Gabriel's toiletry bag is zipped
shut next to his sink. A stick of deodorant, a travel-size tube
of toothpaste with fluoride, a comb. Condoms—an unflinching commitment to safe sex or an act of uncharacteristic opti-
mism, I can't quite decide. In small orange bottles, his migraine
meds—the ones he takes to manage them in the long run, and
the ones he takes when he starts getting symptoms. There's a
third bottle.

I listen for footsteps, for the clicking sound of our door
unlocking. Nothing. I squint to read the label and do a quick
search on my phone.

The internet tells me this particular medication is used to
treat seasonal depression, adult depression, or to help people
quit smoking.

Gabriel, to my knowledge, has never smoked. That's my
thing. It's currently the middle of summer. That leaves only one
candidate: the middle one. The obvious one.

It's not a huge surprise. There was that period of six months,
after we left Émile's world, when Gabriel practically didn't get
out of bed. Well, we didn't have beds, so, rather, there was

a period of six months when Gabriel scarcely crawled out of his sleeping bag. He couldn't work. He barely spoke. I didn't know what to call it at the time, but if that wasn't depression, what was?

I put the pill bottle back in Gabriel's toiletry bag and return to the other side of the suite. Gabriel left his laptop shut on his nightstand. I could try to guess his password, but he's too smart for that. Back when we still kept in regular touch, he told me about apps that encrypt your passwords and save them. He even reminded me to update mine every few months. "You never know," he wrote to me once. "It's easier to prevent an incident than to try to fix it."

So, not his laptop.

What's left?

Nothing.

I've looked through his clothes, through his things, through his pills, and I've come up empty.

Maybe I'm wrong. Maybe he's not hiding anything. Maybe he lied to Harris for perfectly innocent reasons.

I straighten up our suite. It's a habit. Gabriel has depression and I have this—this incessant need for order, this panicked part of myself that calms down when surfaces are clean and every item has found its spot. I pick up his shorts, fold them, and add them to the pile on his side of the armoire. I place his book on his nightstand, tuck a piece of hotel stationery in its pages as a bookmark.

It shouldn't feel good, but it does. The world falling neatly under my control.

What else can I fix?

There's my suitcase, nudged back into its corner this morning. I wiggle it so that it stands parallel to the wall. Next to it is Gabriel's large travel backpack, a model with multiple compartments and a strap across the stomach. It's the kind of item that never looks neat, no matter which position you stick it into. I try folding it in half, propping it up against my suitcase. Each time, it slides back onto the floor.

*Damn it.*

I grab it with both hands. It's almost impossibly light, the materials thin and practical, the whole design optimized for easy movements, except for—

Through the nylon, I feel it: a small object, light but slightly sharp, solid, something Gabriel forgot to remove when we settled back into our suite hours ago. I open the backpack. Whatever the item is, I can't find it: It's lost in a maze of inside pockets, hidden behind a forest of zippers. The bag demands that I start again, that I keep one hand on the outside and feel my way through its insides with the other until my fingers meet on each side of the fabric. Between them is the item, which I pull out and stick under the desk lamp to better examine it and—

I drop it. Like it's boiling hot, or like it's pricked my fingers.

It clatters lightly against the floor.

I crouch to get a better look at it. Not that I need a better look. I know exactly what it is. I'd recognize it even with one eye closed, even with a gun to my head.

There are things you don't forget.

Like: Gabriel bumping into Sabrina Brenner on our first day here. Like: the undercurrent of flirtation that passed between them as they traded apologies. Like: the butterfly hair clip she caressed as she spoke to Gabriel. The tip of her fingers tracing the shape of a wing the same way they might have traced Gabriel's jawline, or the squiggly path of a blood vessel on the inside of his arm.

The butterfly hair clip she wore three days before her death. The same butterfly hair clip that somehow ended up in Gabriel's backpack.

## 27  *THE ONLY TOWN WE KNEW,*
*HUDSON VALLEY,*
*AND OUTSIDE-OUTSIDE*

———

É mile wanted a fire.

The man loved fires. As soon as the temperatures started warming up in the spring, he had us build massive campfires. We'd sit around them while he told stories—pontificated—for hours, until the little kids fell asleep on mothers' laps and the older ones couldn't hold back their yawns. He talked; we listened; he loved it.

That year, he craved it even earlier than usual. Never mind that it was December. Who cared about the seasons? If Émile was ready for spring, then it was spring.

A couple of nights after my conversation with Gabriel, Émile had us all gather around the firepit. He was in a good mood, smiling as he sat close to the fire, wrapped in a fat down coat. There must have been 150 of us, all told. Gabriel and I scored seats at the front, but the crowd was five deep. I didn't want to think about how cold those at the back must have been.

Those days, it was tough to think about the others, generally. Girls older than I was, who had failed to warn me. And the younger ones, of course, whom I was failing in the exact same way. All those girls I couldn't save.

Émile rubbed his hands close to the flames as he launched into a story.

"Once upon a time," he said, "there was a sick baby girl. Her father was a peasant. He sent his sons to collect water from a spring to baptize their sister."

We assumed he'd made up the story, but I recognized it years later in a thick book of Grimms' fairy tales at the public library. It was called "The Seven Ravens." The brothers lose the jug; their father, angry, curses his own sons and turns them into ravens. Years later, the sister, grown and healthy, goes in search of her brothers. She asks and asks and asks—asks the sun and the moon and the morning star until she finds them. Ultimately, she restores them to human form.

"It's the girl who saves the boys," Émile said. "Not the other way around."

He looked at us when he said it, girls aged fifteen to eighteen, huddled to one side.

"She knows they need her help," Émile continued, "and she does everything she can to rescue them."

He was animated, arms in motion, eyes reflecting the glow of the fire.

There was power there. There was allure. Something that transcended time and place, that made you think of the grand tradition of storytelling. He was, in that moment, a spokesperson for generations past. Someone who could see the workings of the world more clearly than any of us.

It was almost enough to make me forget. Well, not *forget*, exactly—there was no forgetting—but almost enough to make me access the place Émile had occupied in my mind, before.

And then.

It was like the flames knew.

One moment, Émile was gesticulating, and the next, he was on fire. His left arm, specifically, was burning.

The flames spread up his down coat, toward his neck. Soon they'd be licking his face.

Émile screamed. Around him, three mothers sprang into action. Émile was big on fire safety. It was part of his whole self-sufficiency thing: He needed us to be able to rescue ourselves, without outside help.

We knew about stop, drop, and roll. As far as we were concerned, Émile had invented stop, drop, and roll. But in his panic, he needed the mothers to help him down to the ground. Their hands guided him through the stop and drop part. Roll, he had to figure out by himself. The mothers could no longer touch him. The flames were everywhere.

Clumsily, Émile rolled.

After a few excruciating seconds, he got back up.

"I'm fine," he said, patting himself as if to make sure.

His coat was charred, but the mothers had acted quickly. The flames had spared his body. Émile had caught fire, and he had escaped unharmed.

I braced myself for fury. Waited for Émile to blame whoever had built the fire—too large, too close to the crowd, too reckless.

But he was in a good mood. And he was embarrassed. So he played it cool. He laughed, like it had all been a big practical joke. Like the air wasn't saturated with the smell of burnt fabric.

"Really," he said, moving his camp chair away from the fire, "I'm fine."

He ran a hand through his hair.

"Now, what was I saying? Before I started roasting myself?"

Just like that, he was back to fairy tales and girls who rescued boys. Nothing could keep Émile quiet. Not even flames. His verbosity defied the elements.

Gabriel nudged my foot with his. He searched for my gaze. I nodded.

For a minute, we had seen it.

The possibility of a world where Émile burned.

———

Gabriel and I talked about the fire under our tree. We talked about it during chores. We talked about it whenever we had a moment.

We talked about the fire, and we talked about leaving.

We had no idea what *leaving* entailed. The idea felt too forbidden to share even with Joan.

But there were ways to begin forming a plan. One day, Joan mentioned a trip she had taken out of town. We asked her how she'd gotten there.

"I took the train," she said, then caught herself. "Do you . . . know what a train is?"

"We're not stupid," Gabriel said.

"Of course not. Of course." She pinched the bridge of her nose. "I just never know . . . But okay. Yes. I took the train. There's a station in town."

"Could we go see it?"

She gave us a look.

Maybe she guessed, then.

But that was the thing with Joan. She never pushed us. She played along.

"We've just never actually seen one," I added. "A train."

Maybe she knew there was so little she could actually do for us. But showing us a train station—that, she could do.

She took us. Suddenly, we knew where the trains were.

We didn't know where they went, or how to get on one. Those parts, we'd figure out when we had to.

I pretended to be her—Émile's little soldier—until the end.

Our last morning together—the only way to get through it was not to think. To allow my escape plans to exist in an entirely different part of my brain.

Two weeks had passed since the incident with Émile. (That's all I knew to call it in my head at the time, *the incident*.) Every night, I'd waited for Edwina to materialize at my bedside.

She hadn't. Every morning was a deferment, a suspended sentence.

———

Gabriel and I cleaned the cafeteria for the last time.

"See you tonight?" he whispered on our way out.

"Yep."

The plan was to leave in the middle of the night.

First, the youngest children went to bed. Then, the older kids. Finally, the adults.

With each minute, my unease grew.

Packing was quick. Gabriel and I barely owned anything worth bringing. Whatever we decided to take with us would fit in the pockets of our thin coats.

Me: a single dollar bill retrieved from the hole in my mattress, and the little wooden *F* Gabriel had carved for me. Gabriel: a stopwatch he had stolen, for good this time. Not that we'd need one, but the stopwatches had made our conquest of outside-outside possible. It made a kind of sense to bring one as a good-luck charm.

When I arrived at the red oak tree, Gabriel was already there. Calm. Resolute, as if he'd already said goodbye.

Me, I was a mess. Émile was behind every tree, in every shadow. My legs were shaking. My thoughts were cloudy. I was all fear, no bravado.

"Let's go," Gabriel said.

He headed not toward outside-outside, but toward the main building. Toward Émile's office and his living quarters.

Gabriel walked up to one of the first-floor windows and bent his arm, positioning his elbow in front of the glass. That part, we hadn't discussed.

"Stop," I whispered.

I turned the knob on the front door.

"He doesn't lock his doors," I mumbled.

Gabriel's face fell.

*Seriously?*

*Seriously.*

We padded our way to Émile's office. Gabriel knew where to go. He had been there, like all of us, on the day of his own test, when he was eight. It was like he didn't need me at all.

"Okay," he said, shutting the door. He looked around. "Guess we should . . ."

He grabbed a pile of papers on Émile's desk and started

scrunching them up, stuffing them at the foot of the bookcase behind the desk. There was no hesitation in his gestures, only resolve.

I remembered what I was supposed to do. From my pocket, I produced a small box of matches, pilfered from Joan's bar.

The match lit up with a small crack.

"Hold on," Gabriel said.

I shook the match. The flame went out.

Gabriel was looking at Émile's desk.

*Right.*

I opened the wooden box, took out all the cash—didn't even count it—and stuffed it in my coat pocket.

Gabriel reached under his own coat. He pulled out a small bottle.

We, the good people of Émile's world, got rid of our trash by burning it. (It's not like we could have relied on the town's regular trash pickup.) We'd all seen the smoke, and smelled it, too. But here's a little thing Gabriel had learned, working as a young man on the compound: It wasn't enough to bring a flame to the pile of garbage. You had to douse the pile in *something* first. This was called an accelerant. There were various kinds, but gasoline—like the gasoline we used for the generators that kept Émile's office warm and his electric car charged—worked the best.

He thrust the bottle into my hand.

"You do it."

I considered it, then shook my head.

"I can't."

"Sure you can."

Gabriel wrapped his fingers around mine, tightened my grip around the bottle.

"It should be you," he said.

He didn't have to say why.

Gabriel intuited it before I did—that the only kind of justice I would ever receive was the kind I would make happen for myself.

I started pouring. Just then, a thought took hold in my mind. Dark, toxic.

Émile was sleeping upstairs. That, I knew.

But maybe he wasn't alone.

Maybe Edwina was inside, too. In Émile's room, doing to someone else what she'd done to me. Standing in the corner. Hands around another girl's limbs.

My mouth opened.

I didn't know, of course. There was no way to know for sure. But it was a distinct possibility.

I held them in my mind. Émile, Edwina. And the other girl. The one being held down.

She would escape, whoever she was. I was sure of it. We, the girls this had happened to—every day of our life was a building on fire. The girl would recognize the blaze for what it was: a chance to escape Émile, to end this terrible moment.

And Edwina?

Edwina was a different story.

She'd want to protect Émile. That was her purpose. She'd want to get him out, away from the flames. She'd breathe in smoke. Edwina would burn, if she had to.

I heard all the possibilities in my head: *Stop, wait. We can't do this.* I felt Edwina's hands around my ankles. The rehearsed expertise of her gestures, her confident strength. How I'd known immediately: She had done it before; she would do it again.

The last drops of gasoline trickled out of the bottle.

"Go ahead," I told Gabriel.

This is how the fire was set, in the end: I poured the accelerant, and he struck the match.

———

Gabriel hadn't lied: As far as accelerants went, gasoline worked. *Really* worked. The flames rose, tall and fierce and hungry.

For about ten seconds, it felt good. It felt *great*. Émile's office. His papers. His *thoughts*, ablaze.

The fire spread to Émile's desk, his chair, his books. It started creeping up the wall, reaching greedily for the ceiling.

"Let's go," I said, but Gabriel was already at the door.

We ran. There was no time to hesitate, no time for sadness.

Once we'd almost reached the edge of Émile's world, we stopped to look back.

"Holy shit."

The fire was alive. Untamable. It had spread not just to Émile's entire office, but to that whole side of the building. A large plume of smoke rose in the air. The flames engulfed another portion of wall, reaching the roof.

It was sick, in every sense of the word.

I turned to Gabriel, expecting to meet his gaze. I thought he'd need it, too, this wordless congress, his feelings bouncing off mine.

But from our corner of the night, Gabriel had eyes only for the fire. He stared at the flames, transfixed. Hypnotized.

I nudged him.

"Come on."

He blinked. We started running.

Right before the last turn, we stopped to look again.

The entire building was in flames. The walls, the roof. They were on the verge of collapsing.

I gasped. Gabriel pulled his coat tighter around his chest.

I'd known setting fire to a building would cause great damage. Obviously. But there was a difference between a fire in your head and a fire in real life. This was so out of control. So *violent*.

Even from a distance, I could see them: three silhouettes in long nightdresses.

Running toward danger. Hoisting something out of the building.

Someone.

The only person there was to evacuate.

Émile wasn't moving. A mother held him by the shoulders, and two women supported his legs. They walked him away from the structure and laid him down on the ground.

I waited for him to lift his head. A hand. A foot. Nothing.

From a distance, Émile didn't look injured. He didn't look betrayed. He didn't look outraged, or sad, or hurt.

He only looked dead.

———

THE SIXTH DAY

I return the hair clip to Gabriel's backpack.

Is this even the right pocket?

Who knows?

Who cares?

I don't realize that I'm going to the lobby until I'm already there. Better this way: I forget to worry about Gabriel. I forget to worry about William Brenner. That's how stunned I am: For a few minutes, I forget to worry about men.

"Could you call me a car, please?"

Behind the front desk, Catalina frowns, but she picks up the phone.

"Of course," she says. "Where are you looking to go?"

*Literally anywhere but here?*

"The nearest town."

Catalina presses a button and tells someone on the other end of the line that a guest has requested a ride to downtown Escalante.

"You can go to the entrance lounge," she says. "The driver will meet you there."

The car pulls up a minute later, so clean it looks brand-new, Ara-branded water bottles in every cup holder.

"It'll be about thirty minutes," my driver, whose name tag says LEON, informs me.

"Sounds good."

The car passes rock formations, a handful of tourists posing for photos. A gas station sprouts along the side of the road.

Then, the town.

I haven't seen a town in almost a week.

My shoulders relax. It's a reflex, something I'll never be able to rewrite: Towns, no matter how small, mean safety. They mean freedom.

Leon drops me off on Main Street. There are low buildings on each side: a grocery, a thrift shop, a couple of motels, and a store that appears to sell everything from office supplies to souvenirs. The sidewalk is so hot that it burns my feet through the soles of my sandals.

"Will you need a pickup?" Leon asks through the driver's side window.

*Good question.*

"I . . . don't know yet."

Leon considers me.

"Just call the hotel if you do," he says. "Someone will come."

I nod.

Leon gives me a little wave and pulls away.

It dawns on me that I haven't brought anything aside from my phone and a pair of sunglasses.

Yeah, well. I've survived worse with less.

A coffee shop comes into view, minuscule but well-tended-to. Its façade is pink and bears the establishment's logo (a prowling bobcat). Inside, the furniture is modern, the walls decorated with artful renderings of bones—very Georgia O'Keeffe.

"What can I get you?" the cheerful, blue-haired barista asks when I approach the counter.

"Coffee. Please."

"Iced?"

"Sure."

I pay with my phone and settle at a table in a corner. Just me, myself, and my three possessions: my cell, my sunglasses, my coffee.

My memories.

Of the night Sabrina Brenner died. Of Gabriel, who wasn't in the suite when I returned. Who switched off the ceiling light as soon as he came back. He's never liked bright lights; it's a migraine thing. But you know who else doesn't like bright lights?

People with things to hide.

More images.

Of Gabriel, who went to wash his hands right away. Who assured me that everything would be okay.

Gabriel, who, the next morning, couldn't tear his gaze from Sabrina's body.

Who said: "Sabrina, we—" and never finished his sentence.

*Sabrina, we had a fight?*

*Sabrina, we did something terrible?*

I take a sip of coffee.

It's good.

Who gives a fuck, right?

But it is.

I'm not going back to the hotel.

Harris made it clear that he wouldn't look kindly upon anyone who left the Ara. Sure. But there is simply no way I'm going back to the suite. I mean, what am I supposed to do?

Confront Gabriel about the hair clip?

Pretend nothing happened? In a few hours, lie down in the bed next to his?

For the first time in my life, I can't imagine sharing space with him.

The feeling is odd, foreign. There was a time when he only had me, and I only had him.

Somehow, that was enough. We made sure it was.

Like at his wedding. Annie was an only child, but each of her parents had multiple siblings, and those siblings each had multiple children, so her side was all aunts, uncles, and cousins. Gabriel's side was me.

His engagement to Annie was short. Those two planned their wedding in three months, with the help of Annie's parents and, crucially, their money.

Annie's inherited wealth was behind every detail: Annie's custom-made dress, Gabriel's lovely tux, the reception at a former brickyard in upstate New York by the Hudson. It should have been impossible to book that venue with less than a year's notice, but Annie's mother pulled some strings, possibly bribed a wedding planner or two, and there we all were, on a gorgeous and muggy afternoon in July, watching Annie walk down the aisle.

Was Gabriel a little too quiet for a happy groom? I'd pushed the idea out of my mind. What did I know? It was the first wedding I'd ever attended. Gabriel must have felt overwhelmed. I couldn't blame him. He had to hold his own amid Annie's boisterous family, her rowdy cousins, her father and his interminable, corny speech.

As dinner was winding down, and while Annie posed for photos with her bridesmaids, I found him off to the side, gazing at the Hudson. I tapped his shoulder, reached for both of his hands. He squeezed them back.

"How do you feel?" I asked.

Gabriel looked in the distance at his bride. Her strapless dress, her bare shoulders, her professional makeup, her hair pinned back on the nape of her neck.

"Really good," he said.

It sounded like the truth. After leaving Émile, marriage was the biggest leap of faith Gabriel had taken. In the yellow light of a New York State sunset, a slight breeze in his hair, he seemed—perhaps for the first time in his life—sure of himself.

"I'm happy for you," I said.

———

I'm exhausted. The coffee is good, but it's not helping.

I take it with me and drain the cup as I walk along Main Street.

One of the two motels beckons me.

A kind, middle-aged woman with a purple T-shirt and visible roots in her dyed blond hair informs me that the Staircase Inn does, in fact, have rooms available.

"This might sound weird," I say, "but can I pay with my phone?"

The woman shakes her head no with a soft smile.

"But we take cash," she says, and directs me to the nearest ATM.

As it turns out, Escalante, Utah, is equipped with at least one ATM that supports contactless technology. I take out three hundred bucks and return to the inn. My new friend takes two of my three bills and hands me a key.

"Second floor," she tells me.

As I start climbing the small staircase, she calls out after me: "I'm Ronda, by the way. Without an *h*. If you need anything."

"Thanks, Ronda."

I don't know what I would have done if the ATM hadn't worked.

Actually, I do, and that's what scares me. I would have begged, borrowed, possibly stolen. I would have asked strangers for a spot on their couch. I would have slept in the desert, outside.

Anything but the Ara. Anyone but Gabriel.

The Staircase Inn is not fancy, but it's clean, with small bottles of bodywash in the bathroom and a welcome basket on one of the nightstands. Inside, bottled water and two granola bars.

I eat both, wash them down with water. Then I take off my clothes, shower, and lie down. I'm naked in a hotel bed; the sheets are wet; my hair drips against the pillow. I don't care.

There's no tension, no tossing and turning. No half dreams. No nightmares. In the Staircase Inn, away from Gabriel, I sleep for what feels like the first time in my life.

## 29 THE ONLY TOWN WE KNEW, HUDSON VALLEY, AND THEN, THE WORLD

FIFTEEN YEARS AGO

We waited for someone to turn up behind the counter, then asked for two tickets for the next train.

"The four thirty-six to New York?" the man said. He was bald, with red cheeks and cold, cold blue eyes.

"Sure," Gabriel said.

I handed over Émile's money. From the pile, the man separated a single bill, then handed me two tickets and a pile of change.

"Platform one," he said.

We sleepwalked down a flight of stairs.

The platform was windy. Cold gusts bit at my cheeks. It felt good, deserved. My hands went pleasantly numb.

I closed my eyes. Flames danced at the back of my eyelids.

I thought about it. Lying down on the nearby grass and surrendering. Waiting for sleep to find me and never let go.

Bile rose at the back of my throat. I ran to a trash can and missed it by a few seconds.

Gabriel stood next to me. He patted my back. When my stomach was done seizing, I opened my mouth, tried to find the words.

*What have we done?*

*What the fuck were we thinking?*

It seemed impossible that we could have erased Émile from the world. That he'd stopped existing at all.

The ground rumbled under our feet. There was a roar like a volcanic eruption.

Our first train. So massive, so fast, smelling of diesel and piss.

We stepped into the last car. At four thirty-six in the morning, Gabriel and I were almost the only passengers.

Suddenly, the ground shifted under our feet. We were jerked forward.

Our train was moving.

We were leaving. For real.

In another life, this was the time for our great liberation. This was when we would have looked out the window, scared but exalted: *We did it!*

But we'd just killed a man. We held on to the luggage rack above our heads and crashed into the nearest seats.

"Tickets, please!"

I handed our tickets to a young man with curly black hair that flopped out of an interesting hat. He punched holes in them using a little tool. This is what I'd learned about the world so far: that it was full of men and tools.

Gabriel put his head on my shoulder. His hair tickled my cheek. A brittle kind of sleep found us.

Whenever the train stopped, I woke up. For a second, the recent past was erased from my mind, and I had to learn our circumstances all over again: the fire, our departure, the train.

Every time the doors opened, I waited for someone to come for us. Not the police. I didn't know enough about the police to fear them. It was the mothers I imagined, a whole army of them swarming the train, ready to mete out our punishment.

I didn't know about the law, about prison, or about the death penalty. But there's a gut feeling that comes with killing someone. You don't need to be threatened with consequences for it to feel terrible.

"Look," Gabriel said, pointing at the window.

It was pitch-black outside. Months later, I realized the darkness had been a tunnel. A disembodied voice said the words "New York, Grand Central." We got off the train. The crowd threatened to pull us away, as though we held no more weight than crumbs in dishwater swirling toward the drain. There was a ceiling above us as tall as the sky.

Gabriel grabbed my hand.

"Let's go this way."

He followed the crowd. Where was he finding it, the ability to orient himself, to do what needed to be done? Why wasn't he rattled? Why didn't he seem even a little bit upset?

The world outside the train was tunnels. We heard more train sounds; we saw some maps, but we weren't ready to figure out a whole new system. We walked around until we felt a gust of wind. Wind, in this underground world, meant stairs, and stairs meant outside.

We eschewed the escalators. Instead, we climbed the nearest stairwell, and climbed some more, and there it was.

New York City.

It was still dark out. Around us, the city rose in a great whirlwind of artificial lights and sounds. Sirens, shouts, the rumble of hot dog carts setting up for the day. Before you could wrap your head around any of these concepts (sirens for what, hot dogs for whom), the city turned your head to yet another sight: someone whose path you were blocking on the sidewalk, a man in a suit swearing as his paper cup of coffee emptied itself on his shiny shoes, steam coming out of the ground for absolutely no reason.

It was more people, more *world*, in an instant than we'd seen combined in our eighteen years.

And it was so *loud*. After a few seconds, it wasn't sound anymore. Just noise.

The man in the suit walked right into me. I stumbled backward; Gabriel caught me. There was no time to be afraid, or angry, or even insulted. There was the cold touch of the man's sleek suit, the wet coffee stain on his sleeve, the prickly smell of his cologne. Tears sprang to my eyes. For a second, there was no room inside of me for Émile or the flames. In all its tumult, the city promised me something: One day, I would not think about the fire at all. I would be rid of my ghosts.

Gabriel grabbed my hand. Together, we started walking.

I reached in my coat pocket. Found something in there, exactly where I expected it.

My fingers closed around it. It had followed me into this new world.

A single dollar bill, the shape of a mouth smeared in lipstick.

THE SEVENTH DAY

A faint tapping sound nudges its way into my sleep until, finally, I wake up.

For a moment, I feel amazing, like my brain has had a massage. Then I remember: the Ara, Gabriel, the Staircase Inn.

I identify the sound, too: Someone's knocking on the door. Pretty impatiently, by the sound of it.

"Just a second!"

My clothes are still crumpled in a corner of the room. I step into my underwear, try to untangle my running shorts. The knocking grows faster and louder.

"Let me in, please!"

The *please* is a formality: The voice on the other side of the door, which I think I recognize as Ronda's, is pissed off and possibly spooked.

"Just a sec!"

"I have a key, honey, and if you force me to use it, I'll—"

"Wait!"

I give up on my shorts, wrap myself in the bedsheet, and crack the door open.

Ronda peers at me. She's holding a newspaper in one hand, a bundle of keys in the other.

"You've gotta go, honey."

"What?"

"Will you just let me in?"

Reluctantly, I step back and—securing the sheet in place with one hand—open the door wider.

"Sorry," I say as Ronda steps in. "I'm not dressed."

Why am I telling her something she can clearly see for herself?

"Then get dressed," Ronda says. "And please leave."

"What's going on?"

Ronda puts her hands on her hips.

"Look," she says. "I don't want any trouble. I'm not going to call the police. I'm just asking you to please go."

"Why would y—"

Ronda thrusts the newspaper under my face.

Here, on the front page—the front page, really?—is a photo of me and Gabriel at the Ara. We're sitting in the dining room. I'm twisted on my chair, looking back in the direction of the camera, while Gabriel is staring straight ahead. Both of our faces are clearly visible. Above us, a headline screams: MAN WHOSE WIFE DIED IN "SUSPICIOUS" CIRCUMSTANCES AND SISTER NAMED PERSONS OF INTEREST IN HOTEL MURDER PROBE.

*Fuck. Fuck. Fuck.* I snatch the paper from Ronda.

"Investigators have identified two persons of interest in the death of Sabrina Brenner at the upscale Ara hotel, a police source has revealed exclusively." Words jump out at me: there's Gabriel's name, "a man who was once a potential suspect in his wife's death in 2014, in a high-profile New Jersey case that remains unsolved." Then, my own name, and a mention of our "troubled childhood" in "an infamous cult." The legalese, of course: Gabriel, the article says, "was never charged with any crime and has always maintained his innocence." Some background on the Brenners: They got married two years ago, "in what was the groom's third wedding." The article describes William as "a successful media magnate," who "was arrested early on in the case, then released due to a lack of evidence."

"The police have apologized for my unfair arrest and investigators are now working diligently to find whoever hurt my wife," William is quoted as saying. "I appreciate their efforts and am confident they won't rest until the person responsible is behind bars."

Ronda repeats what she just said about not wanting any problems. Again, she asks me to leave. Above the headline, the front page informs me that I'm reading the *Escalante News*, the local broadsheet that "proudly serves Garfield County" and has apparently done so since 1982.

"I know I said I wouldn't call the police," Ronda says, waving her phone, "but if you leave me no choice—"

"Okay," I say. "I'll go. I'll go. I'm sorry."

Ronda lowers the phone, and her voice. Now that she's won, it's like she regrets going into battle in the first place.

"I don't know what you're tangled up in, honey, but I do hope it works out."

"Me, too, Ronda."

"Drop your key at the front desk when you're done. I'll see you downstairs in . . . ten minutes?"

I nod. She shoots me a rueful look as she closes the door behind her.

Clearly, William is working with the police. They must have told him they were going to name us persons of interest. How else would he have had time to tip off the local paper, give them a photo and a quote?

I pick up my dirty clothes from the floor and slip them back on.

As far as I know, William doesn't own any papers in Utah, but he must have contacts. He held on to the photo, waited for the perfect occasion to deploy it.

Oh, the glee he must have felt, when the police handed him just that.

At the front desk, I ask Ronda for a phone charger.

"I need to call my hotel for a ride."

"Just use our phone," she says, and points at the landline on the check-in counter.

"I need to look up the number."

Ronda asks me for the hotel's name, types on her keyboard, and dictates the number.

On the other end of the line, Catalina sounds tense. I expect her, too, to banish me from the Ara, but she tells me that Leon will be there in half an hour to pick me up.

"Thanks."

I hand the phone back to Ronda.

"You can wait outside," she tells me.

Thanks to the blistering heat, I have the sidewalk to myself as I sit on the curb and wait for Leon to turn up.

*Persons of interest.*

Here's what I know about persons of interest: They're not suspects. Not exactly. Technically, being a person of interest just means the police want to talk to you. That's one of the many things I learned on TV.

After Annie's death, Gabriel was never named a person of interest, probably because the police knew where to find him, and because he was already cooperating. But a good number of persons of interest do end up becoming suspects. It's a thin line—sometimes almost invisible.

What do the police have on Gabriel and me?

They can't know about the hair clip. If they did, it would be in an evidence room somewhere, not tucked inside Gabriel's backpack.

So, what?

Maybe someone talked. Maybe a guest at the Ara said they saw Gabriel the day he bumped into Sabrina. *He told you he's never spoken to her? Well. That's not how I remember it.* Maybe that discrepancy was enough for the police—especially Harris, who must be desperately looking for a new suspect.

*What the hell do we do now?*

There's the crunch of gravel, and the heat of a car stopping a couple of feet from me.

I get up.

"Hey, Leon," I say as I open the passenger door. "Thank you for coming all this—"

I stop.

There's someone in the back seat.

"Hello," he says.

He's back. Tired, pissed off, but also, it would seem, hopeful. There's a slightly manic edge to his smile—a shark who can't believe he gets to stare down this particular chum bucket.

"Deputy Harris," I say.

He pats the seat next to him.

"Get in."

I do, because I have no other choice. My phone is still dead, and even if it weren't, I'm not sure how long it would take to get an Uber all the way out here.

Leon drives to the end of the street and makes a three-point turn.

"So," Harris says.

I sit in silence.

"I'd like to talk to you," he continues. "At the station."

"And if I say no?"

He shrugs.

"Then you go back to the hotel."

*And then what?*

"We've made an interesting discovery," Harris goes on. "I think you'll want to hear what we have to say."

"Tell me here."

Harris shakes his head.

"No. At the station."

I don't have to say another word. It's perfectly possible for me to wait until Leon drops me back at the Ara, pack my bags, and fly home to New York.

But.

Whatever Harris has—or thinks he has—on me or Gabriel, it's not going away. It's like he said yesterday: He can reach us at home.

Plus.

The image of Sabrina Brenner's hair clip—the golden metal, so delicately bent into its butterfly shape—is burning inside my brain.

This will follow Gabriel home, too.

Fuck. I need to know. I need to peek inside Harris's brain and see if he's bluffing.

It's stupid to do this without a lawyer. I know that. But I've run out of time.

What I must remember is this: I don't *have* to say anything. Harris has nothing on me. If he did, I'd be wearing handcuffs right now. I can go to the police station and sit and listen and tell Harris I want to stop at any time. I can get him to talk without giving him anything in return.

"Fine," I tell Harris. "I'll go to the station."

He smiles.

"Leon?" he asks.

Leon gives him a thumbs-up and pulls over for another three-point turn.

found the paper on a bench in Central Park.

We'd been in the city for four days. Gabriel and I had each gone to look for work. I'd spent the morning trying every diner I could find with a HELP WANTED sign in the window. No one wanted to hire me—officially, because they were looking for people with experience, but also, probably, because I had very little idea of how to conduct these conversations. I was exhausted, hungry, cold. Utterly unprepared for the world.

Two afternoons earlier, after one night in Grand Central and one in Penn Station, Gabriel and I had settled into a storage unit. It was a wild idea that had seemed perfectly logical to us. We'd seen an ad for the storage units on a massive billboard by the Hudson: a drawing of a man standing among what appeared to be all his things—electric guitar, recliner, dress shoes, suits, even a signed baseball—and the words WE'RE HERE UNTIL SHE FORGETS ABOUT THE LIPSTICK ON YOUR COLLAR.

We didn't get it at the time—we didn't know about marriage or adultery. But the implication was that our man's wife had caught him in a compromising situation and kicked him out.

The joke didn't matter. All we'd known, looking at the

image, was that the storage unit looked like—well, a building that could fit a person and things.

So we'd marched ourselves to the storage facility, where a man named Al had decreed he'd let us stay in one of the storage units under two conditions: one, that we not breathe a word of this agreement to anyone, and two, that we pay him a hundred dollars in cash every month.

A hundred dollars. It was so much money. Al had needed the first month up front, too. So, that day—the day of the newspaper—Gabriel and I were in imminent danger of running out of cash.

I needed a break, but I didn't want to go back to the storage unit without Gabriel. So I went to Central Park.

The paper—the *Daily News*—blew open as I walked past. It was the movement of the pages flipping in the wind that caught my eye. I picked it up and sat on the bench to thumb through the pages.

A man named Bernie Madoff was a "confessed swindler." An investigation was under way to see if he could have been caught earlier. Another man named Paterson was the governor (whatever that meant). He thought New York was facing the "largest deficit" in its history, which didn't sound good, but what did I know?

My legs went numb against the bench. Around me, people hurried, chins tucked in the necklines of their coats.

And then I saw it.

ONE DEAD IN "CULT" BLAZE

For a second, my mind conjured the absurd hope that maybe this was a different blaze, a different cult.

But no.

This was *our* fire.

*Our* cult.

*One person is dead and another is injured after a fire devastated part of the compound of a reclusive organization some have described as a cult.*

*Firefighters responded to the blaze last week at 2:33 a.m. News of the death remained under wraps for days due to the group's secretive nature. A county official has now confirmed that one person died of injuries suffered in the fire later that night.*

My throat closed.

Seeing it in the paper made it so real. Émile had died, and now the world knew. His ghost had traveled to New York City after all. I could practically feel his hands on my shoulders, on my back, closing around my neck.

I kept reading.

*The county official says the victim was a twenty-two-year-old female. No public records exist for the woman, but a source says she was known within the organization only as Edwina.*

It wasn't Edwina I'd seen getting pulled out of the building. I knew that for sure. The image was seared onto my brain forever, Émile's body dangling from the mothers' arms, inert, pale. Dead.

But the paper told a different story.

I read it again. And again. And again. Each time, the same result: *a twenty-two-year-old female . . . known within the organization only as Edwina.*

My mouth was so dry. I tried to swallow and failed.

I wasn't entitled to feel shocked. *Shock* implied a certain amount of surprise. I'd known this was a possibility. I'd pictured Edwina on the second floor even as I'd poured the gasoline.

I'd accepted it.

I'd hoped for it, even. Maybe.

And it had happened.

My vision blurred. I wiped tears from my eyes. More came. They stopped abruptly, replaced by a lump in my throat. My fists clenched around the newspaper.

*The organization has been run for years by Émile Blanchard, a mysterious figure who imposes a strict code of silence on his follow-*

*ers. Mr. Blanchard emigrated from France in his twenties and was once an entrepreneur. He is believed to have started the group in 1987. Members now live mostly cut off from mainstream society, with only Mr. Blanchard making occasional contact with the outside world for supplies and PR missions.*

*"We can't investigate," the county official, who requested anonymity due to the fear of reprisal, said. "A young woman died and no one in this organization will say a word to us. If anyone from the public has any information, we urge them to come forward immediately."*

I pictured the scene: A fire truck like the ones I'd seen in the city, pulling up to the compound. Men in gear rushing to Émile's aid, tending to Edwina's body.

And then: A police car. I'd seen them around the city, too. People in uniform doing whatever "investigating" entailed. (I didn't know. I didn't have a TV yet.)

Émile had prepared us for a moment like this. From the time we were kids, he'd told us about the possibility of intruders on the compound. He'd made it clear that we weren't to talk to anyone or show them anything. There were drills. We all had our orders.

Émile.

He was alive. Still in the world. Recovering, presumably. Dealing with the fire, with the destruction of his office. The mothers caring for his wounds, his needs, his life.

They'd done it. Those diligent, cruel, insanely brave women. They'd run into a burning building to save their man. They'd done exactly what they'd been trained to do.

No one would speak to the police. That, at least, was for certain.

---

I walked back to the storage unit.

It made me want to die, what we'd done to Edwina. I know, I know. I'd pictured it, craved it, and still, it made me want to die. All the ways I could do it flashed in my mind: jumping into the frigid Hudson, stepping in front of a bus. New York was full of possibilities in that way.

I waited for Gabriel. Eventually, the door to the storage unit opened with a groan.

"Hey," Gabriel said. "So, I went around construction sites like we said and—"

"Look," I cut in, in a voice that wasn't my own.

I tried to press the paper into his hands. Gabriel held them up. His fingers were covered in some kind of grime.

"Just take it," I said.

He did. I held my breath as his eyes bounced around the pages. When they widened, I knew he'd reached the part about Edwina.

"What's this?" he whispered.

We hadn't talked about Émile. Not once since we'd left.

I took the paper back without a word.

Gabriel dropped to the floor. He raked his grimy fingers through his hair.

"We didn't know," he said finally.

*But I kind of did.*

*And you should have, too.*

*You had the same information I did.*

Gabriel must have followed the same train of thought. Quickly, he switched gears.

"What she did to you," he said.

"It wasn't—"

"I know. But I can't forget."

He picked up the paper again, went back to the article.

"I just can't," he said.

"It was Émile."

"It was both of them."

I wanted to scream. I wanted to tell Gabriel that this was not his pronouncement to make. That what had happened belonged to me.

Gabriel would never understand it, that thing I shared with Edwina—a dark, confused intuition. I'd hated her, but I'd also known that we did what Émile asked of us. We, the girls, the women.

It would have been so easy to convince myself that, in her place, I would have been better. That I would have drawn a line. That I would have refused to hold down another girl, to pin her to Émile's bed.

But I knew. I just knew.

Whatever culpability she held, whatever she had done—if Émile had asked, I would have done it, too.

THE SEVENTH DAY

Leon parks outside the police station. Inside, it's stuffy and quiet. It reminds me of a TV show I watched a few years ago, an eccentric detective investigating the death of a girl, a too-nice receptionist putting out doughnuts for the men.

I follow Harris as he trades greetings with a couple of colleagues—a raised hand, a quick nod. He leads me to a small, drab room, bare walls, carpet, a table and two chairs. Not too different from the one in which I spoke to the New Jersey cops, after they found Annie's body.

Harris gestures for me to sit. He settles on the other side of the table and produces a small tape recorder, into which he speaks the date and time and my name.

"So," he says. "Can you tell me how you came to be in possession of Sabrina Brenner's phone?"

Not necessarily where I thought we'd start, but sure. I don't mind talking about the phone. If anything, I was a model citizen, with the phone. Confronting a coyote to retrieve evidence.

I tell Harris about the desert, the coyote, my shoe.

"When I came back to the hotel, I looked for you," I say. He raises a skeptical eyebrow. "I did! But I couldn't find you, so I gave it to Deputy Calhoun instead."

Harris nods. He takes a sip from a paper cup of water that I didn't notice when we first sat down.

*I'm parched.*

"Could I get some water, too?" I ask.

"In a moment."

Shit. I've watched enough shows to know it's not a good sign when the police won't allow you a drink of water.

"I need to talk to you," he says, "about Gabriel."

I do the only smart thing: wait for Harris to ask a question.

"What can you tell me," he continues, "about Gabriel's interactions with Sabrina Brenner?"

I suppress a twitch.

*Interactions,* plural?

Gabriel told Harris just yesterday that he never spoke to Sabrina. That was incorrect—a mistake or a lie, I'm still not sure. But either way, Harris isn't buying it.

"How were they around each other?" he continues. "How did they address each other? Did you know them to associate?"

*Associate?*

Harris sounds so confident.

*What do you know that I don't?*

"I didn't know them to associate," I say, truthfully.

Harris sighs. He leans back in his chair and studies me for a few seconds.

I know what he's doing. So many people are uncomfortable with silence. They'll do anything to break it. They'll start talking. Spill secrets.

But I grew up in Émile's world, where silence was worshipped. I could sit here all day.

"Listen," Harris says. He puts his hands on the table, leans toward me. "I'm going to level with you." *Sure.* "This could be bad for you. But if you help us, we'll be able to help you. Do you know what I'm saying?"

*I honestly don't.*

Harris sighs again and shakes his head. With a smug little smile, he tells me to wait. When he returns a minute later, he's holding a manila folder, which he places on the table. He's about to open it when he makes a show of being struck by a thought.

"I'm going to give you one last chance," he says, "to tell me what you know about Gabriel and Sabrina. Once I show you this, it's over. I can't help you anymore."

I sit in silence.

"Fine," he says. "If that's how you want to do it."

He opens the manila folder to reveal a small stack of documents. Harris flips through them until he finds what he's looking for, then slides the folder upside down so that it's facing me.

It appears to be a printout of a . . . screenshot of a phone?

It reads "Notes" at the top. Underneath, in a large font, the words "Food Journal."

Below that, in a much smaller font, is a painstakingly detailed account of a person's daily intake.

Toward the bottom, between lunch and dinner, a few lines that don't belong:

Gabriel Miller
6/12
47 Jackson St.

I look up at Harris.

"This, as you've probably guessed, is a screenshot of what we found on Sabrina Brenner's phone," he says.

*What?*

"Now, the code isn't too hard to crack. Gabriel Miller—we both know who this is. Six-twelve—that's Gabriel's date of birth, right? The twelfth of June?"

I don't say anything. Harris doesn't seem to mind.

"And Jackson, of course, is the street on which he lives in Seattle."

I don't confirm, but Harris is right.

"So what I'd like to know," Harris says, "is what are Gabriel's personal details doing on Sabrina Brenner's phone?"

"I don't know."

That's the truth. I have no fucking idea.

That damned phone.

I would never have given it to the cops if I'd known.

They must think I gave it to them hoping to frame William, and overplayed my hand.

Oh my god. Gabriel has no idea about the phone. I never got to tell him.

Harris rests his elbows on the desk, clasps his hands below his chin.

"I'm going to be straight with you," he says.

*Wouldn't that be something.*

"Whatever happened to Sabrina Brenner, I don't think you had anything to do with it. As far as I'm concerned, you're not a suspect. Not at the moment."

*Okay.*

"I think," the cop says, "that your brother—that Gabriel had something to do with it. I know he lied to me about his past interactions with Mrs. Brenner. Obviously. And I also know he lied to me about his whereabouts the last evening she was seen alive. I know he left the dinner table briefly just hours before her death."

Harris closes the folder.

"People lie all the time, of course. Or they get confused. Or they don't remember. That's why I haven't moved on him until now. But the phone makes it clear there's more to his story."

The deputy stares into my eyes.

He's so young. Younger than I am, for sure. He's inexperienced, grandiose, and more than a little bit arrogant.

But he's not bluffing. That's the scariest part: He's not that good, this deputy, and still, he's got something real on Gabriel.

"I think you've been covering for him," Harris continues. "I think you've been covering for him for a long time. And I think it's weighing on you. Is that why you were so upset by the pool two days ago?"

It's not hard to recognize Harris's tone for what it is: a threat.

"I'd like to leave now," I say.

"Like I said, if you help us, then we can help you. But you've got to make the first move."

"I'd like to leave."

Harris takes a deep breath. He holds it for a couple of seconds. I can feel it in the air around us, how badly he wants me to crack, how much easier his life would be if I just yielded.

He exhales.

"Fine," he says.

I get up and walk toward the door. My palms are sweaty; my heart pounds in my ears. But I know what to do. I know what it feels like when the world of crime approaches the edges of your life like a lighter to a piece of paper. It's so tempting to believe that the blaze is inevitable, to picture your world going up in smoke before the first flame even catches.

I need to leave before Harris gets to me.

———

"We'll get a warrant."

I stop, my hand inches from the door handle. Harris gets up from behind the table.

"We'll search Gabriel's stuff. Your stuff. Your clothes, your phones, your computers. Whatever secrets you have, whatever secrets he has, we'll find out."

I turn around.

"I don't just mean about Sabrina Brenner," Harris says. "You know, a lot of people think Gabriel should have gone to prison for Annie Woodward's death."

Oh, it rattles me, her name in his mouth. It really does.

"I've always thought someone ought to look into the case again," Harris says. "Technology has improved so much in nine years. Who knows what would come up if the right detective took it up."

Now he's bluffing. Annie died in New Jersey, a different jurisdiction, two thousand miles away. And Harris has no basis on which to get a warrant. I do know that.

But he's not done.

"You know what I've always thought we should be better at, us in law enforcement? Interdepartmental communication. There was this guy a few years ago—serial murderer. He lived in Massachusetts, but he always made sure to cross multiple state lines whenever he committed a crime. Jurisdictions got crossed. He went undetected for years. So aggravating. I always thought, 'If I join the force, that won't be me. I'll make sure to communicate any relevant information to my peers.' And here we are."

For a second, I consider it. I could break. I could tell Harris everything he wants to know.

I could tell him about the hair clip.

*No.*

I did not come here to renounce him at the first opportunity. Gabriel. The boy I chose to be my brother.

I think about Romulus and Remus, how Gabriel saw us reflected in them.

Here's what I know: When Romulus and Remus disagreed on where to establish the city that became Rome, they didn't draft in a third party to decide. They dealt with their discord between themselves.

I place my hand back on the handle. As I push the door open, I turn to look at Harris.

"Then get a warrant," I say.

And then I do what I've been free to do since this interview started.

I leave.

---

When Leon drops me back at the Ara, it's crawling with guests. They're pulling suitcases behind them, accosting members of the staff, asking for cars. One of the influencers is on the phone, evidently with an airline, asking to be put on standby and repeating, louder than strictly necessary: "My member ID is nine . . . seven . . . three . . ." Madison, on her own call, yells what I imagine to be answers to security questions: "Acoustic guitar . . . Newfoundland . . . Cookies and cream."

Employees, too, are milling around, asking for patience, answering questions in soothing voices. Clearly, people have moved up their departures. They want to leave *now*—not in a few hours, and certainly not in a day or two.

They're desperate to get away—from us, I realize. The two persons of interest.

"Excuse me?"

Catalina is standing next to me.

"Can I speak to you for a few minutes?"

Without waiting for an answer, she ushers me toward a corner of the lobby.

"I'm sorry to have to do this," Catalina says, "but I need to ask you—"

I spare her.

"You want us to go."

Catalina nods.

"I'm sorry," she says.

"Don't be. We'll go."

At this, Catalina is visibly relieved.

"But can you give us one more night?" I ask, and gesture around at the chaos. "I just don't think we can get flights today."

I look at her with my most innocent eyes.

I am not a suspect. I am a mere person of interest. And I am still, despite everything, a guest at this hotel.

"That'll be fine," Catalina says.

I glance at the clock above the check-in counter. It's a little after three-thirty.

One afternoon, one evening, one night. That's the time I have to get the truth out of Gabriel.

After that, he'll head back to Seattle. I'll head back to New York. We'll be lost to each other, possibly forever.

And still, the documentary will happen. Even if I refuse to participate, my absence will become part of the narrative. The cameras will make their demands for a truth, a "coherent story."

If we're not ready to provide what they need, then what?

They'll come for us. The producers, the documentary, the viewers.

Who knows what they'll say: what theories they'll put together, what stories they'll invent?

People can be so creative.

## 33  BLOOMFIELD, NEW JERSEY AND SPRING LAKE, NEW JERSEY

The month before Annie and Gabriel got married, Annie had an idea.

"What if we went to the beach this summer? We could do Spring Lake. I went there all the time when I was a kid."

It was a source of fascination to me, Annie's insistence on addressing us as though we were normal people who *went to the beach*, who *did Spring Lake*.

"Don't you already have plans this summer?" I asked. "Like your own wedding?"

Annie shrugged. We were in the living room of their new house, drinking wine and eating olives. They'd moved to Bloomfield the previous week. There were still unpacked boxes piled against a wall. One of them served as our table.

"I meant we could go after."

It wasn't inconceivable that Annie and Gabriel might include me on a trip.

They wouldn't have gotten together, if not for me.

I met Annie first, at Columbia. A total fluke: We sat next to each other during a film night. (I never attended film night, because the movie club invariably picked French films, and I was, thanks to Émile, allergic to anything related to France. But that night, the movie club found the strength to tear itself from the French New Wave and screened the 2008 *Revolutionary Road* adaptation.)

That was in 2011. I was twenty; Annie was twenty-two. She was finishing her undergraduate degree (data science), and I had recently transferred from community college to the School of General Studies. This was Columbia's track for students with a "nontraditional path" in higher education, which in my case was putting it lightly.

"Nontraditional" could mean you were a single parent, or a veteran, or a newly retired ballet dancer. Or it could mean you'd been raised in a cult, escaped, lived in a storage unit for two years, in a homeless shelter for one, gotten your GED, and found your way to subsidized housing and education.

Time had passed. Gabriel and I lived in an apartment by then. We had beds, a shower, a lock on our door. Every day felt like something we'd gotten away with.

Before the movie started, Annie tapped my shoulder.

"Could you watch my bag? I'm just running to the bathroom."

It was that simple, out here in the real world. This was how people made friends.

After the movie, she asked me what I thought about "Leo," and I pretended to know who she was talking about. As the credits rolled, she stretched and declared: "Well, I'm never getting married."

I said that movie would put anyone off the idea of matrimony.

"It's not even the movie," she said.

"Then what is it?"

We walked to the local pizza joint, where the slices were the size of our faces. On the way, Annie complained about her suitors.

"There's nothing *wrong* with the guys I meet, really. They're just . . . all the same."

By the time we sat down to eat (pepperoni for me, cheese for Annie), it had become clear: The guys in Annie's life were as plain as her pizza. I pictured them: fine young men who shared her pedigree, all well mannered, well educated. All unbearably dull.

"I just want someone different, you know?" she said, blotting her slice with paper napkins. "Someone who doesn't have his future all mapped out."

It was a pattern I later learned to recognize in TV shows, movies. In a world where she had always been provided for, Annie yearned for someone who would, finally, need *her*. Who would turn *her* into a provider—of stability, comfort, opportunities.

I picked a slice of pepperoni off my pizza, tilted my head back to drop it onto my tongue.

"I think," I said when I was done chewing, "there's someone you should meet."

———

From the first date, they moved so fast, Gabriel and Annie. That kind of whirlwind felt foreign to me. I'd started dating, too, around the time Gabriel and I moved into the apartment. But it wasn't a means to an end. I never thought of it as a search with a specific endpoint—a partner, a ring.

It scared me, at first. The idea of intimacy, of partners, of sex. I knew so little.

But suddenly, I had access to a wealth of information. For a while, I treated sex and relationships like one big research project. I went to the library. I borrowed books. I read magazines. Slowly, I started being able to imagine it—me on a dinner date, me in someone else's bed.

That's where I met my first date, in fact—at the library. Others followed more easily than I could have imagined. The apps were starting to get popular, but I eschewed them. I needed to meet people in person—at bars, at school, even at work.

My dating was drinks, movies, drinks, movies, the occasional museum outing. It was waking up in a stranger's bed—a nice stranger I'd gotten to know just enough for this purpose, about whom I didn't feel the need to learn anything more.

Sometimes it went well. Other times it was complicated. Not everyone was kind. Not everyone was nice, fun, or even just good at it. There were things I didn't like. I was discovering them in real time, and I had to figure out how to communicate those preferences. That was a lot of work. And it required people who *listened*, not just to spoken language (although that, too) but to everything else as well: the tensing of a muscle, the sharpening of a breath.

I had no tolerance for people who tuned me out. One particular loser—someone I'd met at a campus mixer for people interested in finance—found out the hard way when I left in the middle of things.

But when it went well—that felt like a magic trick I'd taught myself. My dates and I made each other feel good in a variety of ways, from the moment we met up to the morning after. Every time, I marveled at it: The fact that sex hadn't stopped after Émile. That it wasn't confined to one memory, one room, one man, one girl. That it could be as silly or as deep as I wanted it to be. Sex could mean a hot stranger, body parts finding the right places as if by telepathy, and a midnight subway home. It could mean talking until sunrise, homemade pancakes, and never messaging each other again.

After Annie's death, that carefree feeling was gone. It was easy enough to meet up with someone, to order drinks, to talk about work. But then, inevitably: *So, where's your family from? Oh, you have a brother? Where does he live? What does he do?* I worried the person would put two and two together. *Oh, Gabriel Miller, isn't that—* And which questions would follow, then?

*Well, what's he like?*

*Well, do you think he did it?*

Not mentioning him was an option, of course. But every date started feeling like one massive lie by omission. And to be frank, what happened to Gabriel took a big chunk out of my faith in humanity. When we were younger, it had been easy to convince myself that cruelty was Émile's thing—and that once we left, people would, simply, be better. But clearly, I'd been wrong. On my dates, I kept waiting for someone's worst instincts to take over. I couldn't relax. It became impossible to enjoy myself. So I stopped.

After everything—the loss of Annie, Gabriel's relocation—the shutting down of my dating life felt like the smallest loss of all. I missed the good parts, but not the complications that came with them. There was no great love lost, no thwarted passion to mourn.

Which isn't to say I don't believe in romance. It happens to some people. They meet, and suddenly their whole life makes sense. I guess being in love and being in a rush are very similar feelings.

And they *were* in love, Gabriel and Annie. Early in their relationship, we met up for beers, the three of us. When Gabriel got up to get us a second round, he rested his hand on Annie's shoulder, and I realized I'd never seen him like this. At ease. Comfortable in the world.

He couldn't believe his luck. That someone like *her* would take a second look at *him*.

"I mean, have you seen her?" he asked me once. "She's gorgeous."

She was. Multiple levels of gorgeous. Annie was a natural beauty who took care of herself. Her eyebrows were threaded; her nails were done; her clothes fit just right. She wasn't just elegant or pretty, although she was those things, too. She had something extra. Something that can't be faked, or drawn on, or injected.

I have to imagine it was a thrill, being seen by her.

Actually, I don't have to imagine.

I was picked, too, once.

———

Within six months, in April 2012, Gabriel and Annie were engaged. It was an unstoppable force, this domestic bliss they conjured up out of nothing.

This was the time when, finally, Gabriel's life started falling into place. For a while, when we lived in the storage unit, he'd worked construction. Except, of course, he wasn't in a union, and he didn't have an ID card, much less a bank account, and so what he really did was work the job of some guy who *was* in a union but preferred to outsource his work to Gabriel.

(A few years later, when I started watching the mob show, it hit me: The guy in question had hired Gabriel to free up his time so he could go earn the bulk of his income through illegal means. *Duh.* But he paid Gabriel cash. He didn't ask questions. And he was the most polite person we'd ever encountered. So the arrangement worked for us.)

Then, Gabriel became depressed, and he didn't work for six months. Afterward, we moved to the shelter, and he found jobs as a contractor—legit, this time. It was the logical occupation, given his background at the compound. But it wasn't his passion. It wasn't *Howard.*

While at the shelter (I should say "shelters": one for men, one for women), we got public library cards. Gabriel started attending whatever talks he could, at whichever branches he could get to. He liked learning, and—crucially—the talks were free.

One Saturday morning, Gabriel listened as Howard Auster spoke about Agrippina (the Roman empress) and her fucked-up family. (Where to begin? A despot brother, an uncle who became her husband, a son who had her killed.)

Gabriel was transfixed. He had found the Romans, or maybe the Romans had found him. From then on, any spare time he had, he devoted to them. Gabriel browsed the internet from the library's computers, spent entire afternoons reading Howard's books.

He kept going to events. If Howard Auster was speaking publicly anywhere in the Tri-State Area, Gabriel Miller was in the audience.

Howard started recognizing him. Gabriel was known to ask insanely detailed questions—the kind someone could ask only if they'd read Howard's books multiple times.

One night, Gabriel came back from one of those events completely elated: "During the Q and A, Howard joked that he should hire me as his assistant. I said I'd do it. He took me out for coffee afterward and we kind of . . . spoke for two hours?"

We lived in the apartment—a studio in East Harlem—by then. Life was still fragile, but filled with possibility.

"What did you talk about?" I asked.

Gabriel put down his messenger bag. He carried it everywhere, and it was invariably filled with books.

"A bit of everything, I guess? His work, his next book, and, like, my life. Our life."

*Our life?*

We didn't talk about our life. Or rather, we talked about it on an as-needed basis, like when we applied for the apartment or did paperwork. But it wasn't the kind of narrative that made for a pleasant, professional talk over coffee.

"What did you tell him?" I asked.

Gabriel was rifling through his messenger bag.

"Just the basics," he said. "You know. Émile. How we grew up."

When he finally gazed up from his bag, he looked slightly worried.

"I didn't go into details," he said. "About . . . anything."

"Okay."

"He was just easy to talk to. Apparently, people care about that stuff."

*They do?*

"Anyway, he said he's going to think about it," Gabriel said. "The job."

"That's good."

Gabriel smiled. He really was happy. Who was I to ruin that for him?

"I mean it," I said. "Well done."

Howard emailed him the next day. He wanted to give things a try. Gabriel was hired on a part-time basis for a trial period of three months.

Howard was inspired. Three months after this initial offer, Gabriel went full-time.

Thus, the three great loves of Gabriel's life were assembled: First the Romans. Then Howard. And finally, a few months later, Annie.

———

Gabriel and Annie's wedding was planned for July 2012, on the first Saturday of the month. I supposed that left time for a trip to Spring Lake later in the summer.

"Maybe," I said, the night of the wine and olives, when Annie suggested we go to the beach.

"Could be fun," Gabriel contributed.

That was how he rolled, back then: agreeing with everything his fiancée said. He was young, smitten, silly.

But still.

"Don't you want to go on your honeymoon by yourselves, you weirdos?" I asked.

Annie took a sip of rosé.

"Oh, we are," she said, setting her glass down. Annie was the one who taught me how to hold a wineglass properly, with the tips of my fingers around the stem. "We're going to Cabo for a week. This would just be a little extra."

Those were the days. Of good times—so many of them. Of *little extras.*

"Fine," I said. "I'll request the time off work."

In addition to my classes, I was waitressing at a diner on Seventy-seventh and Broadway. This was my second place of employment. My first, in our earliest days in New York, had been another diner, close to Penn Station. The manager saw me crawl in one afternoon, covered in dirt and despair, and hired me as a food runner. He realized how green I was, meaning he was free to pay me cash, less than minimum wage. The wait-staff, too, saw my situation as an opportunity: I didn't know they were supposed to tip out food runners, and no one decided to enlighten me.

My new manager paid me properly. And she gave me the time off to go to Spring Lake.

Our rental house (paid for by Annie) was a fifteen-minute walk from the beach. We couldn't see the ocean from our windows, but we could smell it in the air: briny, salty.

Spring Lake gave me my first taste of a hot, sticky, mosquito-bite-y, citronella-candle-y American summer. I didn't know this was what the season looked like for thousands on the East Coast. As far as I was concerned, we'd invented the whole formula: breakfast on the deck, afternoons on the beach, ice cream at night from a local store called Fancy Cow, chunks of chocolate and nougat rolling between my tongue and the roof of my mouth. That irresistible ease, bug spray on top of sunscreen, my hair in lazy braids and buns, everything tacky with humidity: our skin, our clothes, the bloated doors of our rented home.

In the mornings, Annie and I walked into town for bagels and takeout coffee, while Gabriel worked. He'd barely taken time off for his wedding and honeymoon. That week in Spring Lake, Howard was revising the first half of a new manuscript, and Gabriel had pledged to remain available.

Still, there he was. There we were, all three of us. At the beach.

I'd never seen the beach before. In the city, I'd never made it to Coney Island—the idea of roller coasters held no appeal for me, and it was far, and I was forever short on time and money. Gabriel and I did know how to swim. We'd made the effort to learn at a public pool, a specialized class for adults, the two of us mastering a hesitant breaststroke.

By the time we arrived in Spring Lake, Gabriel had seen the beautiful beaches of Cabo. He'd told me all about the ocean, his first dip in water that didn't smell of chlorine.

I was beginning to feel left out.

But there was no time on the first day. Not after driving out, missing our exit a couple of times on the highway, unpacking, and going to the grocery store. ("Do we have to go now?" I asked, desperate to make it to the beach. To which Gabriel replied: "Do you want to eat tonight?")

After dinner, once Gabriel and Annie went to bed, I walked down our empty street. It was quiet, dark, stunningly suburban.

The good people of Spring Lake kept the most beautiful lawns I had ever seen.

On the streets of Spring Lake, I was alone. The quietude was broken only by the slap of my flip-flops against the sidewalk. I crossed a small park, walked over a bridge, made a right turn, went a few more feet.

And there it was. The ocean.

I got closer. Removed my flip-flops, stepped onto the sand. I registered its grit between my toes, the way in which it yielded under the arches of my feet.

I felt like the only person on earth. By myself on the darkened beach, the moon glowing just for me. The ocean was calm; it produced only small waves, accompanied by faint lapping sounds.

I walked to the edge of the water, let it lick my feet. My toes flexed. I waded farther in, up to my knees.

Out of nowhere, I was pulled in. The water had seemed so flat, so peaceful—I didn't expect it to drag me forward. As quickly as I could, I retreated to the shore.

But I wasn't done. Absolutely not.

I wanted more of it. A real swim, a full beach day. I wanted waves and seagulls. I wanted to nap in the sun, read a book, get sand stuck in its pages.

The next day, I was ready.

"Beach?" I asked after Gabriel wrapped up a call with Howard.

"Let's do it," Annie said.

We lugged three beach chairs up from the basement and carried them, backpack-style, to the sand.

"We can sit here," Annie said, pointing to an empty patch next to the lifeguards' giant chair.

A problem suddenly occurred to me.

We'd brought things with us. Wallets, books, phones. And in order to go into the water, we'd need to leave those things behind.

"Go ahead," I told Annie and Gabriel. "I'll look after our stuff."

"I don't think we have to worry about that here, Frida," Annie said.

Technically speaking, I knew that was true. I'd seen our fellow Spring Lake residents. It didn't take a detailed examination to confirm that Gabriel and I were the most broke people in a ten-mile radius. Well, *I* was—Gabriel's status had of course changed when he'd married Annie. Still. Whatever we had, it was hard to imagine that anyone in town would find it worth stealing.

Yes, and. There are fears you can't intellectualize. Old reflexes you let go of only when the world has shown you, over and over again, that you are safe.

I wasn't there yet. My phone, my wallet, my credit card, even my ID: They all felt infinitely precious to me.

Gabriel considered me, then the ocean.

"You've got your book, right?" he asked.

I pulled it from the pocket of my chair-backpack. Out of the two of us, Gabriel was the more voracious reader, but I wasn't too far behind. That book—I still remember it—was a novel called *The Beginner's Goodbye*. It was about a man with a sister and a dead wife, and I didn't know to find it foreboding.

"Yup," I said. "I'll be fine."

Gabriel gave his bride a gentle nudge. They walked toward the water.

I'd read five pages of *The Beginner's Goodbye* when a shadow fell on the paper, along with fat drops of water.

"Come on," Annie said, out of breath. "It's really fun in there."

"I'm good."

"Don't you want to at least try it?"

I closed my book. When I opened my mouth to speak, all that came out was a sigh.

"I'll stay with our stuff, if you're that worried," she said.

How much did Annie know about our past? Not a lot. I'd checked. When she and Gabriel first broke the news of their engagement to me, over cocktails at a hotel bar, I waited until

Annie excused herself to the bathroom, and whispered to Gabriel: "What have you told her, about . . . us?"

Gabriel knew what I meant. *Have you told her about the fire? About Edwina? Do you intend to?*

*I know love makes people stupid, sometimes.*

"She knows about Émile," he'd said. "And she knows we were homeless. I think that's enough."

And it was. Enough for Annie to know that I'd grown up with almost nothing. Enough for her to understand, on the beach, that this phase of my life had left me with an understandable wariness about losing what I finally had.

"I know this is stupid," I mumbled.

"What?"

As I searched for a polite way to tell her to drop it, Gabriel called from the water.

"Frida! Come on!"

For an instant, he was magnificent. Goofy, unafraid. Ecstatic. He had a wife, a job. The sea parting at his feet.

Damn it! I wanted a taste of it. Maybe our stuff would disappear. Maybe I'd lose everything. Maybe losing everything was preferable to staying safe on the sand while everyone else was having fun in the waves.

I ran. The water was cold and awesome in every sense. There was no need to swim; standing was enough of a challenge on its own. The water had no boundaries, no respect. It was ready to grab me, spin me around, spit me back out.

The nerve! The gall of nature! I loved it.

Something coiled around my ankle. I flinched. Inside my brain, a record scratched.

That feeling—what was it? A braided bracelet around my wrist, blue and brand-new, secured in a tight knot. Something to tell us apart, me and all the others.

That, I'd come to realize, was what the blue bracelets were for: to mark us. Those who wore them were over eighteen. To Émile, a girl with a blue bracelet was fair game. Ditto, the separate dorms from fourteen to twenty. They were there to keep us among ourselves: just the girls and Émile, no room for questions, secrets we were too ashamed to share. The exclusive company of other girls, our shared quarters, also set the scene for inevitable quibbles, primed us to turn against one another. At fourteen, Émile closed off our minds. At eighteen, he got started with us. At twenty, once he'd established this new normal, he released us to the company of other men.

But I was no longer in Émile's world. I was in Spring Lake, New Jersey. When I reached down for the thing in the ocean, all I pulled out was a piece of seaweed.

Maybe there were no monsters in these waters. Maybe nothing lurked under the surface at all.

A tall wave formed on the horizon. Gabriel grabbed my hand.

"You've got to dive under it!"

It came, and I dove—not deep enough. For a few seconds, I was tossed around like lettuce in a salad spinner. My body whirled. I knew not to swim, because I couldn't tell which way was up. All I could do was trust that I would float upward.

I broke through the surface. Gabriel's gaze locked on me, concerned.

"I'm okay!" I shrieked. "I'm okay."

I *was* okay. This was our world: it was possible to *almost* drown, to *almost* get in trouble. Disaster was no longer inevitable.

I made my way to Gabriel. We waded back in a bit together. Gabriel stopped, turned to look at the beach. In my memories, the image freezes for a moment: Gabriel and me in the waves, Annie on the sand. Separate from us. In a different world.

And then, we were all moving again. Gabriel yelled something I didn't catch in Annie's direction. She rose from her chair and ran to join us in the surf.

As soon as I enter our suite, I feel Gabriel's presence.

I find him on the patio, hunched over his laptop. When he sees me, he snaps it shut.

"Where have you been?" he asks.

I've been so busy agonizing about him that it didn't occur to me that he should have been agonizing about *me*, too. I didn't come back to the hotel last night. My phone was dead. He should be panicked. Hell, he should be filing a missing-person report by now.

But he isn't. He's . . . mildly concerned, if anything.

"Now you care?" I ask.

"What do you mean?"

"I was away all night."

He frowns.

"I looked all over for you," he says, defensive. "I asked Catalina if she knew where you'd gone. She said you took a car into town. Your stuff was still here, so I knew you hadn't left. And your phone was going straight to voice mail."

"It's dead."

"Well, if you charge it, you'll see that I tried to call you a dozen times."

Something about his tone, his cool rationality, sends me over the edge.

"All night!" I shout. "You didn't think that something might have happened to me?"

He rubs his forehead.

"Why are you yelling at me?"

*Because I don't understand anything you're doing, and it's starting to scare me.*

Gabriel spares me from having to respond. "We need to talk, anyway. I mean, there's something I need to tell you."

He stands and sets his laptop down on his chair.

"The police," he says. "They . . . Do you want to sit down?"

I shake my head.

"I already know."

"You do?" he asks.

"The person of interest thing?"

He nods.

"I saw it in the paper," I say.

His mouth sets in a resigned line.

"I saw it online," he says.

I whisper: "This is so fucked."

He takes a step toward me, tentatively. The awkwardness around us is inescapable, like the windless heat right before a storm. We're still scarred from our fight, our throats still raw from the words we hurled at each other.

That fight. I feel like it happened a hundred years ago. Back when Gabriel's lies to Harris were my biggest concern.

Before I found Sabrina's hair clip.

Before Gabriel's name showed up on her phone.

"Let's sit," I say.

Gabriel doesn't seem to hear me.

"Why are they doing this?" he asks. "What's their endgame? They have nothing on you or me and—"

The sun is shifting, climbing to its highest point above the patio. A ray lands brightly on Gabriel. His face is half-lit-up, half-hidden in the shade.

"Gabriel," I say. "Please, will you sit with me?"

He looks at me like he's just noticed I'm here.

"What?"

I need to know. I need to just come out and say it.

"Your name was on her phone."

Gabriel shifts. His face disappears in the shade.

"What did you just say?"

"I spoke to Harris. He came to town, asked me to come to the station. It doesn't matter. The point is, he says they found your name on Sabrina Brenner's phone. And your date of birth. And your address."

"And you believe him?"

*Frankly, yes.*

"Come on, Frida. The cops are allowed to lie. And even if it were true, it doesn't mean any—"

I step back inside the suite.

"Where are you going?"

He follows me. I walk over to his backpack, pick it up, unzip the inside pocket.

"This," I say, and take out the hair clip. "This is why I believe them."

Gabriel blanches. His hands ball into fists.

Here's what I know, in this moment: He's tall, and he's always—always—been stronger than me.

And a dead woman's hair clip is in his bag.

And he's a person of interest in her murder.

As am I.

"Okay," he says. "Let's talk."

"I'm listening."

He holds up a hand.

"Not here."

I frown.

"I can't . . . here," he says, gesturing at our surroundings.

"Then where?"

"Outside," he says.

Of course.

Where there are no eavesdroppers, no witnesses.

In the desert, where no one can hear you scream.

I squeeze my eyes shut, then release them, trying to shake the Etch A Sketch of my brain back into a blank slate.

This is Gabriel. The person I've known the longest. In a way, the only person I know outside of myself.

I grew up next to him. He shared my most brutal years. If I was a feral puppy, released, starving and unschooled and primed for abuse, into the world, then he was my littermate.

"Let's go," I say.

I'm still wearing yesterday's clothes. I slip the hair clip into the side pocket of my running shorts. It's the only thing that feels real right now.

Maybe I'm more prepared for this than I thought.

Maybe, in a corner of my mind, I've been bracing myself for a long time.

There was a firepit in the backyard.

"We should make s'mores," Annie said on our fourth day.

She had just looked up from her magazine, a special edition of *People* dedicated to true-crime stories that had "shocked America."

"Never had those," Gabriel said.

Annie tilted her head to the side, like, *It figures.*

"You?" she asked in my direction.

I shook my head no.

"Next time we go to the store," Annie declared, "we'll get supplies."

She loved that stuff. Introducing us to new things, walking us through our many first times. First comic books, first black-and-white cookies, first ice rink. I think she got a genuine thrill from it.

It had been hard for me to wrap my head around Annie and her upbringing. After our movie club–and–pizza night, I thought she was sweet. I built her up in my mind as a *nice girl.*

She *was* nice, but not like that. Annie was fierce and clear-headed. Her father ran a chain of copy shops. One day, she would take over the family business. He'd once hired her on a part-time basis, so she could—well, spy on other employees for him.

"Kind of gross," she'd said, wrinkling her pretty nose after she'd explained the situation to us.

Indeed. But who was I to judge? People did what they had to do for love, for money, for survival.

It was hard for me—and, I presumed, for Gabriel—to gauge exactly how rich Annie's family was. Sometimes she seemed like the wealthiest person in America. At other times it was hard to imagine that America was filled with anything but Annies.

Materially, she had wanted for nothing. Private schools, tutors, vacations. Anytime I tried to run through the list in my head—the list of all the things Annie had enjoyed that I hadn't—I had to start over, lower the standards: parents, a bedroom, food.

But she wanted to invite us in. From the moment she'd met Gabriel, she'd yearned to be the person who'd show him the world. Someone who bought graham crackers, marshmallows, and chocolate bars. Someone who asked her brand-new husband, as our last dinner in Spring Lake drew to a close, like it was nothing: "Do you want to start the fire?"

It took my breath away.

It really did.

Gabriel paused. He swallowed.

Then, as if he'd surrendered to something: "Sure."

He turned to me.

"Wanna help?"

*Are you out of your fucking mind?*

But I couldn't very well say that in front of Annie, so I followed him to the backyard.

I gritted my teeth as we each picked up a couple of logs from the garden shed.

"You good?" he asked.

I nodded. We'd had a good week. A good *life*, finally. No need to ruin everything with a fight.

But still. I was angry.

*Wanna help?*

So unnecessary. He knew I didn't. And he was perfectly capable of building a campfire by himself. Why drag me into it?

There was an unspoken rule between us. We didn't force each other to process things faster than we were able to.

It was an agreement we'd come to back when we still lived in the storage unit. Right after they caught Émile.

Here's how it happened.

They didn't get Émile for the girls.

Émile knew what he was doing. The girls were eighteen. There was no evidence left of what he'd done to them. To us. Only the word of a few women, all of them bad witnesses, since they'd spent their lives in a cult.

No. The girls were not trouble.

In the end, it came down to taxes. Émile—according to the newspapers—hadn't filed a tax return in years. He owed hundreds of thousands of dollars to the government. If convicted on all charges, one article said, he faced up to fifty years in prison.

Émile was forty-nine years old when he was arrested. A conviction meant he would, in all likelihood, die behind bars.

That didn't mean anything to me. The fact of Émile's suffering was just that: a fact.

And if, by some miracle, he didn't die in prison, he'd be deported back to his native France after his release.

A small consolation prize: Gabriel and I did have something to do with his arrest. The fire had brought police to the compound. It had blown the doors to Émile's building wide open for them—literally and figuratively. The cops had found documents (I pictured them stored in a trunk or a chest of drawers, somewhere far enough from Émile's desk that they survived the blaze) that constituted probable cause. They'd obtained search warrants, and things escalated from there until Émile pleaded guilty.

"At least he won't hurt anyone else now," Gabriel said the day we found out.

This was a part of us I'd come to hate. So resilient. Such survivors, all the time.

It infuriated me.

Two mornings later, Gabriel couldn't get up.

"Come on," I told him.

"Can't."

"Migraine?"

Gabriel grunted that his head was fine.

"Let's go, then," I tried again.

He turned to face the wall. Frustration coursed through me. But it occurred to me—just in time, just as I was about to erupt—that whatever was happening to Gabriel, he couldn't control it.

Émile's arrest meant that this was it. That there was nowhere left to return to. That the only life available to us was this one, and it was barely a life at all.

Gabriel was sick with this new world. The one he had journeyed to just for me.

I owed him.

So I worked. Gabriel didn't.

I bought food for two with money for one. I washed our clothes in the storage facility's sink. I bought more ibuprofen. I heated up soup on a camping stove. I played music for him on the portable radio I'd purchased from the dollar store.

This went on for six months.

It was love. It was, simply, what we did for each other.

So why couldn't he give me a break, with the campfire?

Maybe he couldn't face it without me.

Maybe fire was something we'd always have to take care of together.

Gabriel dropped his firewood next to the pit. I did the same thing. Then he showed me how to do it, the kindling first, the tinder second. I hated every minute of it. In a corner of my brain, we were back at the cult—a boy building a fire for Émile, all of us gathering around the flames.

Annie, oblivious to all of this, was in the kitchen, putting plates into the dishwasher.

"Ta-da!" she said when she came out, nudging the door open with her hip, balancing a platter with both hands.

In addition to the usual—according to Annie—graham crackers, marshmallows, and chocolate, she'd set out a few extra fixings: peanut butter cups, cut-up strawberries, white chocolate chips.

"Why don't we enjoy the fire for a bit," she said, setting the platter on a small patio table. "Then, dessert."

I sat in one of the Adirondack chairs arranged in a semicircle around the pit and stared into the fire. This thing. Organic, almost alive.

*What if I put my hand in, what if my sleeve caught fire, how hot would my skin get, would it hurt would it blister would it bubble would it foam would it—*

"I'll be back," Gabriel said, and got up.

He made it look like he'd left something inside, or was going to the bathroom. But I knew. This was someone whose grief had once pinned him to the ground for six months. He couldn't stand it, either—sitting by the fire, with nothing to look at but the flames.

Annie, leaning back in her own Adirondack chair, was swirling her leftover rosé from dinner.

"So," she said. "Are you . . . seeing anyone?"

I chuckled.

"No one in particular," I said. "Everyone in general."

"Good. That's good."

Annie grew serious then. Her inquiry about my dating life, I realized, had been a warm-up—a gentle nudge to set both of us on the road to deeper confessions.

"Listen," she said, gazing down at her glass. "I know that we never talk about . . . things."

"Things?"

"Life. Before we met."

*Ah.*

Annie looked up from her glass. The fire cast its glow on her face.

"What was it like?" she asked, whispering even though it was still just the two of us. "After you left?"

The silence that followed was interrupted only by the occasional pops and cracks of the fire.

Annie placed a hand on my arm.

"He never talks about it," she said. "We're married. He's going to be my husband for the rest of my life. Or his life. And I can't get him to tell me."

I opened my mouth, but I was stuck.

*What was it like, Annie, to be born in a cult?*

*To leave?*

*To exist in the aftermath?*

*Well.*

*Here's what it was like, being homeless: Every time we tried to do something, we bumped up against some complication. We could sign up for a P.O. box at the post office, but we needed a primary address to do so. Ditto getting a cell phone. We could shower for free, but only in other boroughs (which we couldn't travel to without subway cards), and only during work hours (we needed to work to afford subway cards).*

*And there was the big one: We didn't have birth certificates or Social Security numbers. As far as the government was concerned, we did not exist.*

*Then Gabriel got sick. Not his body, but his mind. So I took care of him. Of us. Back then, I would wake up at night, drenched in sweat, frantically awake with the knowledge that this life—our world—was hanging on by a thread. Me. I was the thread.*

*By the time Gabriel got better, in December 2009, I knew things had to change.*

*We needed help.*

*There are things I can't explain to you, Annie. Like how, by then, we'd been out for a year. Émile had pleaded guilty to all charges. If he suspected we'd had anything to do with Edwina's death, he'd clearly failed to leverage it into a proper plea bargain. That made me feel like it was safe to crawl out of our hiding place.*

*Edwina's death: I will never tell you about that.*

*Do you hear me?*

*You couldn't waterboard it out of me.*

*There was an organization. I'd seen people lining up outside for meals. I joined them whenever I could. One Sunday, I spoke to some-one who said they could help.*

*This was a kind of help that would be meted out only in small, imperfect ways. It required patience and bravery, two resources I was running out of. But it was help.*

*I moved into a homeless shelter, Gabriel into a different one. On paper, we weren't related, so we couldn't stay together. It was back to the dorms, girls on one side, boys on the other.*

*I missed him.*

*It took so much work, Annie. So much work to put together two existences from scratch. We tried, and tried, and tried again.*

*A social worker entered our lives. Then, a woman from an advo-cacy group that helped people who had left, or needed to leave, various cults. Together, they tracked down a former follower of Émile. In a previous life, she'd been a nurse, so Émile liked to have her present during the births. She was there when Gabriel was born and, six months later, when it was my turn.*

*That woman signed a document. Gabriel and I waited. We filed more documents. At the end of this trail of paperwork were our Social Security cards.*

*That was the most tangible sign I'd ever received that we might claim our spots in society.*

*We got IDs. We opened bank accounts.*

*If it occurred to Gabriel to track down his birth parents, he didn't say it. I didn't bring mine up, either. Those total strangers? What could they have done for us? I mean this literally. Yes, we were resent-ful, angry in ways we couldn't have parsed out. But we also had no concept of how parents were supposed to act in the real world. If we had known, then maybe we would have grieved for the normal, loving childhoods that had been taken from us. But we didn't know, and so there was nothing there for us to miss.*

*After a year in our respective shelters, we moved into an apart-ment. We paid what we could, and the city covered the rest.*

*We had proper beds, twins that we pushed to each side of our liv-ing area. We had regular access to food, showers. It was like our bodies came out of survival mode. Every problem they'd been holding on to for the past two years rose to the surface. My shoulder hurt. Gabriel had hives. I needed glasses. He needed to get a true hold on his migraines.*

*We fixed ourselves, one body part at a time.*

*We got a small TV, the cheapest we could find. I watched it all the time. The news, sitcoms, medical dramas, police procedurals. Life was easier to understand distilled into the pithy, snippy language of Hollywood writers' rooms.*

*In addition to TV, I took up smoking. Carmen, another waitress at the diner, was always asking me if I wanted to go out for a smoke. I said no, no, no, until I said yes.*

*It's fine. I like smoking.*

*And then, well, you know this part, Annie. I transferred to Columbia.*

*I'm good with numbers. One day, I think—and it sounds absurd for me to say it even in my head, but this is what my life is like now— I'll get a job somewhere. Maybe at a bank. I understand that stuff. Funny, right? After never having any of it, I understand money. Sometimes I think there's a clarity that comes from looking at things as an outsider. I had to figure it out for myself—this world. Same with bank accounts and interest rates and stocks and bonds. No one walked me through it. I didn't grow up with it. And so it slotted into my adult brain, unpolluted by the confusion of youth, the incomplete, incorrect bits of knowledge and bias we inherit from the people we love.*

*I know a thing or two about that.*

*I once revered a man who made up a lot of shit.*

*He did introduce me to math, though. In his office. That's where my affinity for numbers became obvious.*

*Oh, and while we're at it, Annie. As long as we're talking.*

*I'm weird about fire. Gabriel is, too. We can't tell you why. But I wish there was a story we could share with you, so you'd know there are some activities we're not suited for.*

*Like this. Like s'mores.*

———

I didn't tell Annie any of that.

Instead, I did what she'd asked us to do. I gazed at the fire.

I'm sure she could see the flames reflected in my eyes. Maybe, if she looked close enough, she'd see them spread all the way into my brain. Maybe she'd see the original embers, the ones that started them all, in my memories.

"It's complicated," I said finally.

She shrugged.

"Okay," she said.

"It's not that I don't want to tell you."

"I get it."

*But you don't.*

Annie cleared her throat.

"Anyway," she said, and got up, clapping her hands, "time for s'mores."

She went back inside the house and returned with Gabriel.

"Now, here's how you do it," she said, stabbing a marshmallow onto a stick. "I like mine burned, so I put it into the fire and let it—"

She demonstrated as she spoke, thrusting her marshmallow into the flames. Then she pulled it out, still burning, and blew on it. It was partly charred—unappetizing, really, but Annie seemed delighted.

"Then, you take a graham cracker and some chocolate—"

She showed us the whole architecture, the weird chocolate-sandwich-between-crackers of it all. With her free hand, she slid the singed marshmallow off her stick and onto the chocolate. She put her stick down, closed off her s'more with another cracker, and held it out to Gabriel.

"First bite," she said.

That was a thing they did, a theory they'd built up in the shared language of their love: The first bite of any given food was deemed to be the best. If someone asked for a taste of someone's food, they had to wait until that person had taken the proprietary first bite. Conversely, letting someone else have the first bite was a sign of deep care, a privilege passed down.

Gabriel crunched down on the s'more. He closed his eyes and chewed.

"Not bad," he said. "Not bad at all."

He held out the s'more to me. I waved him away.

"I'll make my own."

I set out to work. Marshmallow, stick.

"You don't have to burn it if you don't want to," Annie said. "You can just hold it close to the flames and wait for it to heat up."

But I burned it. Oh, I burned it. Stuck it right into the fire, pulled it out, and watched the tiny flame singe the white surface, wrap itself around the marshmallow's soft, squishy, gelatinous body.

After a few seconds, I blew out the flame. I mirrored Annie's gestures, laid a piece of chocolate on top of the cracker, slid the melted marshmallow off the stick, completed the sandwich.

*First bite.*

Food was so intense, in those days. After years of Émile-mandated grub, followed by years of whatever would fill our stomachs for as little money as possible, our meals offered endless possibilities. The first time I had a cheeseburger—a proper one, with a thick patty and a brioche bun and rings of red onions on top of the meat—my jaw got sore from all the chewing.

At first, the s'more was all textures. The snap of the cracker giving way to the cool, smooth chocolate. Then the warm gooeyness of the marshmallow. It was hypnotizing, that initial resistance followed by total surrender. Like a magic trick you conjured with your teeth, a little voice somewhere immediately chanting, *Let's do it again, again, again.* Physically impossible not to go back for one more bite, and another one after that.

And then, the tastes. Of course, the tastes. They were perfect. Sweet, perhaps *too* sweet, but unapologetic, overt in their own excess. *What else did you expect? I'm a candy sandwich.*

Only after I swallowed my third bite did it occur to me to speak.

"Wow," I said.

Annie gave me a satisfied nod.

We went back for more, trying different combinations: a peanut butter cup instead of plain chocolate, strawberries between the chocolate and the marshmallow. But I returned to the original. Nothing extra was needed.

After all this time, this was what fire could mean: a graham cracker yielding to chocolate, marshmallow melting on your tongue. The pure, pure magic of those days.

———

THE SEVENTH DAY

Gabriel and I make our way toward the edge of the hotel compound. Our heads are bowed, our steps swift. We've each grabbed a water bottle from the minibar—our only precaution.

"Hey!" someone yells in our direction.

I think I recognize Catalina's voice. She must be outraged. We dared to leave our suite—we, the two persons of interest, to whom she so graciously granted one last night in paradise.

At the periphery of my vision, I spot a group of people: a dejected Fabio, a suspicious Madison. William Brenner, too, still here, still free.

I quicken my pace, put a hand on Gabriel's back. Not that he needs it. He's walking so fast I can barely keep up with him.

The desert opens before us.

"This way."

My feet know where to go. I know this place, its slopes, its hidden crevices.

Maybe my confidence is undeserved. The last time I ventured out here, the desert coughed up a dead woman's phone. It gave me hope, but look where it got me: in an interrogation room, a police deputy's urgent gaze on me, outrageous claims spurting out of his mouth. Gabriel's name on Sabrina Brenner's phone.

I point to the hiking trail Ethan took us on yesterday. Gabriel nods. We keep walking in silence.

It's impossibly hot, in a way that makes me think I've never experienced actual heat before. I drink a few greedy gulps of water as we pass the point where Ethan ended yesterday's hike. Soon, we're standing at the top of a hill, under a rock formation that forms a canopy over our heads.

I look at Gabriel for the first time since we left. His fore-head is slick with sweat. He wipes it with the back of his hand. I know—I *know*—one of his eyes is blue, but from where I'm standing, they both look black. The effect is uncanny, like he's a version of himself I've never met before.

"So," I say, "what do you want to tell me?"

Gabriel screws the cap back onto his water bottle. His ges-tures are slow, precise.

"There's something you should know," he says.

His voice is so low I can barely hear him. I try to meet his gaze, but he stares somewhere above my shoulder.

"Sabrina and I . . ." he starts.

This is it. What he tried to tell me in our suite, the morn-ing after we saw Sabrina's body. Already, Gabriel couldn't bring himself to meet my eyes. He started: *Sabrina, we—*

I never learned the rest. Gabriel changed the subject. Decided to keep something from me.

"Sabrina and I," he tries again now. "We've been—we had—"

"What? What is it?"

"Something happened," Gabriel says finally.

My mouth is dry. I swallow with difficulty, bite my tongue in the process.

"What was it?" I ask.

He gives me a pained look.

"Between us," he says. "Something happened."

"Between you and . . . Sabrina?"

"Yes."

"What? What happened?"

"We were . . ."

His cheeks are bright red.

"Gabriel," I say. "What is it?"

He lets out a frustrated sigh.

"We were . . . seeing each other," he says.

"Huh?"

By which I mean: *What the fuck?*

"You and Sabrina? What?"

He nods stiffly.

I need to make sure I understand correctly.

"You were . . . having an affair?"

"Well, technically, I wasn't," he says. "Having an affair. She was having one. With me. I guess. If you can call it that."

I bring a hand to my forehead.

"How is that . . . What? How is that even possible?" I make a sweeping gesture in the direction of the hotel. "You were right here. I was right here."

He winces.

"Not always."

They come to me now: those moments, throughout our stay, when I lost Gabriel. When he went back to our suite while I stayed by the pool. The hike he missed, on our third day. During our last dinner before the murder: *I'm just going to grab a sweater.* All those times I thought I caught him gazing into the distance.

He wasn't gazing into the distance. He was looking at *her.* Admiring her from afar.

Is that right?

I turn the idea over in my mind.

Do I believe him?

*Can* I believe him?

And if I do, is there more to this?

Gabriel sits on the ground.

"Come here," he says, and pats the dirt next to him.

I hesitate.

*Really? It's Gabriel.*

I sit.

He nods in a silent *thank you*.

"It started on the first day," he says. "I don't know if you remember, but I bumped into her on the way to—"

"I remember."

"There was . . . something about her. I mean, she was gorgeous, of course. But it wasn't just that."

I search for a more comfortable position on the ground. When I speak next, I choose my words carefully, to keep him talking.

"How did you go from bumping into each other to . . . whatever happened?"

Gabriel sighs.

*Did you love her?*

*Have you been . . . grieving for her?*

*Or did something else happen—something darker?*

*This story you're about to tell me—how does it end, exactly?*

Gabriel opens his mouth, then shakes his head.

I put my hand on his. It's a gamble. He's nervous, embarrassed for reasons I haven't figured out yet. But he doesn't pull away.

"Tell me," I say.

He nods. He opens his mouth again. This time, he speaks.

## 37 ESCALANTE, UTAH

THE FIRST, SECOND, THIRD, FOURTH,
AND SEVENTH DAYS

Here's how it unfolds, in Gabriel's telling.

On the first day, on his way from the swimming pool to our suite, Gabriel bumps into this woman. He's noticed her. Everyone has. He doesn't expect her to notice him in return—or if she does, it will be for the wrong reasons. Because he's tall, shy, and awkward. Because his eyes don't match. I've always suspected that Gabriel might be beautiful, but I've never known for sure. His face has been a part of my world for so long. It just *is*, for me.

Obviously, people also notice him because he's Gabriel Miller, whose wife died in circumstances just a little too strange for comfort. It happens. It has happened too often.

But Sabrina Brenner notices him in a way that feels good. He swears she does. Her hand lingers on his arm. Above the lenses of her sunglasses, her eyes—her beautiful green eyes—search his. She smiles at him in a way that lights up her whole face.

"I'm not some sicko," Gabriel tells me under our rock canopy. "I don't start imagining things the moment a woman looks at me. So I didn't think it was anything, at first."

But then. That night, the first night, Gabriel and I go for one last drink after dinner. Espresso martini for me, a pineapple-based mocktail for him. I leave our spot at the bar for a few minutes, to go to the bathroom. In that time, he sees her, by herself, on a stool at the opposite end of the counter. She spots him, raises her hand in a little wave, and—looking left, then right, maybe checking for her husband—approaches him.

Under the canopy, Gabriel's voice takes on a hypnotic quality. It's not hard, hearing him talk, to imagine a scene as though I'm living it through him. I know how he speaks, how he breathes. I know how he reacts to most things.

Or at least I think I know.

Maybe there's a whole other Gabriel lurking under the surface.

But it's my version of him I picture chatting with Sabrina at the bar.

They talk for a few minutes. She's at the Ara with her husband, but he's been working a lot. He always works a lot.

Here, she looks a bit sad.

"This trip," she said. "We were supposed to spend time dealing with our—"

She catches herself. A pink flush creeps up her delicate cheekbones.

Maybe she doesn't want to bore him. Maybe she realizes it would be unbecoming to tell a stranger—this young stranger— what she was supposed to do with her old husband. Maybe she feels disloyal toward William.

"Where are you visiting from?" Gabriel asks, to change the subject.

"New York," she says.

Here, I imagine Gabriel's jaw tightens.

"I used to live in New York," he says.

"Oh, really? Where were you—"

Sabrina notices someone in the distance. Gracefully, she detaches herself from the bar on which she was leaning. Her hand is on his arm again.

"It was good talking to you," she says.

She takes off before Gabriel can tell her that it felt good for him, too.

A few seconds later, I return.

"So what did I miss?" I ask, completely fucking oblivious.

Gabriel gives his mocktail a little swirl.

"Nothing," he says.

———

The next day, Gabriel and I go to the pool.

Sabrina Brenner and her husband are there, too. Gabriel keeps them in a corner of his eye. William has on linen pants and a matching shirt. Sabrina is wearing a white bikini and has wrapped a red cover-up around her waist. She's reading a book—Gabriel leans forward to get a glimpse of the cover, an oil portrait of a melancholic woman. William scrolls on his phone.

About an hour in, Sabrina and William get into the kind of quiet argument couples know how to have in public. They're sitting at the edge of their respective chaises, feet on the floor, backs hunched. Their brows are furrowed, their movements abrupt. William speaks, punctuating each syllable with a little shake of his closed fist. Sabrina touches her husband's arm, but he gets up, grabs his things, and goes.

She stays behind. Slides a finger under the lens of her sunglasses, presumably to wipe off a tear.

Gabriel has talked to this woman—this beautiful, friendly woman—twice in his entire life, but her sorrow moves him.

"She was sitting there," he tells me. "She looked so sad."

*So you noticed it, too. This thing between the Brenners, like a frayed rope on the verge of snapping. It wasn't just me. It wasn't in my head.*

I don't say this.

If I speak, Gabriel might catch himself. He might stop talking.

Wherever he's going with this, I need to hear it.

Eventually, Sabrina leaves the pool, too.

Something wakes up inside Gabriel. He can't let her go.

"I'm going to go back to the suite," he tells me.

"You okay?"

"Just hot. I need to sit in the AC for a bit."

I nod. It annoys me that Gabriel can't seem to spend one full day by my side. But even I have to admit it *is* horrendously hot by the pool.

"Want me to come with you?"

"No," he says, maybe too fast, but I don't notice. "I mean, I'll be fine. Enjoy yourself."

Gabriel tugs his T-shirt back on and hurries away.

He doesn't have a plan. If there is to be another run-in between him and Sabrina Brenner, he needs fate to engineer it for him. She's not in the lobby. Not in the dining room, which is closed. She must have gone back to her suite, but—isn't her husband there? Would she go back to him so soon after a fight?

It occurs to Gabriel that he doesn't know anything about this woman.

He's about to give up when he spots her. She's walking into the lobby, coming from the direction of the entrance lounge. Maybe she just needed to take a walk. Maybe she needed to be alone for a few minutes. In any case, when she sees Gabriel, her face brightens.

"Oh, hi," she says.

Gabriel says hi back. Sabrina stops. Her voice shakes a bit, but in Gabriel's presence, she seems to relax. Once again, they're chatting. About the desert, the heat, the hotel. Mindless things.

"Listen," Gabriel says, then hesitates. He doesn't know what he's trying to ask, or how to ask it. In the end, he settles for: "Is everything okay? Are you okay?"

Sabrina looks at him as though it's been months since anyone has asked her that question.

"I'm . . . fine," she says. "My husband—he's under a lot of stress. I get on his nerves sometimes." She gives a forced chuckle, runs her hand over her already-smooth hair. "Wives and husbands, you know?"

Gabriel nods.

He knows.

"If you need anything," he says. "Just . . . I'm here. My sister and I, we're staying in suite twenty-nine."

Sabrina's hand drops from her hair.

"Your sister?"

"Yes. I'm here with her."

"The woman you're with, that's your sister?"

Gabriel confirms. He doesn't explain. Doesn't say, *Well, not really. She's my . . . something. We grew up together.*

Something like electricity travels between him and Sabrina.

It gives him a kind of courage he hasn't felt in nearly a decade.

"Hey," he says. "Do you maybe want to . . . sit with me, or something? We have a patio. It's nice and quiet."

Sabrina doesn't point out that all the suites have patios, and that they're all nice and quiet.

She nods.

"Hold on," I say. "You really said this? 'Sit with me, or something'?"

It's a detail, I know, but it feels important to me. Something about the credibility—can I imagine those words coming out of Gabriel's mouth?

Actually, yes.

I've been on enough dates to know this is not what quality flirting sounds like. And Gabriel? I don't think he ever was a smooth talker.

He cringes.

"I know. But it worked."

Sabrina follows him back to our suite. Gabriel speed-walks past our beds, which are made, thank god—housekeeping came while we were away. For a second, the whole affair looks sordid. But then, those two are on the patio, and everything seems to click into place.

Meanwhile, I'm leaving the pool and heading into the desert, water and crackers in hand, to rescue a coyote.

"So," Sabrina says, taking one of the two chairs, waiting for Gabriel to settle on the other. "Where are you visiting from?"

He tells her about Seattle. He's free not to explain why he moved there; it's clear she doesn't recognize him. In fact, he finds that Sabrina Brenner is a blank canvas on which he can repaint himself. In her eyes, he can be whoever he wants.

It feels so good. So freeing.

Sabrina asks him questions, and he answers. "What do you do?" He tells her about the Roman Empire. It is an extraordinary kind of bliss, telling a beautiful woman about the Roman Empire. "How did you get into that?" He tells her about books, about the internet, about films. "How's Seattle? I've never been." He tells her about the weather, how he actually likes rain. Not everyone understands liking the rain, but Sabrina does.

She tells him things, too. She was born and raised in New Jersey. Gabriel keeps his expression blank. He doesn't tell her he used to live there, too. With Annie. In fact, he doesn't tell Sabrina he was once married. She doesn't ask for that information, and he doesn't volunteer it.

How old was she, when Annie died? Thirteen, at most fourteen. It's not surprising that she doesn't place him. Gabriel, to her, is simply the kind stranger she happened to bump into at a luxury hotel.

Sabrina tells him about her mother, who owns a hair salon. About her string of stepfathers. "None of them turned out to be the dad who stepped up," she says with a wry little laugh. Gabriel says he's sorry.

"It's okay," she says. "It is what it is."

There's something brave and resilient about her. Someone who social-climbed but never forgot where she came from.

Gabriel and Sabrina sit in silence for a moment.

Then: "You must be thinking I'm nuts," she says. "Telling a perfect stranger my life like this."

"I'm not thinking that," he says.

Maybe he's not thinking at all.

A quiet supplication hangs between them like mist.

*Please. Please, keep telling me your life.*

"I used to work at a bar," she says. "This cocktail bar for rich people. Well, rich men, mainly."

That's where she met William Brenner. He was a customer.

"The first time he came in, he left me a two-hundred-dollar tip and his number on the receipt," she says, and beams. "I was smitten."

A lot of people think she married him for his money, she says, but she really was. Smitten.

He took her to Broadway shows, to old New York steakhouses.

"Sometimes, he did these extravagant things," she says. "Like out of a movie."

Once, on her day off, he invited her to the opera. In the afternoon, while she was getting ready, the intercom buzzed. She rented a room in Chelsea back then. Her roommate called out for her. When Sabrina stepped into the living room, a massive box was waiting for her, with a silver bow tied around it and the name of a French *maison de couture* in elegant white letters.

"It was this incredible dress," she says. "Black velvet. Silk princess gloves." Her fingers trace an invisible line from her hands to above her elbow, as if she can intuit that this young man—with his bathing suit and his flip-flops and his hunched shoulders—does not know what princess gloves are.

"You know what really got me?" she says. "He remembered the shoes. Black stilettos. They were in the box, with the dress. It's like he thought about it, you know? And realized I wouldn't own anything nice enough to go with it?"

Sabrina chews her lip.

"That blew my mind," she says. "I think that was when I knew I'd marry him, if he ever asked."

Which he did, three months later, at a French restaurant called La Grenouille. He slid the ring—a diamond the size of a cherry tomato—across the table.

"It was a small wedding," she says. "At his house in the Hamptons. It was his third time, so."

Gabriel nods politely.

"You want to see a photo?" Sabrina asks.

Gabriel doesn't really want to see a photo of the beautiful Sabrina marrying William, but she seems excited, so he acquiesces.

Sabrina's not an idiot. She chooses a photo that shows her by herself, without her husband. She's the most radiant third wife the world has ever seen. Her dress is tasteful, but in the taken-in waist, the slight bouffant of the skirt, the bouquet of closed-up peonies, Gabriel senses the excitement of a first-time bride. *I don't want to go full princess*, the outfit seems to say, *but when am I going to get another chance?*

"So beautiful," he whispers.

When he realizes he said this out loud, his face burns.

"I'm sorry," he says.

He doesn't know where to look.

With a smile, Sabrina puts him out of his misery.

"It's okay," she says. "Thank you."

She puts away her phone.

"Anyway," she says, "he's a nice man. Just a bit . . . difficult, sometimes." She pauses. "We came here to work through things. It was my idea. Do you know what I thought, when we arrived? We got assigned suite number six. And I thought, 'Six, that's my lucky number.' It really is. But, you know. There's only so much a lucky number can do."

Gabriel wonders, but doesn't ask: *How difficult?*

*Does he hit you?*

*Are you afraid of him?*

He thinks but doesn't say: *I would be so much better, if you gave me a real chance.*

Instead, he asks: "So, what have you been reading?"

She tells him about the book he saw her with at the pool, which turns out to have been *Madame Bovary*. "It's about this terribly romantic woman," she says. "She marries this complete bore of a guy. I don't think there's anything wrong with dreaming of romance, but the world will punish you for it."

"What happens to her?" Gabriel asks. "The woman?"

"I don't know yet," she says. "The book was published in 1857, but somehow I've avoided spoilers for two centuries."

She thinks.

"I don't think it's going to be good, though."

A shadow falls over her face. Gabriel feels a vital need to change the subject.

"Do you read a lot of classics?"

Sabrina becomes animated again.

"I used to, when I was a kid. Then I stopped when I was a teenager."

*Around the time the stepfathers entered her life.*

"I got back into it after I married William," she says. "I quit my job at the bar when we got engaged. He said I didn't need to work anymore. So I had a lot of free time. He has a wonderful library."

Gabriel realizes he could sit here for hours, listening to her talk. *Watching* her talk. He's not in love, exactly. You can't be in love with a woman you've only spoken to three times. But he is mesmerized. In thrall.

Sabrina checks her watch—a shiny gold thing with the name of a French brand Gabriel would recognize if he watched the mob show as assiduously as I do—and gets up.

"I should go," she says.

Gabriel follows her back inside the suite. She puts a hand on his arm again.

"Thank you," she says. "For your kindness."

In this moment, Gabriel realizes what's so special about her.

Sabrina Brenner is one of the most beautiful women he's ever seen. Yet she acts as though his attention were a gift. Like she's been starved for it, and she's grateful for this man finally turning his eyes to her.

It is an absolute miracle.

Sabrina puts her hand on the door handle. At the last second, she seems to reconsider. She walks the five steps that separate her from Gabriel. This time, her hand lands on his shoulder. She leans toward him, and, swiftly, but with care, presses a kiss to his cheek.

It means so little, at their respective ages—Sabrina's young, younger than he is, for sure, but she's not *that* young—a kiss on

the cheek. Sabrina will forget about it in a few seconds, he's sure
of it. But to him, it's a gift he didn't know to yearn for, a turn of
events he wouldn't have been able to imagine.

Gabriel doesn't say it like that. He recounts the kiss chastely.
"She gave me a little peck on the cheek," he says. "It took me
completely by surprise."

His body language fills in the blanks for me. His pupils are
dilated. He wipes his—presumably damp—hands against his
shorts.

The door shuts behind Sabrina.

Gabriel knows he should be happy that it happened at all.
He should treasure what he has, the memory of this woman's
lips on his skin.

But he sits on his bed in the empty suite, his knees weak with
need. He wants more, more, more.

———

Which leads him to the third day.

On the third day, Gabriel and I are scheduled to go for a
hike. But first, breakfast.

Of course, the Brenners are there, too. This time, no argument. They're sitting in complete silence. William doesn't even
look at his wife. He stabs at his scrambled eggs, turns the pages
of his newspaper brusquely. The paper bristles each time he flips
over to a new section. When he turns his attention to the sports
pages, they rip between his fingers.

Sabrina plays with her yogurt parfait but doesn't eat. She keeps
her eyes on her food. Her manner is muted, like she's sorry for
even being present. Like she wants to pay back the world for the
air she dares to breathe.

"It broke my heart," Gabriel says. "And it made me angry,
too. I just felt like I should do . . . something."

"So, what? You ditched me?"

Gabriel closes his eyes for a second.

"I wasn't trying to . . . make anything happen. I just—"

"It's okay."

"No. Wait. I need to explain this."

He searches for his words.

"Do you have any idea," he says, "what kind of hell dating is, for me?"

Back when we still wrote to each other, visited each other, he'd occasionally hint at some kind of romantic (or, at least, romantic-adjacent) life. "I had drinks with a woman who works at such and such"; "I watched that show with [insert stranger's name]." It wasn't much, just enough to keep me from asking further questions. But now I realize that I don't know, really, how much intimacy was involved, if any.

"Has there been—I mean, have you not—"

What am I trying to say here?

*Have you not been with anyone in nine years?*

*I don't just mean sex. Has there been no warmth in your life? No companionship?*

He waves his hand in the air.

"There was a woman . . . seven years ago, I think? And a couple other ones after that. But I mean, nothing that lasted. Nothing good."

Gabriel shakes his head.

"I still try, sometimes. But I never know what to expect. I'll meet up with a woman, and all she'll want to talk about is Annie. Or she has a podcast. Or she just wants to tell me she knows I killed her."

He swipes a hand across his face.

"With Sabrina . . . I wasn't planning to seek her out, or anything. But it had been so long since anyone had looked at me like that. Like I was . . . worth looking at. This is going to sound so stupid, but I wanted to be there for her. And I knew she wouldn't talk to me if you were here. So, yeah. Sorry. I guess."

"It's fine."

*Just tell me what you did.*

So, on the third day, at the breakfast table, as we're fueling up for a hike, Gabriel tells me he feels a migraine coming on.

"Do you want me to stay with you?" I ask.

Once again, he dismisses me.

"No, no. Go hike. One of us should get to see the desert."

"You sure?"

He nods.

"I'll be fine."

I leave. Gabriel stays in the dining room a little longer. He watches as the Brenners get up from their table. By the time he comes back to our suite, I've already left.

Gabriel wanders the hotel. He checks the lobby, the pool, the entrance lounge, even the spa. Sabrina is nowhere to be seen.

He retreats to our suite.

"I felt so stupid," he says. "Like what did I think was going to happen?"

Gabriel is about ten minutes into his pity party when he hears a knock.

He opens the door.

It's her.

The polite friendliness of the previous day, the apparent wholesomeness of a kiss on the cheek—all that's gone.

A fire has been lit inside Sabrina Brenner.

"Can I come in?" she asks.

He doesn't say yes. Doesn't need to. He steps aside, and she walks into the room.

Gabriel starts: "Can I get you any—"

"I didn't come here to talk."

I hold up a hand.

Gabriel's going too fast. I'm trying to picture it, this scene straight out of an old movie, the kind where the actors have real faces and even realer chemistry. Where the most mundane scene can turn into the most erotic moment.

And it happened to Gabriel?

Really?

"Are you making this up?" I ask.

For a second, he looks offended.

"Sorry," I mumble. "Keep going."

"She kissed me again," he says. "Not on the cheek. And then—"

He pauses.

"One thing led to another," he says.

"Is this your polite way of saying you had sex with her?"

"Yes."

This is a lot to process.

I try to see it from her point of view.

Why does she do it, Sabrina Brenner?

In the story Gabriel just told me, why does she show up at his door, hurried and willful, with a clear plan in mind?

She's been married to William for two years. He's a jerk. So much worse than a jerk: He's violent, coercive, controlling.

But sleeping with Gabriel—that's something she decides to do for herself. It's a part of her life that has nothing to do with William.

She does it for control. She does it because it's something she can do.

"Jesus," I whisper.

"I know."

"So this whole time, you were . . ."

The words float between us.

*Flirting. Making out. Having sex.*

*With Sabrina Brenner.*

*The murder victim.*

"I liked her," he says. "I really did. I didn't know her that well, but that was okay."

This whole time, Gabriel kept this secret.

He kept it when Sabrina's body was found, and he kept it throughout the murder investigation. He kept it when he talked to Harris. He had so many chances to tell me, and he passed up every single one of them.

Something occurs to me.

"Is that why you lied to Harris?"

Gabriel nods.

"I panicked," he says. "I mean, what are the chances? I sleep with one woman, and she's found dead?"

He doesn't need to say *again*. It's implied.

"So what about her phone?"

Gabriel rubs his forehead.

"After we . . . were together," he says, "she asked me for my address. I guess she figured that writing to me was safer than texting. William might see texts. He would never see a letter."

"And yet she wrote down your contact information on her phone."

"Not in full. Right? Did Harris tell you that?"

I nod.

"She said my name was safe, because she could just pretend it was the name of an author she'd heard about."

I can see it: Sabrina typing Gabriel's name in her Notes app, hiding it in her food diary. " 'Miller,' " she might have said. "Very literary."

Of course, she doesn't know about Gabriel's past. She doesn't realize that his name means something to thousands of people. Sabrina couldn't imagine that her husband—the media tycoon, the tabloid man—would know exactly who Gabriel Miller is.

"I didn't give her my number or anything. I think she wrote down my street, and—something else."

"Your date of birth."

"Right. She's into astrology. She wanted to do my birth chart, something like that. Maybe send me a card for my birthday."

*And.*

"Twelve Jackson Avenue, right? That's your address?"

Gabriel says yes. Smart Sabrina. The twelve in Gabriel's date of birth did double duty.

The excuses write themselves: if Sabrina had pretended that Gabriel Miller was an author she was interested in, then maybe "Jackson" is the title of his book and "06/12/1990" its publication date.

I think.

"And the hair clip?"

"She wanted me to have it."

I tilt my head. *Really?*

"It was in her purse," Gabriel says. "She gave it to me after . . . everything. Said she wanted me to have something to remember her by. She was sure William wouldn't notice it was gone. She said that's not his style, to notice things."

I tsk.

"I gave her something, too," Gabriel says. "A spare key to our suite. I wanted her to have somewhere to go if she . . . needed to be safe."

*Seriously?*

*Well. You always did move fast.*

"The cops didn't find it?" I ask.

He shrugs.

"If they did, they wouldn't know it's a key to our suite. It's just a key card. They all look the same."

*Okay. Sure.*

Another thing.

"When you left the dinner table," I say, "the last evening before she died, did you really—"

"I didn't really need a sweater, no. When I saw her leave with William right after they had their appetizers, I figured something wasn't right. I followed them at a distance back to their suite. William didn't see, but Sabrina did."

"Are you sure?" I ask.

"What?"

"That William didn't see?"

"Yes."

He's so self-assured. So naïve.

*Can't you see, Gabriel?*

*Don't you understand?*

*If everything you're telling me is true—if all this did, in fact, happen—then William knew something was going on. And he saw you. He put two and two together.*

"Anyway, I overheard her telling William she'd forgotten something. She told him to go ahead, that she'd be right back. Next thing I knew, she was running up to me. It wasn't much at all. She kind of hugged me. She kissed me. But it was—you know. Important."

I know. I've seen enough movies. The stories people tell themselves, when they're in love. Or, maybe not in love, but infatuated. Every moment, every detail, seems like the most important thing in the world.

"Yesterday," I say. "When we spoke . . ."

*And by "spoke," I mean "argued."*

"You could have told me," I say.

"I could have."

"Why didn't you?"

"It was . . . complicated. I almost did, actually. Tell you. But I couldn't figure out how, and then we were yelling, and—"

*You. You were yelling. And throwing stuff.*

"The point is," he says, "I didn't know how to explain, and I didn't want to make it sound like something it wasn't."

There's another uncomfortable detail I need to broach.

Logistics, always: It seems ridiculous to care, but at the end of the day, they're out to get you. Everything that happens in life is logistics. You don't *leave a cult*; you walk to the nearest train station and board the first train. You don't *commit arson*; you pour gasoline and strike a match.

You don't *sleep with a murder victim*; you welcome her into your suite, unzip her dress, run your hand on the inside of her thigh.

"Did you use a condom?"

Gabriel gives me a look, like, *Are you high?*

I know, I know, but: logistics.

"If you didn't," I say, "they'll find your, um—DNA on her—"

"I used a condom."

*Well, that was smart, at least.*

There's a long silence.

It all hovers between us, the first day, the second day, the third day. The illicit romance. A whole little drama that unfolded right under my nose.

Allegedly.

I sigh.

"You don't believe me," Gabriel says.

He sounds dejected.

"I do."

But he knows I don't.

Or, rather, I don't know if I do. It sounded so real when he recounted it just now. And also so convenient. A way to explain it all—the lies, the phone, the hair clip. An unimpeachable narrative: The only person who might challenge it is dead.

"We should leave," I say.

It's the only conclusion. Whether I believe Gabriel's story or not, we should absolutely get out of here.

"No," Gabriel says.

I shoot him a look.

"Why on earth would you want to stay?"

He folds his arms across his chest.

"Because I didn't do anything. You wouldn't—"

"We stayed because we didn't want to attract Harris's attention," I cut in. "But that ship has sailed. We're persons of interest, Gabriel."

"I don't care," he says, defensive. Almost angry. "I'm not guilty, and I'm not going to start acting guilty."

"But you already are!" I explode. "You're lying to the police. You're hiding things from me. Gabriel, this is serious. William Brenner is angry. He's rich, he's powerful, and the police know they've pissed him off. They need to catch someone. And you—you're the perfect way to make all their problems go away."

Gabriel stands.

"I can't believe this," he says. "I thought you'd be on my side."

"I am on your side!" I yell.

I stand, too, and slap dirt off my shorts.

"I'm trying to keep you out of prison," I say. "Gabriel, do you not realize how serious this is?"

"You think I don't know?"

There's a mean tinge to his amazement, like I'm so stupid he can't believe his ears.

"Trust me, Frida, I know exactly how serious this is."

Gabriel turns away from me. He surveys the desert. I've been thinking of our perch as a hill, but—it occurs to me as I gaze down into the void beneath us—"cliff" might be more accurate.

"I let people chase me away once," he says slowly. "I'm not

running away again. Let them come at me. Let them charge me. I don't care. I'm innocent."

"And you think innocent people never get convicted?"

Maybe he'll hate me for being honest with him. Maybe what I'm about to say will banish him from my life forever. But I need him to hear me out. I need him to get the hell out of here.

Maybe I need to lose him in order to save him.

"Two women," I say. "That's a lot for one man."

He whips around.

"What the fuck did you just say?"

"I'm sorry," I say. "I don't mean it like that. But it is how other people will look at it. The police—"

"Go away."

His delivery is sharp and irrevocable, the falling blade of a guillotine.

"What?" I try.

"Leave me alone," he says. When I don't move, he screams: "Go! Before you say something else you'll regret."

His voice shakes. Once again, he looks away from me. He's the one who ordered me to leave, but he doesn't want to witness my departure.

*Oh, Gabriel.*

*It's like you don't know me at all.*

I take a couple of steps forward. Now I'm standing next to him. At our feet, a drop. At least fifteen feet; enough to make me feel dizzy when I look down. Enough to make me feel like I need to hold on to something, or someone.

But no.

There's something I need to do, and I need to do it on my own.

"I told you to leave," he says.

"Gabriel."

*If I convince you to believe me, then will you go?*

"I know you didn't kill Sabrina."

That part's not true. But I need to tell one lie to get to the truth.

The truth: I have no idea who killed Sabrina. Up until yesterday, I didn't think Gabriel capable of doing something like that. But now I don't know.

I don't think he planned it. That's one thing I can say. But things happen. Accidents happen. Maybe it's not murder, but it's *a killing*. It's *homicide*. All those words that suggest lesser degrees of intention.

The truth:

"And I know you didn't kill Annie."

Gabriel lets out a bitter exhale.

"You said that already."

I shake my head, select my next words carefully in my mind.

"FREEZE!"

Deputy Harris has his service weapon raised in front of him. He's not alone. He and his colleagues are making their way up the hiking trail in the manner of an invading army.

"PUT YOUR HANDS UP!"

Gabriel has a frightened, dazed look, like he's been startled awake from a nightmare.

"Put your hands up," I whisper, and raise my own palms in the air.

Before Gabriel can follow suit, Harris is on him. He twists Gabriel's arms behind his back. I trip dangerously close to the edge of the cliff.

"Don't move," Harris snarls. Gabriel's body is completely slack, but Harris doubles down anyway. "I said don't move, motherfucker."

Harris wrestles handcuffs onto Gabriel's wrists. His colleagues—I recognize Deputy Calhoun, plus the other cop I saw at the Ara, and four more who must have come as backup—stand behind him, forming a human barrier, like they're worried Gabriel will make a run for it.

"You're under arrest for murder," Harris says, his mouth to Gabriel's ear, and gives him a sharp nudge. I expect the usual warnings to follow: "You have the right to remain silent"; "Anything you say can and will be used against you"; "You have the right to an attorney." But Harris is seething.

"Were you trying to kill her, too, you piece of shit?"

He nudges his chin in my direction. *Oh.* He means *me.* I realize what the scene must have looked like to him: Gabriel, his suspected murderer, with another woman, at the edge of a cliff. Seconds away from a fatal shove.

"I don't know what you're talking about," Gabriel manages through gritted teeth.

"SHUT UP!"

Harris seems to catch himself. "You're under arrest," he recites again, "for the murder of Sabrina Brenner. Anything you say can and will—"

"Wait," I say.

I know it's stupid, to think that I'll get through to him, but what else am I supposed to do? Watch Gabriel get taken away?

"He didn't do it," I try, pitifully, ridiculously. "You have the wrong—"

Harris takes one hand off Gabriel to shove me aside.

"You," he says. "Stay out of this, or you're coming with us, too."

"Do you have any proof?"

My question is like kindling to the blaze of Harris's anger. With one hand still on Gabriel's wrists, he brings his face right up to mine.

"Were you trying to protect him? Huh? Did you think it was clever, making up all that stuff about William Brenner?"

He's clearly expecting an apology of some sort, or for me to insist, *No, no, I swear, it wasn't like that, I wasn't trying to do anything.* But he's too angry to wait for a response. With his free hand, he snatches what looks like a plastic bag from the hand of his nearest colleague.

"Is this good enough for you?" He's shoving it against my chest. I can't see what's inside, but I hear the rustle of plastic. "The fucking murder weapon?"

"Kenneth," Deputy Calhoun says. "That's enough."

As she takes the bag back from Harris, I see it: Slipped inside a translucent evidence bag is a rock. A rock that used to be white and is now almost entirely stained with blood.

I blink.

*White marble chunks from Italy*, Catalina said on our first day, when she gave us the tour. She was standing near one of the decorative planters, running the tips of her fingers on the rocks. *You won't find them anywhere else in the region.*

This white rock like a red flag. It could only have come from the hotel. In time, it will be tested, but it's pretty clear whose blood it's covered in.

Harris is taunting Gabriel again.

"Did you really think we wouldn't find it, in your fucking backpack?"

*Wait.*

*Wait.*

In his *backpack*?

I looked inside Gabriel's backpack just yesterday. All I found in there was the butterfly hair clip—the one I'm still carrying around in my shorts pocket.

But no rock.

"Let's go," Harris says, and leads Gabriel away.

ELEVEN YEARS AGO   |   AND THEN TEN YEARS AGO
AND THEN NINE YEARS AGO

We had so many good times. Gabriel, Annie, and me.
  Then the garden of earthly delights did what it always does. It started to spoil.

Can I be honest?

When I introduced him to her, I never thought those two would end up getting *married*. I figured they'd do what they needed to do and move on.

Gabriel had just turned twenty-two when they tied the knot. Annie was twenty-three. In a sense, their ages don't matter, but neither of them was fucking *ready*.

One evening, a year into their marriage, Gabriel showed up at my place. When he'd moved in with Annie, I'd signed a lease for a new studio on West 133rd Street, tucked between a park and a barbecue restaurant.

Gabriel stood at my door, finger on the doorbell, looking flushed. His messenger bag was strapped across his chest.

"Can I crash with you tonight?"

I didn't have time to ask what had happened. Iryna, my new manager at the diner, had just called me to ask if I could work a half shift—Carmen was supposed to work that night, but her kid had chicken pox.

"You're vaccinated, right?" Iryna had asked on the phone.

As of three years ago, yes, I was.

"I have to go to work," I told Gabriel. "Here's a key. Speak later?"

He nodded, looking dazed.

When I returned at three in the morning, he was lying on the couch with the lights on. I showered and changed. Sharing space with him still felt like the most natural thing in the world.

I sat on the floor, my back against the couch. Gabriel started to shift to free up some room for me, but I stopped him.

"Why don't you tell me what happened?" I said.

I knew he'd find it easier to speak if I wasn't looking at him. He sighed.

"We had a fight."

"About what?"

"It's complicated."

"Try me."

There was a silence, then, he conceded: "Money."

*Money?*

*Yeah, well. I can't say I'm too surprised.*

When Gabriel and Annie moved in together, I had . . . reservations, shall we say. Okay, fine. I didn't think it was a good idea. Not even in the lovely suburb of Bloomfield, New Jersey, in a cute two-bedroom house. Yes, I know: romance, whirlwind, young people. But I was a brutally pragmatic person. I didn't know how they'd make it work, financially. Gabriel was a writer's assistant. Annie had just started working as a regional manager at her father's company. He couldn't pay her *too* well, lest the other employees riot. Annie's family helped them, but still.

It seemed so precarious, this suburban lifestyle they were jumping into without a plan. Like a child's idea of real life.

"There's just . . . never enough, somehow," Gabriel said. "I don't know. I guess we're bad with that stuff."

"Okay. Well, that happens."

I didn't know what else to say. In TV shows, couples often fought about money. It seemed to be part of life.

What I didn't understand was how the fight had gotten so bad that Gabriel had ended up on my doorstep.

"Does Annie know where you are?"

Gabriel sighed again. In my peripheral vision, he fingered his phone, then placed it facedown on the couch.

"It's fine," he said. "I texted her hours ago. She hasn't replied."

"Maybe you should go home to her."

He sat up.

"You want me to leave?"

I craned my neck to look at him.

"No," I said. "That's not what I'm saying."

Gabriel settled back down.

"It's not just the money," he said.

*Ah.*

"I forgot we had plans, the other day. She waited for me at a restaurant for two hours. Tried to call me, too."

"Where were you?"

"At the library. Doing research."

"About?"

"Roman emperors of the Flavian dynasty."

I wasn't an expert, but I imagined I wouldn't have been thrilled if I'd been bested by Titus or Domitian in my husband's list of priorities.

"And a couple of weeks ago," Gabriel continued, in full-confession mode. "For her birthday. We were trying to make plans, and I said I'd cook up a feast. She misunderstood my tone. I was joking."

"About making her dinner?"

Gabriel held up a hand.

"You kind of had to be there," he said.

*Still*, I thought. *What could possibly be funny about that, you idiot?*

"When she came home, I was . . . sitting on the couch, reading and eating saltines out of the box."

Despite myself, I laughed.

"You'll work it out," I said.

I really believed that. Yes, I knew about their troubles, financial and otherwise. And I knew they argued. But I couldn't picture things being dire. Couldn't imagine Gabriel or Annie screaming, slamming a table, throwing things.

I'd only ever seen them in love. Their fights existed in an unknown, invisible part of their world. That made them easy to discount.

———

I loved Annie. And also: I'd gotten to know her as an actual person. Not just a whimsical young woman dropped into my life in a flurry of wedding planning, beach vacations, and s'mores.

She was a whole human being. She was fun, spontaneous, smart.

And she was flawed.

Maybe Annie felt judged for getting married so young. Maybe she was insecure in her own choices, and so she felt the need to justify them constantly. But her behavior shifted after she and Gabriel got married. She started making harsh, sweeping statements about her friends: "I look at my people who aren't married, and I'm like, What do you get from this? Jumping from one person to the next? Don't you want to build something?" Or: "I'm so glad to be done with the whole dating circus, sleeping with strangers, lying to myself that it's okay, that I'm not selling myself short. I like to be on solid ground, you know?"

Oh, I knew. But as someone who was very busy *jumping from one person to the next*, who had never touched anything resembling *solid ground*, I couldn't very well relate.

I never confronted her about her insensitivity. Because she was family. Because we needed to get along. Because I loved her.

Still, she irritated the hell out of me.

Fine—it was more than that. Her little asides hurt me. I felt judged. I didn't want to defend my life, my choices.

Every outing with her became a challenge. I'd come home with all my bitten-back quips lodged in my throat like so many fish bones.

———

In most situations, none of this would have been a big deal. Couples fight. People change.

But sometimes things get complicated.

Once Annie realized that Gabriel crashed at my place that one time, she started venting to me about their fights. I think she figured that if I was getting his side, then I should hear hers, too.

"Did he tell you," she said on the phone one day, "that he didn't do anything for my birthday?"

"Yeah. That sounded bad."

"He said he would cook and then he said it was a *joke*."

"Honestly, he fucked up."

There were texts, too: *Your brother is late again* or *Can you tell your brother to stop LYING* or *I know you guys didn't grow up with much* [Gee, Annie, you think?] *but he is BAD at sharing and needs to do better.*

Again, I agreed. I'd doubted Gabriel was ready to be any kind of long-term *boyfriend*, let alone a husband.

He and Annie went into counseling—a fact I was informed of separately, by each party.

If it helped, I didn't see it.

*Your brother is AWOL again*, Annie texted me one evening. *Any idea where he went?*

*Probably the library*, I wrote back.

*Your brother came home drunk last night.*

*In his defense, Annie, we didn't have a drop of alcohol until we were twenty. And it's not like we ever had a partying phase. Our tolerance is abysmal.*

*Your brother needs to get a grip.*

*I'm sure he does.*

Etc., etc., etc. In Annie's pissed-off texts, he was always "your brother," never "Gabriel."

My brother did not get a grip.

In fact, he fucked up majorly, one night.

He didn't even realize.

It was Annie who told me.

know what I saw. There was no rock in Gabriel's backpack yesterday.

Meaning: Gabriel is being framed. Someone entered our suite, found his backpack, and put the rock there.

It's not hard to guess who.

William.

But how?

It hits me as I follow Harris, Gabriel, and the other police deputies down the trail.

*I gave her something, too.*

*A spare key to our suite.*

It wouldn't have meant anything to the cops, the spare key card, if they saw it. But it would have meant everything to William Brenner.

William must have felt Sabrina pulling away from him. He watched her so closely, always. Her whole world was under his control. Despite what Gabriel just told me, I'm sure of it: William spotted Gabriel in the background when he and Sabrina made an early exit from their last dinner together.

When I saw them fighting during Sabrina's final moments, what did William say?

*Stop lying to me.*

He knew. William. This viciously proud man. He realized his wife was cheating on him, he confronted her, and then he killed her. Then he turned his attention to the other man.

William decided to end Gabriel's life, too, in a whole other way.

That's why he took a photo of us at dinner. That's why he tipped off the *Escalante News.*

That's why—I realize now—he planted Sabrina's phone for me to find.

Of fucking course. He had it. He looked at it, set it aside, held on to it. If it contained any evidence incriminating him, he removed it. And then, he set his plan in motion.

William couldn't give the phone to the police directly. Coming from him, the evidence wouldn't be credible. And he'd have some questions to answer: *How did you find the phone? How long have you had it? Why are you only giving it to us now?* Much cleaner if it came from someone else.

And William knew that, if I found the phone, I'd deliver it straight to the cops. So he put it in the part of the desert only I frequent. The coyote's den.

Sabrina was wrong about her husband. It's not that it's not his style to notice things. It's that he notices only the things he cares about. The things that might benefit him. Like: A woman going by herself into the desert, hovering near a coyote's lair. By the pool, in the dining room, a woman casting suspicious glances in his direction. A woman *waiting* to get her hands on anything she thinks might provide evidence of his abuse.

And all of this is why—when the timing was just right—he planted the murder weapon in Gabriel's bag.

I picture it as clearly as if it were unfolding in front of my eyes: William waiting for Gabriel and me to set out for the desert, sidling up to our suite as soon as we'd left. Pressing the key card against our reader. Maybe he doubted, for a second or two, that the door would open. But it did, and William was vindicated.

All he had to do was check our luggage tags. Once reassured

that the backpack belonged to Gabriel Miller, he tucked the rock in there, careful not to leave fingerprints, probably handling it through a tissue or a T-shirt.

Meanwhile, Gabriel and I were in the desert, talking about Sabrina. About affairs and strangers and the things people do when no one is watching.

Then what? Cops need warrants to go inside hotel rooms. William would have known that. So?

So, he took the backpack out of our suite. William knew we weren't around; he'd just seen us leave for the desert.

And then? What did he do?

Maybe he placed the backpack in the lobby or right at our door. Or maybe he was more brazen about it. Maybe he marched the backpack straight to Harris. I can almost hear him say it: *Look, Deputy. Look what I found.*

If that's how it happened, when Harris asked William how he'd come into possession of Gabriel's backpack, how did William explain it?

Easy. One option: play the hurt husband. Admit to one misdeed to cover up another, bigger one. *My wife . . . she was cheating on me with this guy. You're the one who told me, Deputy. His name is on her phone. I miss her so much. I needed to know if he had any of her things. Anything to remember her by. I asked a member of the staff to let me in. They kindly obliged.*

Maybe he did, in fact, ask a housekeeper to let him in, in case Harris felt the need to confirm. This *is*, after all, how the world treats William Brenner. Especially the deferential world of luxury resorts, where money buys favors and opens doors.

And that's *if* Harris asked. A cop who is offered key evidence on a silver platter won't necessarily question its provenance.

So Harris reached inside the backpack and plucked out the bloodstained rock. *He just went into the desert*, William would have said. He might even have pointed. *That way.*

And *voilà*.

We're at the bottom of the trail now. In a few minutes, Gabriel will be thrown into the back of a police car. They'll put on the siren, even though there's scarcely any traffic on these roads.

Gabriel walks a step ahead of Harris. Head bowed. Compliant. The deputy's grip tight around his wrists.

My brother, who did almost everything right. Who left a cult. Who stopped drinking when it turned out he did, in fact, have a problem. Who remembers his meds—the migraine ones and the depression ones. Who takes care of himself. Who tries and tries to iron out his mind, even if that means staring at a journal he can't seem to fill. He takes the journal on vacation. He keeps it in his nightstand drawer.

That's who he is. Someone who grieves and struggles against himself and goes back for another round.

But not a murderer.

We've reached the police car. Harris places a hand on Gabriel's head as Gabriel folds himself into the back seat. I try to catch his gaze, but the door slams shut.

Harris walks to the front of the car. His colleagues get into their own vehicles. They drive away. I can almost feel it, the tear in the fabric of our existence as Gabriel gets taken from me.

My brother. Lost to the world.

Mine to save.

———

I know what I need to do.

*No. No.*

*Please don't make me go back in there.*

My mind is a beehive.

For almost nine years, I've done my best to leave this part of my brain alone.

The part that schemes. The one that knows how to get away with dreadful things.

I hate it.

But I need it now.

A beehive like any other: Approach at your own risk. Poke your hand in, feel the heat of—

And here they are. A thousand stings. A thousand memories, each coming back with a burning stab.

What do I know about murder?

Well.

Probably everything there is to know.

Everything *useful*, certainly.

It's a knowledge deprived of assumptions. Sharpened in the tricky, humbling world of logistics.

The kind of knowledge that comes from experience.

ALMOST NINE YEARS AGO

When my phone buzzed at eight one Saturday morning, I answered groggily. I'd graduated the previous May and was almost five months into my job at the bank, meaning I'd worked until two the previous night.

"Annie? Is everything okay?"

"No!" she yelled. I held the phone away from my ear. There was no need to put her on speaker, she was so animated. "I'm on my way to the city. We need to talk. He's done it this time. I'm done with him. DONE!"

"What's the—"

She hung up.

I pinched the skin between my eyebrows. That was it for sleep. I dragged myself into the shower, put on jeans and a black T-shirt. (How I wished I had a sense of style. After the drab clothes of Émile's world, after the years I had spent doing my laundry in a sink, I badly wanted to figure it out, this boldness, this artistry that enabled some people to put together Outfits with a capital *o*. But it never clicked.)

There were dishes in the sink, dust on my shelves, streaks on my mirror. I needed to wash my sheets. A pile of unopened mail sat on the kitchen counter.

I typed a text to Annie: *Can we go to a café or something?*

But I knew there was no way she'd say yes. Annie did what she wanted to do, however she wanted to do it. I deleted the text without sending it.

That was my first lucky break, not sending that text. If I had, what would she have written back? Something damning, like: *No. You'll want to hear this in private. Better for all involved.*

I straightened up my studio as best as I could, but Annie must have been driving like a madwoman. She knocked just as I wrestled my comforter out of the duvet cover.

"Coming!"

I opened the door to find a disheveled, clearly distressed Annie, dressed in leggings, a loose T-shirt, and clogs. She wasn't wearing any makeup. I was pretty sure it was the first time I'd seen her without even a bit of concealer on.

She walked straight to the couch. As soon as she sat down, she buried her face in her hands. It was like she didn't even see me, or the mess in my studio, or anything that wasn't in her direct line of sight.

"Can I get you some water?" I asked. "Or maybe some coffee?"

"Your brother," she said.

She looked up.

"I think you should sit down," she said.

So I did. On a barstool across from the couch.

"Last night," she said, "Gabriel came home drunk. Again."

*Damn.*

"Does he have a . . . problem?"

She nodded.

"Probably," she said. "And it's like you said. Abysmal tolerance. He goes to the bar thinking he'll have a couple of beers to unwind. What he doesn't realize is that two beers for him is like seven vodkas for me."

*Well, he never was good at math.*

"But that doesn't matter," Annie said, her voice shaking. "I really don't fucking care about that right now. Sorry."

She took a deep breath, then held it for a couple of seconds before exhaling.

"Last night," she said, "after he came home, he was talking. None of what he was saying made sense, at first."

"Okay . . ."

"Then he started repeating this one thing. I couldn't hear him—he was on the bed, half talking into a pillow. And then I thought I'd misheard him. But no."

Annie was staring blankly above my shoulder. There was something desperately searching in her gaze, like she was looking for a marker at sea.

"He was saying . . . It sounded like . . . No, it didn't just sound like it. That's what he was saying: *'I killed her . . . I killed her . . .'*"

I stopped breathing. Stopped thinking. Stopped doing anything but sitting there, listening to Annie.

*I killed her.*

*I killed her?*

"I mean, it sounds like he was wasted," I said, my voice wobbly.

"No," Annie said. "I mean, yes, he was, but it sounded so . . . real. Like it was coming from somewhere deep, you know?"

She held up a finger.

"And then he started saying something else. A name. 'Edwina, Edwina' . . . Just over and over again."

*Gabriel.*

*Fucking hell.*

*Don't you know? That people like us don't get to get wasted? That we need to know what we're saying and who we're saying it to, at all times?*

But it was unfair to think that way. Whatever was happening to Gabriel, he wasn't choosing it. If anything, *Edwina* was the reason he was drinking so much.

Annie reached into her purse—chic, olive-green leather with golden metal embellishments.

"We don't know an Edwina," she said, riffling through her things. "It's such an odd name. It got me thinking."

From her beautiful handbag, Annie pulled out a sheet of printer paper.

"I remembered reading something, years ago," she said. "It was in a newspaper, but I found the article on the internet."

Annie held the sheet in my direction, clearly waiting for me to take it.

I stepped off my barstool.

I don't remember walking toward her or grabbing the sheet of paper.

What I do remember is the feeling, like falling from a great height.

At the top of the sheet of paper was the headline, a scream from the past:

ONE DEAD IN "CULT" BLAZE

And underneath it, every word, every punctuation mark, exactly as I remembered:

*One person is dead and another is injured after a fire devastated part of the compound of a reclusive organization some have described as a cult.*

My eyes scanned the rest of the page. I didn't want to look up at Annie. Didn't want this moment—this moment when I was looking at the piece of paper in my hand—to end. Whatever would come next, I wanted no part in it.

*A county official has now confirmed that one person died of injuries suffered in the fire later that night . . . a twenty-two-year-old female . . . known within the organization only as Edwina.*

Two fingers appeared at the top of the page. Annie folded the piece of paper in half and put it back in her purse.

"I know it sounds nuts," she said. "Trust me. At first, I thought I was going crazy. I tried to calm down. Then I got angry again. That's when I called you. But . . ."

She massaged her temple with the tip of her index finger.

"December 2008," she said. "That's when you left, no?"

I didn't say anything. Didn't even move.

"And it's the right . . . cult, right? Gabriel mentioned a guy named Émile."

Annie gave me a sad little look.

"I'm sorry, Frida. Did you . . . did you even know? About the fire?"

I struggled to keep my expression neutral.

"Yes," I said after a second. "I knew there was a fire. But . . ."

"And you left soon after that?"

*Oh.*

Gabriel hadn't clued her in on the details—or timing—of our escape.

"I didn't want to believe it at first. Didn't want to think Gabriel could be . . . responsible for something like this. But what else is there to think?"

"Well—"

She spared me having to think of what to say next by continuing: "He never wants to talk about that part of his life. And I never know how to ask. He's so guarded. Guess now I understand why."

She kept mumbling. Smart Annie. Righteous Annie. She'd taken the information she had and drawn a new picture in her mind: In her version of events, Gabriel had set the fire on his own. Then he'd realized he'd killed Edwina, after which he'd decided to flee and taken me with him.

Annie sighed. "I . . . I have to tell someone."

*What?*

"Don't you want to talk to him first?"

"I can't," she said. "I wouldn't feel . . . safe."

"But—"

"But what?"

*But nothing.* She was being perfectly logical. If you suspect someone committed a murder, or a homicide, or whatever, and you just busted them, then they're the last person you'll want to tell.

"He's your husband," I tried.

Annie considered the ring on her left hand. It was a very

simple band, gold-plated. The only design Gabriel was able to afford, and he'd had to save up. Annie could have bought something fancier using family money, but she'd stuck to this one.

"I know," she said. "But if he— I mean, that's game over."

Of course.

That was how it worked, in Annie's tidy, clear-cut world. If you did something bad, then you went to prison. If harm was done to you, then you went to the police, and that harm was acknowledged. There were people who did bad things and people who didn't. Gabriel fell into the former category, Annie in the latter. And that was that.

"I understand."

I did. And I understood, too, that Gabriel had let her down in a million ways. He hadn't treated her the way she deserved to be treated. Their meet-cute, their quick wedding, their supersonic drive on the highway to domestic bliss—it was all supposed to add up to a certain fairy tale. He hadn't delivered that. And now he was, maybe, a man who had killed a woman.

Perhaps Annie, on some level, hoped she was wrong. But she wouldn't take my word for it. Only the cops'. She needed the police to look into it and tell her.

"Have you spoken to anyone else?" I asked. "About this?"

She shook her head.

"I went to you first. You're his— Well, you're close," she said. "I think you're the person closest to him. You know him better than I do."

A wife's admission of defeat. It hurt her because it was true. It had never stopped being true.

The loneliness of Annie, on my couch. Unable to speak to her own husband. Unable to tell her own friends. I pictured them: young, unburdened, golden. Unattuned to so many of life's complications. Maybe they'd warned her about Gabriel. *This guy, really?* Maybe they'd known Annie could have done better. Married someone worldlier, more stable, certainly more established.

Annie wouldn't have wanted to tell her friends they'd been right. That the whirlwind had been just that, a whirlwind. That a whirlwind is, after all, just another name for a tornado.

She stood up.

"I thought you'd understand," she said.

*Oh, Annie.*

"Why?"

"Because you're always so . . . good."

"I am?"

"Oh my god, Frida." She grasped her head between her hands, a pantomime of exasperation. "You're like, the most moral person I know. Honestly, it's annoying sometimes."

I shook my head, unable to meet her eyes. *Moral?*

"I get it," she said. "I have this inherited wealth, and I'm spoiled, and everything I have is an offense to you."

"That's not—"

"But now my husband—the guy I'm *married* to—confessed to a fucking murder in his sleep and you want me to keep quiet about it?"

I stood, too. A red light was flashing in my mind.

"I'm not telling you what to do," I said. "But please. Just take a moment to think about this."

She snatched her purse from the sofa and headed for the door.

"I can't believe you," she said. "Honestly. I thought you were better than this. Better than . . . him."

But I wasn't.

I never was better than Gabriel.

———

We hadn't killed anyone on purpose. That, I knew.

Almost six years had passed since the fire. It was entirely possible that no hard evidence was left, though I had no way to be sure of that. (The container of gasoline—that was the bit I kept going back to. I remembered tossing it. Had it burned? Or had it drifted somewhere in the chaos, and was it waiting, tangled in some tall grass, half-buried in some nearby woods, to ruin our lives?)

Even if no solid trace of our actions remained, there was always secondary evidence: witness accounts, not just from former cult members, but also from the man who'd sold us our train tickets, and the conductor who'd checked them. Men from Émile's world could testify that Gabriel knew where to find the gasoline. And the women—they knew about Émile and what he did to the girls. They knew the part Edwina played. How hard would it be to present those facts as motive?

We hadn't killed anyone on purpose, but it wouldn't be impossible to convince a jury that we had.

And then what?

The rest of our lives in prison. Apart from each other.

After all that. Just when things were starting to fall into place. I'd worked so hard.

Maybe I was worried about nothing. Maybe the criminal justice system wouldn't come for us.

Still, someone would know. Annie.

She and Gabriel were going to divorce. That was a guarantee. She would tell people about him. She would tell people about the fire. There would be questions, research. Annie's incorrect assumption that Gabriel had acted alone wouldn't hold up for long.

People would find out.

People we knew. And also strangers. Journalists. There might be articles. A book. A movie.

People would know that I'd stood, holding a container of gasoline, knowing Edwina might be upstairs. Accepting that possibility. Pouring the accelerant, regardless.

That part of me would be revealed to the world.

The part that chose destruction. That *embraced* it.

———

How do you take a secret out of someone's head?

You can't.

No, really. I've thought about it every which way.

There was a place she loved.

The waterfall in Paterson, New Jersey, where her parents had taken her as a kid. On the weekends, especially when Gabriel was away, Annie loved driving out to Paterson and running in the nearby park. She'd run to the top of the waterfall—there was a bridge overlooking it—and gaze at the foaming water for a few minutes before running back to her car. She was the one who reminded me about it.

"I can't believe you're taking his side," Annie said, on her way out of my apartment. "It doesn't matter."

"I'm not taking his side," I tried again. "It's just, Annie—you're so upset."

She pinched her temples. "Tomorrow."

"What?"

"You're right. I'm upset. No one will believe me if I go to the police now. So, I'm going to go home. I'm going to sleep. Tomorrow, I'm going for a run. And then, I'm going to the police."

Her tone grew more confident with each word. It was like she needed to hear herself. Like saying it out loud made her plan more real.

I opened my mouth. Before I could speak, she cut in: "I've made up my mind. I'm not asking for your permission. This is just a heads-up. I didn't want you to find out in the press or whatever."

She placed her hand on the doorknob.

"Think about it," she said. "Think about what he did." And then she said it again, that phrase: "It's game over. For me. It should be for you, too."

It was all a Gabriel problem, for her. In her mind, none of this had anything to do with me.

We went back and forth a few more times, but there was nothing I could do. Her mind was made up. Annie was going to tell the authorities what she knew. She was going to tell everyone.

And she was leaving me no time at all to think of a solution.

It was like with Gabriel's migraines, when I stole from Émile to buy pills.

My brother was in danger.

(I was in danger.)

I had to make it stop.

It was that simple.

The next morning, I rented a car. That part of my scheme wasn't perfect, but I didn't have a choice. I didn't own my little Fiat 500 yet. I could have taken a train, but that would have meant surveillance cameras, not to mention hundreds of potential witnesses. Besides, I wasn't planning on being seen. I wasn't planning on giving the police any reason to look at me so closely they'd come to learn about my rental car.

Here's the truth about committing murder: There are no perfect crimes. Only lucky ones. Only a hundred cursed stars aligning just so.

I drove to Paterson Great Falls. Always in my inconspicuous clothes, my utterly forgettable jacket and baseball hat.

And then I waited for her.

They say that suicide happens in the moment. That if someone is considering ending their life, but you can get them to delay their impulse for even five minutes, the likelihood that they will go through with it drops dramatically.

The same goes, I have found, for murder.

It all happens in the moment.

That morning, at the top of the waterfall, I wasn't sure I'd do it. I was split, sixty-forty. Then Annie was there, and I knew why I'd come, and it happened in flashes, my mind untethered from my body: step out onto the bridge behind her, put my palms to her back, underneath her shoulder blades, shove her over the edge.

If it hadn't worked on the first try, I wouldn't have tried again. But it did.

My little body, stupidly strong for no reason. That's how I'd been since girlhood. My ropy little legs, my buff little shoulders.

It was easier than I'd thought it would be. The act itself. In those brief, incandescent seconds, my mind was clear: I had a plan, and I'd executed it. That was a language I spoke fluently.

But it never felt good. At no point did I get any pleasure from it.

In fact, I came close to following Annie down into the falls.

The possibility crossed my mind like a bird darting across a window.

I thought about it for one second, then two, then three, and then I didn't jump, and the impulse went away.

All that was left to do was go home.

All that was left to do was live with what I'd done.

## 41 ESCALANTE, UTAH

THE SEVENTH DAY

What I did to Annie flooded my psyche like water inside a sinking ship.

My nose is full, always, with the smell of the waterfall and the woods that morning. The wet earth, the yellowing tree leaves. The sweet smell of decay that signals the height of fall. I can still feel the droplets of water on my face, the tiny particles of foam that landed all over me, even in my mouth, as I pushed her over the edge.

There was no dramatic *splash*, no telltale *splat*. A waterfall comes with its own sound, the kind that swallows up a person.

Another thing the waterfall absorbed: my ability to sleep. I didn't even go to bed that night. For days afterward, I expected to collapse from exhaustion.

Never. For almost nine years, aside from a few, rare exceptions, I have slept in fits and starts, no more than three hours at a time.

It has felt fair. Deserved.

I lost parts of my mind. The ones that knew peace. I became someone who sees a nightmare in every shadow. Who had a panic attack after witnessing the arrest of William Brenner, because I saw myself in his place—the handcuffs around *my* wrists, a police officer leading *me* away.

Even my thing with the mob show. I liked it well enough before Annie's death. But after? I *needed* the mobsters. All of them well dressed, lovable, *human*. So many of them murderers. They killed one another. Killed people they loved. Killed their own friends, their own relatives. They buried bodies. Dismembered them. And then?

They went on with it. Went home to their families. They laughed. They cried. They *lived*.

I felt like they understood.

They, too, did what they had to do.

———

How *did* I get away with it?

Logistics. It's all about logistics.

You don't *commit murder*. You complete a series of steps at a certain time, in a certain place.

Every scenario has a weakness. This was true for me. It must also be true for William Brenner.

If I think about what I did wrong—and what I did right—then maybe I can decode his mind, too. Maybe I can save Gabriel.

I see them like parallel lines, my lucky breaks and William's.

Mine: I didn't anticipate how much the place of Annie's death would play in my favor. Bodies of water, as it turns out, are hard and expensive to search. Detectives did look at the falls after Gabriel reported Annie missing, but she was still in the water at the time. They only found her two weeks later, when she surfaced, having drifted several miles downstream. The water had done its damage by then. It was impossible to determine a cause of death.

William's: that Sabrina cheated on him with a man who was once accused of murder. The perfect suspect for the cops to sink their teeth into.

Sometimes, though, the unexpected is just that: a key factor you overlook, because you don't know what you don't know.

For me: I did not expect that people would latch onto Gabriel as a suspect the way they did.

It was my fault entirely.

I'd been out in the world for almost six years. I was catching up as quickly as I could, but I didn't know about *It's always the husband*. It didn't occur to me to imagine a world where the person most likely to kill a woman is the man she chose to marry.

By the time I realized, it was too late.

I understood. It wasn't Gabriel, but it was a lot of husbands, a lot of the time. The assumption that he had killed Annie wasn't unfair, just incorrect.

And there was that small broken bone at the back of Annie's throat. The hyoid bone. When it breaks, the fracture is often indicative of strangulation. That's not what happened with Annie. I never wrapped my hands around her neck. It was the fall, it was the water, it was the fish. It was whatever happened to Annie after I left her.

But it completed the picture of Gabriel's guilt perfectly, in people's minds.

William overlooked something, too.

*Me.*

He underestimated me, my nosiness. And of course, he assumed Gabriel was the one who'd killed Annie.

He doesn't know I searched Gabriel's backpack just yesterday. Doesn't know that I know he planted the rock.

William has no idea how many hours I've spent thinking about evidence and the ways it disappears.

———

When I returned from the waterfall, I changed the clothes I'd been wearing. My shoes, too. I didn't think anyone had seen me, but I didn't want to take any chances. Didn't want to risk the police looking in my closet and finding an outfit matching an eyewitness's description. Didn't want them to look at the soles of my shoes and find a particular kind of dirt caked in the grooves, which just happened to match the soil at Paterson Great Falls.

I stuffed my cast-off clothes and shoes in a dumpster a hundred miles away. Then I took my rental to a car wash before returning it.

And that was it.

When Gabriel called me to say Annie had gone missing, I had to play along.

I hated lying to him. But that, too, was part of the punishment.

When the cops requested to speak to me, I agreed. They asked about Gabriel and Annie. Did they fight? Had Gabriel said anything to me? Did I have any reason to think he might be involved?

Sometimes. No. No.

I didn't lie. I didn't volunteer any information. I answered the questions, and then I left the police station.

I'd had time—not a lot, but just enough—to get ready, to plan.

William Brenner? He didn't come to this hotel planning to kill his wife.

That wouldn't make sense. Here? In a place both public and secluded?

No. Sabrina's murder was committed on impulse.

They were arguing. Sabrina defended herself. That must have taken William by surprise. Maybe she was galvanized by meeting Gabriel. Maybe my brother reminded her that she wasn't alone in the world.

That's the part of the argument I witnessed. Then I went away. The fight must have continued.

Maybe Sabrina threatened to divorce William.

It's so easy to picture, now that I've seen the murder weapon. The rock tells me everything I need to know.

"I'm going to leave you," Sabrina says, in this version of events. "The second we come home. I'm getting a lawyer, and then I'm getting a divorce."

William opens his mouth, but Sabrina continues, indomitable.

"Oh, I know," she says. "You'll ruin me. You'll take everything I have. I won't have anything left after you're done with me. But you know what? It will be worth it. I'd rather sleep under a bridge than in your bed for even one more night."

She walks away.

Maybe she picks up her pace. Maybe she tries to run away from him, in the end.

She doesn't see it happen.

She doesn't see her husband, stunned and outraged. Doesn't see inside William's mind as he pictures it: the divorce settlement, always public to a degree. People will talk. Court papers will leak. He knows this better than anyone. He has made a career out of airing other people's dirty laundry.

Sabrina doesn't see him panic. She doesn't see him hobbling after her. Doesn't see him realizing he'll never catch up to her. She doesn't see herself the way he sees her, slipping out of his grasp, his secrets tumbling out of her pockets.

Sabrina doesn't see William bending to retrieve one of the decorative rocks from a planter by the pool. A white marble chunk from Italy.

Maybe he doesn't think it will do much damage. Maybe he thinks it will just knock her out. Stop her long enough for him to bring her back to the suite, nurse her back to health, win back her affections.

Maybe he forgets that he was once a promising baseball player. Maybe he forgets about muscle memory, about the hours his body spent learning how to throw.

Sabrina doesn't see him hurling the rock, aiming for the back of her head.

In this scenario—and maybe that's why I want to believe in it—Sabrina doesn't know it's happening until the last, blinding second.

She doesn't die afraid. It's the last thing she thinks, in this version: When her loved ones are told—her mother, maybe, and friends from her former life—she would like them to know that she wasn't scared.

In my head, she dies hopeful.

She dies running toward a better life.

The Ara is in sight, this uncanny valley of beauty. Gabriel will have reached the police station by now. Are they taking his photo? His fingerprints? Is he sitting in the same interrogation room I sat in just yesterday?

He needs me to think faster. Be better.

Picture it: Sabrina collapses. William doesn't realize what just happened. He waits for her to move. When she doesn't, he walks up to her. Maybe he whispers, "Darling?" He puts a hand on her arm. Shakes her, gently at first, then harder. He panics. Sabrina bleeds, bleeds, bleeds.

Head wounds bleed profusely. When we were kids, a girl slashed her scalp on the corner of a table in the cafeteria. While a mother sewed her skin back together, we were recruited to clean up. The cafeteria looked like—well, a crime scene: blood on the table, on the nearby chairs, on the floor.

Maybe William is smart about this. Maybe he doesn't touch his wife's body. Maybe he picks up the murder weapon, handles it cleanly, between two fingers, brings it back to his suite, hides it, and washes his hands.

But I don't believe it. Because he's not a planner.

He's not like *me*.

He is angry, abusive, messy.

And so I have to imagine that William, in his frantic state, touches at least some of the blood. Maybe he puts his fingers to his wife's head wound. Maybe his hand goes from her body to his. Maybe the blood gets on his shoes. Maybe it gets on the clothes he was wearing that night: his dinner suit, his white button-down shirt.

Where did he put them? His murder clothes?

No dumpster here. And it's not like he could've handed them off to the hotel's laundry service.

William stashed the murder weapon *somewhere*. He held on to it until he could deploy it in the perfect way, at the perfect time. As he did with the phone.

This is what those two items tell me: that William Brenner has found a hiding place.

Where is it?

Somewhere the police wouldn't have been able to access without a warrant. Obviously.

William's hotel suite?

Maybe. Except the cops would have needed a warrant to search it, *unless* they had William's permission. Which they would have asked for at the very start of their investigation. And which William would've had to give, if he wanted to appear willing. Cooperative. *Innocent.*

That's what happened with Gabriel. I was there when the police showed up for that first search in New Jersey. "Mind if we take a look?" an officer asked. His tone was casual, but the question was a test: *And if you mind, may I ask why?*

Gabriel allowed the police inside his house. He had nothing to hide.

Of course, the cops didn't find anything. They returned after Annie's body was found, this time with a warrant.

They asked Gabriel to wait outside. For three hours, they searched the house, bagging Annie's hairbrush, dusting doorknobs and windowsills for fingerprints, collecting DNA samples. After that, Gabriel was allowed back in.

That part, people can't get over. Somewhat understandably, I suppose.

"He never lost access to the house," one person wrote on Reddit about a year ago. "Two weeks is an eternity when we're talking about evidence. Think of all the stuff he could have gotten rid of. They might as well not have searched it at all."

"It's not just the house," someone else commented. "Think about their electronics. Their garage, their car."

I come to a halt.

*Their garage.*

*Their car.*

Oh my god.

The weakest part in my own plan.

The thing that could have done me in. If someone had seen it. If anyone had said anything to the cops about the make, model, or color.

My rental car.

The papers had all the information the police needed. My name, my address, my signature.

*Holy shit.*

Their car.

That beautiful red rental, gleaming in the desert heat, the purr of the engine when William pulled up to the entrance lounge. A car fit for the man who once wooed his wife by sending her a couture gown and princess gloves. A reminder of how charming he could be, back when he was courting her. Love-bombing her.

The cops must have overlooked the car until it was too late and William had lawyered up, blocking any chance of a warrant.

Where *is* his car?

The Ara offers valet parking only. Clearly, it keeps its own fleet of cars nearby, too. When I asked Catalina to call one for me yesterday, my ride showed up within a minute, air-conditioned and with bottles of water at the ready.

So there is a garage.

Where?

I've taken enough steps around this compound to picture its map in my head: the entrance lounge, the main building with the lobby and the dining room, the row of suites. Nothing but the desert around us.

Which leaves only the ground beneath my feet.

William Brenner's vehicle must be hidden below this very hotel.

But where's the entrance? I haven't seen it.

From a distance, I circle the property.

Nothing.

*Think.*

The Ara would never stoop to the brutally utilitarian aesthetic of regular parking garages, with a barrier and a large EXIT ONLY sign.

No. The beautiful minds who designed this hotel would have figured out a way to hide it. In fact, they might have boasted about their ingenuity online. A hidden parking garage entrance—this is exactly the kind of novelty a place like the Ara would highlight. Exactly the sort of feature they would show off to, say, a group of influencers whose stay they're comping in exchange for visibility.

*Please let me be right about this.*

I look up "Ara hotel hidden parking entrance." Nothing. Maybe I need to stay closer to home. "Ara hotel Madison."

Our very own influencer in chief's YouTube channel crops up. Unfortunately, she doesn't have any video labeled "INSANE garage opening" or "Check out INVISIBLE garage door at luxury resort." Instead, she has an "Ara hotel tour pt 1," an "Ara hotel tour pt 2," and, of course, an "Ara hotel tour pt 3."

*Jesus Christ, Madison.*

I try the first video. It's forty minutes long. *Are you kidding me?* No time to watch it in full. I swipe the cursor to the right and watch Madison's tour unfold at high speed in a preview window. Nothing that looks like a garage. "Ara hotel tour pt 2" is mostly devoted to the spa.

Something catches my eye in the last third of "Ara hotel tour pt 3." Was that a car?

*Yes.*

I scroll back a minute and let the video play at normal speed.

"And look at this, you guys—how cool is that?"

Madison turns her camera. On the screen, Catalina swipes something—a key card—in front of . . . one of the lanterns that dot the Ara's pathways, in which a reader is evidently camouflaged.

Where are they standing?

It's impossible to identify their location going by the lantern alone. There are dozens of those around the compound. I keep watching. In Madison's video, the ground moves. A patch of the desert—a hidden, trap-style door—rises at an angle through the air. Madison faux-gasps as she adjusts the angle of her camera.

That's when I spot it.

The magnolia.

The absurdly beautiful tree that somehow manages to stay

alive in this desert. The one I've admired more than once by the pool.

It's hovering at the top-left corner of the frame. Just its branches. Catalina and Madison aren't standing by the pool, exactly, but it's a reference point. They're right at the edge of the compound. On a spot I think I can access from the desert, without passing through the heart of the hotel.

In the video, Catalina ushers Madison down the sloped entryway to the garage.

By the time I stuff my phone back into my pocket, I'm already running.

THE SEVENTH DAY

With my shoulders hunched, I make my approach. *I'm not here. I'm not here.* There's the top of the magnolia.

From my spot, I sprint to the lantern I think I recognize from the video, press my key card against the reader. I am nothing but the most frenzied kind of hope. I wait and wait and wait until—

Nothing.

I try again.

Still nothing.

*Duh.*

This is a quality establishment. The guests' cars are kept safe, under lock and key. Some kind of special access card is required to open the parking garage.

I need it. I need the precise card Catalina used in Madison's video.

With my eyes on the ground, I dart to the lobby. I'm vaguely aware of guests around me, but they step out of my path. A shield of infamy separates them from me—the person of interest whose brother just got arrested for murder.

Do they even know about Gabriel's arrest?

No time to speculate. The door I'm looking for is off to the side, with a discreet engraved panel marked STAFF ONLY. It's the door behind which Calhoun disappeared just yesterday, when she went to get a glove.

I push it open. It reveals a break room with a table and chairs, a row of lockers, a microwave, a coffee machine with a small pile of discarded pods next to it.

The stunned gazes of Catalina and two of her colleagues—including the one who discovered Sabrina's body—greet me.

*What the fuck*, they telegraph with their silent outrage, *are you doing here?*

I'm used to this. Thinking on my feet, making up excuses.

"I'm sorry," I say. "But." The first sentence that pops into my brain: "William Brenner is in trouble."

Okay, that's not true.

Yet.

"I mean, he's having trouble. Breathing. He's in the entrance lounge, asking for help."

Catalina's face falls. She springs from her chair. *Not Brenner again*, she must be thinking.

"He's been under a lot of stress." I follow the three employees as they sprint out the door. "Hopefully, he'll be okay."

It's like they don't even hear me.

I let myself back into the break room.

I have maybe a minute until they realize William Brenner is not in the entrance lounge, and not asking for help.

*Quick.*

I look on the table, riffle through balled-up napkins, check under an abandoned lunch box. There's a pen and a notebook. I flip it upside down and wait for a master key card to tumble out.

Nothing.

*Come on.*

The row of lockers. I try a door, then another, then a third one. They're all locked.

I listen for the sound of footsteps. How long have I been in here?

More important: What am I missing?

At the back of a door, hanging from a coat hook I didn't see when I first walked in, is a jacket.

I grab it by the collar with greedy hands. There's a badge pinned at chest level. In the hotel's custom font, it spells out a familiar name: *Catalina*.

*Yes.*

*Yes.*

My hand ransacks the pockets. Nothing on the right-hand side. I try the left. Nope. I'm about to put the jacket back on its hook when I feel it: something rigid, tucked in an inside pocket. *Please, please, please.* My fingers slide in, clutch a rectangle of plastic, and pull out—

Well, just that. A rectangle of plastic. It's completely blank. Doesn't say MASTER KEY 1 or FLOOR KEY 3 or anything at all.

I put the jacket back where I found it, leap out of the room, and slam the door behind me.

———

Catalina and her two colleagues are absent from the lobby. Most likely, they're in the entrance lounge, looking for William, or maybe checking his suite. I keep my gaze down, avoiding a guest here, another person there, on my way out.

———

Back to the magnolia I go.

I press Catalina's key card against the lantern so hard I worry the glass will fissure.

But it doesn't. Instead, the ground rumbles.

*Yes.*

The secret door lifts through the air.

Slowly.

So slowly.

*Come on. Come on.*

Any minute now, Catalina will come running.

I pick up a rock. If I'm about to do what I think I'm about to do, then I'll probably need a rock.

The door is still moving when I crawl into the garage.

It's dark inside. I blink and wait for my eyes to adjust. Even the Ara can't do anything about the smell of fuel and motor oil that permeates every parking garage in the world. The structure around me is subterranean, with cement walls and the same kind of squeaky flooring I recognize from the storage unit of my early adulthood.

"Hello?"

No one's here.

Not even the Ara would bury a security guard underground twenty-four hours a day. Besides, the cars are safe in this locked garage. We're in the desert, connected to civilization by a sole access road. It's not like anyone can discreetly steal a vehicle from this hotel.

*Keep moving.*

Using my phone flashlight, I check my surroundings. I'm flanked by rows of cars. Here, five identical black SUVs, presumably the hotel's. Next to them, a white Jeep parked on a spot numbered twenty.

Okay. Okay. The cars are organized by suite number. If I could just remember—

Six.

Sabrina's lucky number.

I make my way down the parking spaces. Twenty, nineteen, eighteen—next row. I make a turn, then another, until—

*Fuck.*

I must have brushed too close to one of the parked cars. One of them—an Italian sports car, white with a couple of thick green stripes on the hood—is screeching so loudly I can feel the vibration in my teeth.

*For god's sake, shut up.*

The car keeps blaring in outrage. There must be security cameras all around me. If no one was watching before, they're certainly paying attention now.

In a minute, two at most, I'll be busted.

I run down the last row of cars.

Finally, a few spots from the wall, I spot it.

William Brenner's rental. So red. So recognizable.

I try a door: locked, obviously. The keys are nowhere to be seen. They're probably in a safe, back inside the hotel. Which also explains the absence of a security guard.

I take a step back. Raise the rock to shoulder height. I tense every muscle in my body and hurl it forward.

And then I duck.

The rental's alarm joins the Italian sports car's in a frenzied chorus.

When I stand up, the rock is on the ground. It bounced back. There's barely a nick in the window.

Car windows are built pretty solidly these days.

I try again.

Nothing.

*Damn it.*

My arm is getting tired. My *mind* is getting tired. Both alarms are screaming. I glance in the direction of the entrance: Still nothing. Just more cars, and a wall, and—

*Yes.*

I step away from William's car for a second, run to the fire extinguisher, and yank it from its spot.

*One more time.*

I lift the fire extinguisher. Shoulder burning, eyes shut, I hurl it at William's window.

When I open my eyes, the fire extinguisher is halfway inside the car. The window has shattered—enough that I can wrap my hand in my T-shirt and punch off a few big pieces.

I reach through the shards, unlock the door, brush the glass off the seat, and get in.

Okay. Okay.

There aren't that many hiding spots in a car. I check the glove box. Nothing. I crawl into the back. Nothing. I check under the seats, lift the floor mats. Nothing.

Back to the front. I sweep my hands over the dashboard, check for nooks, crannies, hidden levers.

Nothing, nothing, nothing.

The trunk.

The fucking trunk.

Quickly, I wiggle my way to the back again. *Think:* Everything I know about the world, I learned on TV. It comes to me: a funny scene in a sitcom, in which a woman accidentally locked a baby in a car. She had the opposite problem of mine: The trunk was open, and she needed to get back inside. I laughed as I watched her slither in through an opening in the back seat, which connected the trunk to the rest of the car.

I fold down the center section of the back seat. Then I play the sitcom scene in reverse: put my hand in the opening, then— tilting myself at an impossible angle—half of my shoulder.

My hand paws at the air on the other side. This is a modern car; there should be a release handle to open the trunk from inside. (Another thing I learned on TV—thank you, *SVU:* In every car manufactured to be sold in the U.S. since 2001, there's a release handle.)

I reach for everything, manage to grab nothing. Keep searching, hit my fingers against the top of the trunk, until finally—

There's a piece of plastic, shaped kind of like an IUD. I wrap my fingers around it and pull.

The trunk pops open.

It feels like every miracle all at once.

I free myself from the car's entrails and jog to the trunk.

It's completely empty.

*Fuck.*

I hit the car with my closed fists. Tears—of rage, of exhaustion—roll down my cheeks. *Gabriel.* I run my hands all over the inside of the trunk like I'm demanding more. Like I can't believe that after all this, all these efforts, all this *scheming,* the car's letting me down.

The rental car.

It has to be the rental car.

*Wait.*

I'm feeling something.

Under the fabric that lines the trunk is a groove. A rectangular groove, the outline of a . . . compartment.

My Fiat is old. But modern cars have that, don't they? Additional storage space below the rear trunk? Somewhere someone could stash a—

I tear the fabric from the sides, throw the liner behind me without looking back.

And there it is. At the center of the earth. Below the hotel, deep in the desert's belly.

Here, in the storage compartment of William Brenner's trunk, is one of his white button-down shirts.

Covered in blood.

"PUT YOUR HANDS IN THE AIR!"

I smile. Deputy Calhoun is back. Catalina is trailing her, of course.

They're furious. They know me for what I am: a liar and a thief.

I'm done fighting.

I do exactly what Deputy Calhoun is screaming at me to do.

I raise my hands in the air. One, the left, is empty.

The other—the right—is holding William Brenner's shirt, covered in his dead wife's blood.

———

THE SEVENTH DAY

Catalina is very sorry.

She gives me the first of many apologies as we watch Calhoun lead William into a police car. From the looks of it, he's going voluntarily: He's not wearing handcuffs; she's not placing her hand on his head and lowering him into the back seat. It's not a formal arrest. But I can picture Calhoun standing at the entrance to his suite, holding up the blood-stained shirt. I can picture William's face falling, a carefully constructed structure collapsing inside his head.

He must know that this is the end of the road. That charges will follow. That this is the part when he starts talking and angles for a deal with the prosecution.

There is always a deal, for men like William Brenner.

Catalina apologizes again.

"It's fine," I tell her.

Really. I assure her she couldn't have known. That William worked very hard to make Gabriel, and me by association, look guilty.

I don't tell her, of course, that she didn't mistake me for anything I'm not.

Everyone froze for a moment after I handed William's shirt

to Deputy Calhoun. So damning: his monogram on the cuff, dark stains mottling the front and sleeves. She frowned, then started a couple of sentences that she never finished.

"We'll have to take this to get analyzed," she said. "But in the meantime . . ."

The end of that sentence was implied: *In the meantime, we'll reopen our case into William Brenner.*

*In the meantime, it's pretty clear what the analysis will say.*

I return to our suite.

"Did you want me to help you book a plane back?" Catalina asks.

I shake my head.

"I'll wait for him," I tell her. "I'll wait for my brother."

She nods and leaves me alone.

I start packing. By the time I'm done, the only trace left of my presence is a butterfly-shaped hair clip, golden, on Gabriel's nightstand.

Sabrina wanted Gabriel to have it. I'm not giving it to the police.

The butterfly is his to keep.

And then I wait.

After a few hours, the door opens.

It's him.

"What— I mean how . . . ?"

He holds up a hand.

"He confessed," he says. "William confessed."

I have so many questions, and they all die somewhere between my throat and my lips. Only one of them wriggles out.

"His lawyer?"

Gabriel shrugs.

"His lawyer was on a flight to Salt Lake when it happened."

*Wow.*

*He must have felt cornered. He had played all his cards. He knew what he'd done.*

*I get that.*

When Gabriel steps further inside the suite, he's wearing an expression I've seen before—in a news segment, on a harrowed man clinging to his panting cat, moments after the animal was extracted from a burning house. A desperate kind of relief.

"Frida," he says. He opens his arms. Before he can do it—pull me close, hug me, collapse—I take a step back.

A memory seizes me.

Those six months when he was sick. The two of us, back in the storage unit. Gabriel was in his sleeping bag, facing the wall. His back was to me. I'd pictured my hand running along his spine and, with the same clarity, a knife digging between his ribs.

In that moment, he'd been mine to take care of. Mine to keep alive. A wounded animal I could choose to revive or finish off.

"There's something I need to tell you," I say.

Before I can lose my nerve, I do.

I tell him everything.

---

When I'm done, he takes a deep breath. Then another, even deeper. He's not in control. The breaths are the only response he can conjure up, his body trying to exorcise something.

"Get out," he says, finally.

I don't fight him, but he keeps talking as though I've tried to justify myself—as though I've done anything other than pick up my suitcase and head toward the door.

"Get out," he says again, "or I don't know what I'll do."

---

I retreat to the lobby.

Fifteen minutes go by. Then thirty. Then an hour.

Maybe I'll never see him again.

That would be fine. Painful, of course. But *painful* is what I deserve.

And then he's here.

From what I can tell, he has showered and changed. I did the same thing earlier. We're both in jeans now, he in a white T-shirt, me in a black blouse. He's wearing his big travel backpack—that fucking backpack—on one shoulder.

I almost expect him to pretend like I'm not here, but he walks up to the ottoman on which I'm sitting.

His expression is unreadable.

"Come with me," he says.

And so I do.

———

We leave our bags in the lobby. Gabriel leads me outside to the entrance lounge. Where I spoke to Harris on the fifth day. Where I tried to get him to focus on William Brenner, before the hotel closed around us like a trap.

We sit on a bench, in the shade of a sail canopy.

Gabriel looks at me. I can't meet his gaze for more than a second.

"I don't know what to say to you," he whispers.

The emptiness hangs between us. Maybe there is nothing left to say, nothing left to do.

Unless.

"I'll confess," I tell Gabriel. "I'll tell the police it was me."

After all this time.

After I got away with it.

But it's the only decent thing to do.

Gabriel shakes his head.

"Don't," he says.

"But—"

"I've lost enough people."

He looks somewhere beyond me. He looks, I think, at all his ghosts. The world we left. Simon. Edwina. Annie. The parents we never knew. Émile.

"You don't get to take away the only person I have left just to put your conscience to rest," he says. "You just don't."

His words silence me like a blow to the head.

"I know," he continues. "I know that William probably saw me that night. I know it's what started the argument."

He swallows with difficulty.

"I heard voices, when they were arguing. I did. And I went in the opposite direction."

His gaze settles back on me. I force myself not to look away.

"She died because of something I did," he says. "I do know that."

"It wasn't your—"

Gabriel shakes his head in a silent *Don't.*

*Just don't.*

———

### THE AFTERMATH

For three months, I don't hear from him.

He goes back to Seattle. I go back to New York.

I get up. I drink my coffee. I walk Charlie. I make some trades.

I don't go climbing. I don't go to my pottery workshop. I don't see the few people I can realistically call my friends.

I leave my car in the garage. No more country roads for me.

The documentary producers email me, asking for a date to shoot my interview. I ignore them.

Every hour, I think that this could be it. The moment when Gabriel decides to go to the cops and tell them everything he knows.

It feels so real. The idea that Gabriel will report me, that a wave is coming to swallow my life. I expect the police to show up at my apartment, to ambush me in Central Park.

Before it's too late, and because I need to know, I call Deputy Calhoun. She owes me. I get to ask questions.

"The coyotes," I say on the phone. "Did anyone ever go to help them?"

There's silence on the other end of the line. I can picture her perplexed expression.

"It's important," I tell her.

"The coyotes are fine," she says. "The mom was rescued with her pups. She's recovering. In time, they'll go to a sanctuary."

"That's good."

I hang up.

The feral puppy inside of me settles a little.

I walk past my old diners. The first one, the second one. I walk through Grand Central. I walk through Penn Station.

I even walk past the storage facility.

Early one morning, I walk to the river.

I'm on a mission.

The single dollar bill. The one I took—stole—from Émile, half a lifetime ago. The one I kept.

It's almost nothing. But it is here, in my wallet, following me wherever I travel. This tiny part of my life that hasn't let go.

It has to happen at dawn, before the streets fill with passersby. It has to happen a few feet from my apartment, the nearest part of the Hudson I can access on foot.

There's a handful of runners out already. I don't mind them; they don't mind me. Most don't even seem to see me, this anonymous woman in jeans and a T-shirt, face bare, hair in a ponytail, kneeling by the water, something fluttering in her hand.

I've thought about burning it. Taking scissors to it. Burying it somewhere upstate, stomping on it, spitting on it.

None of those options felt right.

I crumple the bill and dip my fist in the water. It's cold, and it's gross, and I'll have to scrub my hand two, three times once I get home.

For now, I hold on to it. Émile's little secret.

I think of a quote I read somewhere in a Kerouac book, the one about the road, about his friend. (A friend who—I couldn't help but notice—breaks his thumb on his girlfriend's face at some point in the story.) Something about how if you drop a rose in the Hudson River, think of the places it'll visit, think of its travels to the ocean, "think of that wonderful Hudson Valley."

I think of that wonderful Hudson Valley. Slowly, I open my

fingers. The water doesn't wait. It rushes in, lifts the dollar bill from my palm, carries it away from me.

Slowly, the dollar bill floats away.

No.

It doesn't. Not after a couple of seconds.

The dollar bill bobs up and down. It floats.

I wait for the Hudson to take it from me, but the water won't do it. And so I sit on the bank and watch it, this tiny piece of paper, the imprint of lipstick faded but still visible to me in the morning light.

In time, the paper will disintegrate. The water will reduce it to nothing. Émile's dollar bill will cease to exist. The lip print will disappear for good.

Not today.

Today, I go home.

I brace myself for the end. I say a hundred goodbyes, but no one comes to get me.

Then, an email.

FROM: millerg61290@gmail.com
TO: fridanilsen126@gmail.com
*We should go back.*

I don't understand. I'll go anywhere he wants to go, but I don't understand.

FROM: fridanilsen126@gmail.com
TO: millerg61290@gmail.com
*Where? To Utah?*

FROM: millerg61290@gmail.com
TO: fridanilsen126@gmail.com
*To Émile's place. World. Whatever. We should go back.*

I don't ask why. I only ask when. Gabriel flies in the following week. We meet at Grand Central and board our train without a word.

We have never been back. There's never been anything there for us to return to.

When we get off the train, I think I see our younger selves on the platform. I'm eighteen, throwing up in a trash can, sick with the image of the man I think we've just killed.

I have so many questions for Gabriel.

*Do you remember the way?*

*What's your plan?*

*Why on earth do you want to go back there?*

But I don't say anything. The silence isn't mine to break.

Our feet find the way. We walk through the town. Joan's bar is gone. The pharmacy endures. This completely standard convenience store, once the most confusing place we'd ever visited.

The road is still there. In fact, it looks like it's been retarred recently.

We walk in silence.

It's fall. The trees on either side of the road have yellowed. Around us, the smell of humid earth swirls through the air. For a second, I'm brought back to the day of Annie's death. I feel the spray of the waterfall on my face, the burn in my arms as I shove her over the bridge and into the water.

Bile rises at the back of my throat. I swallow it back.

This isn't about me.

This is about Gabriel, and whatever he needs to find at the end of this road.

It takes me by surprise. The compound. Time passes faster for adults than it does for children; distances, it turns out, are shorter, too.

Somehow, most of the buildings are still standing.

The old church. The cafeteria. The dorms. The stamp of abandonment is everywhere: Whole sections of walls are missing; the church's roof has half collapsed. Ivy has grown on every structure. The ground is covered in weeds.

We walk the property. Underneath the decay, Émile's world is frozen in time. There are still a few bowls—dirty, rusted—in the cafeteria. Some beds in the dorms. Animals have poked holes in the mattresses and nested there. It smells like a pet store, and, in parts, like death.

At the back of the cafeteria, we find it. The Secret Place.

A broom closet.

The door has rotted off its hinges. Inside, the closet is covered in dust, dirt, animal droppings.

This is where we met.

We don't step back inside.

Amazing, the stories we tell ourselves. The fears we conjure up in the dark.

We're not children anymore.

———

We walk to Émile's building.

Here it is, still.

Almost completely charred.

They never tried to rebuild it, by the looks of it. Émile must have settled elsewhere in the time between the fire and his arrest.

We stand near it. I swear I can smell smoke, the strangely salty scent of burnt wood and plastic.

Is this where it began?

Did our lives melt together in the fire? Did the embers keep glowing under the pile of ashes? Did a force enter our lives that night, something that couldn't be extinguished, no matter how long we waited?

Or was it all ordained, somehow?

There's a fable I hate.

The one about the scorpion and the frog. A scorpion asks a frog to carry it across a river; the frog agrees. The scorpion hops on the frog's back. While they're in the water, the scorpion stings the frog, condemning them both to death. When the frog asks the scorpion why it did it, the scorpion's excuse is essentially: *Because I'm a scorpion, and this is what scorpions do.*

It's all so flat. Scorpion has no morals; scorpion has no choice; scorpion stings.

No.

I was never a scorpion.

Whatever I am, I became.

There's a sound at my side—soft, muffled. Gabriel has his face in his hands. His shoulders twitch.

He's crying.

I let him.

Then, in a movement so swift I don't register it until I'm in his arms, he pulls me to him. It's a forceful gesture, desperate, raw. My lip bumps against his shoulder. His arms are clasped around me, constricting my rib cage. I can breathe, but barely. There's just enough air for me to start crying, too.

*If he squeezed a little harder,* I think, *then that would be it.* I can almost hear my spine snapping like a twig.

But he doesn't squeeze harder. He sobs. It's almost silent at first, then he puts his voice into it. Here we stand, Gabriel's weight almost crushing me, the great force of his grief, of his sorrow, pushing me into the earth.

We cry together.

Slowly, his incoherent sounds separate into words. I can't make them out. "Done . . . hoo." I pull back a couple of inches, enough to let him speak properly. Still holding on to me, still far too close for me to look into his eyes, he says it: "I would have done it, too."

I go still.

"I would have done the same thing," he says through his tears. "If she'd told me instead of you. I would have done it, too."

My mind leaves the moment, surrenders to this alternative chain of events. In another world, Annie brings her discovery about the fire, about Edwina, to Gabriel. He resolves to kill her. He lies in wait at Paterson Great Falls. When the time comes, he shoves her over the barrier.

But this isn't the world we exist in. Annie came to me. I did it.

I will forever be the one who did it.

"I would have," Gabriel says, his sentence cut short by wet, desperate sobs. "I would."

I don't try to argue. Gabriel knows himself. He knows what he's capable of. He has spent years wrestling with his own mind.

That's why he couldn't believe me, when I told him, over and over again, that I believed in his innocence. That I knew—really knew—he hadn't killed Annie.

He couldn't believe it himself. In a corner of his mind, Gabriel always saw the possibility of his own guilt.

Whatever we recognized in each other all those years ago, it's here. Burned into the ground underneath our feet. It's in the roots of the trees, in the air around us.

A time-bending force. Two kids grasping at the future, two adults wrapped in the tight vines of their past.

It's love, in the end.

Love is the scorpion.

G abriel and I meet outside the studio.

It's a small space, rented by the producers for the day. I traveled down from the Upper West Side; Gabriel came from the Village.

He moved back a month ago. Didn't tell me until he was already there, in his new apartment, surrounded by boxes.

I don't think he did it for me.

I think, after nine years, he had nothing left to hide from.

We see each other sometimes. Often enough that even when the time between our meetups starts to stretch, I don't worry that he's truly gone.

I sleep at night now. Not as blissfully as I did at the Staircase Inn. But, for better or worse, I fall asleep and wake up on roughly the same schedule as the rest of polite society.

Two weeks ago, Gabriel told me, over coffee, that the time had come.

"I'll let them know we're ready," he said. "The documentary people."

"Okay."

I didn't ask him then, and I haven't asked him since.

*What are you going to say?*

I don't know.

I just don't.

———

The studio is on the first floor of a building with tall windows and a marble entryway. Two women greet us—one tall, one short, one all in black, the other in a red turtleneck and jeans. Our two wonderful filmmakers. Nicky and Sandra. They have been patient, diligent, professional. They've remained determined to tell Annie's story from Annie's point of view, take the focus away from the speculation, train our collective gaze back on the woman who died.

"Have a seat," Nicky tells us. "We're almost ready for you."

Gabriel and I sit in a small waiting room. For some reason, there's a TV in a corner, airing a shockingly loud rerun of *The Jerry Springer Show*.

We wait. A young man, also dressed in black, from his patent-leather combat boots to his sleeveless sweater, comes to get Gabriel, then me. Our faces are powdered, our hair slicked and sprayed.

"This way!"

Sandra waves us over to the back.

Looking like the best versions of ourselves, we make our way to the filming area.

"Why don't you sit on the left," Sandra tells Gabriel. Then, turning to me: "And you'll take the right?"

We take our assigned seats.

"Okay," Nicky says, settling behind the camera. "I'll be filming, and Sandra is going to be asking you guys questions off-screen. If there's anything you don't want to answer, or if you need a break at any point, just let us know."

Gabriel and I both say okay.

He was the one who said we should do it together. The interview. Nicky and Sandra would have preferred to speak to us separately, but Gabriel said no. We would speak together, or not at all.

I didn't ask why that was so important to him. I just showed up.

He could do it. If he wanted to. He could tell Nicky and Sandra everything I told him in the desert.

They wouldn't be able to resist, of course. Our responsible filmmakers. They're pros, but they're only human. They would air it, and it would turn into the true-crime event of the year.

A red light flashes on Nicky's camera; Sandra perches on a stool, printed questions in hand, and I know I'm not in control. At the end of the day, at the end of the decade, I've left it all up to Gabriel.

If he talks, I won't fight it. That's been my deal with myself since I told him. If Gabriel opts not to keep my secret, I'll play along. I'll tell the cops. I'll show them.

But I don't think he's going to do it.

It's a feeling I have. Something like trust, but heavier. Essential. Gabriel didn't come here to give me up.

This is who we are. People who sit together and talk. People who set fires. I pour the accelerant; he strikes the match. We leave under cover of darkness. We find homes. We start over together. Again. And again.

We learn to swim. We run into water. We hide things from each other. Between the two of us, we hold the world's greatest truths.

We hold hands at a wedding. We watch a coffin disappear into the ground. We make it through winter, through depression, through twenty-three years. We say goodbye; we don't see each other for an eternity; we meet again. We hold on to each other.

This is what we've become. What we always were.

The only thing we ever knew how to be. A family.

# ACKNOWLEDGMENTS

When I finish drafting a novel, I never write "the end" at the bottom of the manuscript. That stage never feels like the end to me. On the contrary, it's a beginning, the start of a new phase during which I will welcome other people onto the page, after months of wandering there on my own.

It's a vulnerable thing, showing work when it's still in flux. It also happens to be my favorite part. I've been lucky to work with people who are extraordinarily good at their jobs, who have made me feel completely at home on the page, and who have worked miracles to help my work find its readers.

And so, I extend my most heartfelt thanks to:

My editor, Jennifer Barth. Thank you for always being right. Thank you for your patience, your kindness, your belief in my work, and your incredibly sharp insights.

My agent, Stephen Barbara. Thank you for being such a great reader, for your enthusiasm, and for your attentiveness. When I tell people you're the best agent in the business, I truly mean it.

Reagan Arthur: Thank you for believing in this novel, and for inspiring me to make some big changes.

My friend Abby Endler, an encyclopedia of crime fiction and an endlessly generous supporter of its authors. Thank you for everything.

The amazing team at Knopf and Vintage: Jordan Pavlin, Elora Weil, Brian Etling, Ellen Whitaker, Micah Kelsey, Gabrielle Brooks, Beth Lamb, Erinn Hartman, Laura Keefe, Dan Zitt, Katie Punia, Heather Dalton, Rita Madrigal, Casey Hampton, Felecia O'Connell, Kate Hughes. And David Litman, for designing the beautiful cover.

The amazing team at InkWell Management: Alexis Hurley, Jessie Thorsted, Hannah Lehmkuhl, Lyndsey Blessing, Sidney Boker, and Laura Hill.

Kathleen Carter, for her work on public relations. And to the scouts who have supported my work.

My husband, Tyler Daniels, for making good on his vow to read my drafts, and for answering my many, many, many, *many* legal questions. Aren't you glad you went to law school?

My parents, for their constant support and their love of books. It's a thrill to be able to share all of this with you. My in-laws, who hype me up constantly and forgive me when I forget to tell them important news. My grandmother, who knows everything there is to know about U.S. publishing and waits diligently for my work to be translated into our native French.

My friend Holly Baxter, who unleashed the writer in me. (Look what you've done!)

My French friends, who remain amazing and witty and supportive and incredibly good-looking: Morgane Giuliani, Clara Chevassut, Lucie Ronfaut-Hazard, Ines Zallouz, Camille Jacques, Xavier Eutrope, Geoffroy Husson, Swann Ménage, Baptiste Thiéry.

My friends Christine and Zak Opperman, for their support and excellent company. My friend Nathan McDermott, also for his support and excellent company, and for the horror movies.

My therapist, who still keeps me sane.

The authors who blurbed my debut thriller, *The Quiet Tenant*: Megan Abbott, Alafair Burke, Kimberly McCreight, James Patterson, Alex Segura, Brad Thor, Paul Tremblay. And generally, to all the writers who have made me feel included and welcome in the world of crime fiction. Thank you for your kindness and grace.

To the Bookstagrammers, BookTokers, podcasters, and readers of all kinds: a massive thank-you.

A wise man once told me, when I was starting out, that this is supposed to be fun. I think about this multiple times a week. Thank you, Tim O'Connell.

This might go without saying, but "the mob show" referenced in this book is *The Sopranos*. I really, really love *The Sopranos* (for completely innocent reasons).

The scene Frida remembers involving a character wriggling her way inside a locked car is from the sitcom *Mom*, and the scene in question is brilliantly acted by Allison Janney.

The Italian novel in translation that Frida reads by the pool is *The Solitude of Prime Numbers* by Paolo Giordano. I read it a long time ago, at a beautiful hotel in the desert.

## A NOTE ABOUT THE AUTHOR

CLÉMENCE MICHALLON is the author of *The Quiet Tenant*, a *USA Today* and international bestseller and nominee for the Dashiell Hammett Prize. She's also a freelance journalist whose work has appeared in *The New York Times Book Review, Time, The Independent,* and more. Clémence was born and raised near Paris, has lived in New York since 2014, and became a U.S. citizen in 2022. *Our Last Resort* is her second thriller. She can be found on Instagram at clemencemichallon and on X at Clemence_Mcl.

## A NOTE ON THE TYPE

This book was set in Janson, a typeface long thought to have been made by the Dutchman Anton Janson, who was a practicing typefounder in Leipzig during the years 1668–1687. However, it has been conclusively demonstrated that these types are actually the work of Nicholas Kis (1650–1702), a Hungarian, who most probably learned his trade from the master Dutch typefounder Dirk Voskens. The type is an excellent example of the influential and sturdy Dutch types that prevailed in England up to the time William Caslon (1692–1766) developed his own incomparable designs from them.

*Typeset by Scribe,*
*Philadelphia, Pennsylvania*

*Designed by Casey Hampton*